Penguin Books

Flight into Camden

David Storey was born in 1933 and is the
third son of a mine-worker. He was educated
at the Queen Elizabeth Grammar School at
Wakefield and the Slade School of Fine Art.
He has had various jobs ranging from
professional footballer to school-teaching
and showground tent-erecting. He is now
both a novelist and dramatist.

Among his publications are *This Sporting
Life*, which won the Macmillan Fiction Award
in 1960 and was also filmed; *Flight into
Camden*, which won the John Llewellyn Rhys
Memorial Prize and also the Somerset
Maugham Award in 1960; and *Radcliffe*.
These were followed by *A Temporary Life*,
Edward and *Saville* (1976 Booker Prize).
His plays include *In Celebration*, which
has been filmed, *Home*, *The Contractor* and
The Changing Room. Most of these are
published in Penguins.

David Storey lives in London. He was married
in 1956 and has four children.

David Storey

Flight into Camden

Penguin Books

Penguin Books Ltd, Harmondsworth,
Middlesex, England
Penguin Books, 625 Madison Avenue,
New York, New York 10022 U.S.A.
Penguin Books Australia Ltd, Ringwood,
Victoria, Australia
Penguin Books Canada Ltd, 2801 John Street,
Markham, Ontario, Canada L3R 1B4
Penguin Books (N.Z.) Ltd, 182–190 Wairau Road,
Auckland 10, New Zealand

First published by Longmans, Green 1960
Published in Penguin Books 1964
Reprinted 1977, 1979

Made and printed in Great Britain by
C. Nicholls & Company Ltd
Set in Linotype Juliana

To Barbara

I

We buried my grandfather the second week before Christmas. It wasn't cold, but there was a light drizzle and all of us had come in thick clothes. My mother and I shared an umbrella.

The priest from the Old People's Home stood on a small board at the end of the grave. The rain blew in his face and gathered in fine drops on his forehead.

'Man that is born of a woman hath but a short time to live, and is full of misery,' he said, then screwed up his eyes as he began reading through the cellophane cover on his prayer book.

My father stood with Michael.

Not all of my father's family were there. My grandfather, in spite of silicosis and a severe spinal injury, had had nine children in his eighty-six years; two had died. But the family didn't keep in touch. It might be Christmas itself before they'd all heard of his death. As it was I hadn't seen my grandfather since I was a girl, when he'd lived with us for a year at the beginning of the war.

We gathered round the hole like workmen. It was difficult not to push one another off the boards, which had been laid unevenly over the yellow clay. The spaces between the plots were only broad enough for people to walk in single file.

No one looked grieved, except my father and perhaps my Uncle Jack. None of the men wore full black, but had black silk triangles or armbands on their overcoat sleeves.

Michael merely watched the coffin. It was poised at the

lip of the grave, and the four bearers held the ropes lightly, as if it contained no weight. They stood with their feet wide apart, avoiding the clay. The rain had collected in small pools on the waxed lid and round the name-plate, on which was engraved: 'Arthur Frederick Thorpe. 1871–1957.' I wondered how I might have guessed that Michael was the only man there who was not a workman. With his hands clenched and hanging in front of him, he had the same stiff miner's stance as my father. But he was not as stocky, and was taller. His was the only face that bore no apparent emotion. My mother watched him, even during the prayer. She was content with him, that her son was so apart.

The others had their eyes on the coffin waiting for it to be lowered. After leaving the children behind at the church, some of them had relaxed, and now they began to move restlessly as the box disappeared into the cavity and the priest bent down, reciting, and picked up the trowel. The soil drummed on the lid.

Beyond the grave was a privet hedge, then a large compost heap with dead chrysanthemums sticking from it, then an old brick wall, whitened with salt, leaning in towards the cemetery. Above it, banked up on shale, was the beginning of the goods yard, whose tall wall we'd passed flanking the lane up to the cemetery.

'I heard a voice from heaven,' the priest murmured, 'saying unto me, "Write: from henceforth blessed are the dead . . ."'

It was a line of trucks, being released one by one, that Michael was now watching. His eyes followed the journey of each one until it disappeared beyond the high wall. But his head didn't move. His body was still and rigid. A group of men, shrouded in heavy macintoshes, stared down at us between the actions of releasing each truck. Above their heads was the top half of the Lazenby mill chimney. It was black and very tall, one side glistening like steel in the wet.

The priest looked at us, then said, 'Lord have mercy upon us.'

'Christ have mercy upon us,' some of us answered.

'Lord have mercy upon us.' He began the Lord's Prayer.

At the end of the drive the four black-coated taxi-drivers were waiting round the bonnet of the hearse, their hands pushed deep in their pockets. For a minute brown smoke came out of Lazenby's chimney, then suddenly stopped. The detached cloud floated like a sail over the yards and then the cemetery.

Two graves away, behind my father's back, a blackbird was standing in a puddle on the grass verge, its feathers puffed up, raising a small flurry of water. Its body seemed to spin round in its cloud of spray. Suddenly it stiffened, its feathers like quills, its head bobbing up, and its beady eye darting. Then its feathers collapsed, and it hopped on to the far grave. Looking round, it turned its eye up towards the sky; then crouched and flung itself into the air, flying low over the gravestones with its warning chatter. The small crowd broke up.

I walked between the graves to where Michael was already waiting on the gravel footpath.

'Our Alec should have been here,' he said. 'My dad feels let down about it.'

'Why didn't you sprinkle some soil on the coffin?' I asked him.

He didn't answer. We waited silently. The others threaded their way towards us, the women swiping the yellow clay off their shoes against the grass verges. My mother's umbrella waved from side to side as she tried to keep her balance in the narrow grooves between the plots.

'There you are, Margaret,' she said, and came to hold the umbrella over me as though it were she who were seeking some protection.

'What did you think to it, Michael?'

'I'm glad it's over,' he told her, smiling.

'Well, it's over,' she said, wondering at him. 'I only wish our Alec had been here. It doesn't look right – just one of us missing like that.'

'I don't know why you should want to force him to come,' I said, but she didn't reply. She turned to listen to one of my aunts speaking to her over the heads of the family.

'Come on,' my father said.

My Uncle Jack came to join us. He was the only one at the funeral who had come alone: he was separated from his wife. My mother put her arm in mine.

My father walked in front, with Michael and Jack. For the first time they were all talking. The priest walked alone near the front of the group. The bearers were returning to the hearse to collect the wreaths and when we reached the ornamental gates a screen of sacking was being put round the grave by two men in overalls.

At the other side of the lane was a children's playground. It was nearly dinner time, and strangely quiet, full of boys in school uniform, sitting or standing still on the swings and roundabouts, all of them still, smoking. They talked quietly, leaning earnestly over their cigarettes. We got into the second taxi. I watched the boys now through the rain-marked window. A cousin I hadn't seen for several years walked by and got in front beside the driver. Somebody said, 'Come on, then. We mustn't be late for it.'

'Where's your Alec, then?' my uncle asked.

'He couldn't get.' My father shook his head apologetically. 'It took Michael, you know, all his time to get leave from the university. And our Alec lives at Maudsley now. It's near thirty miles away.'

'And Nora's got two kiddies,' my mother said. Alec was the youngest, and the only one to be married and living away from home.

'Aye. You lose contact when you're away. I know it only

too well.' He looked with curiosity at Michael, and spread his hands over his knees to keep his balance on the fold-up seat.

'Oh, we see him often enough,' my father said. 'It was just one of those days. He's working up to be a chemist. At that big works there. . . .' He tried to remember the name.

'Aye,' Jack said. He was a bricklayer. He glanced again at Michael. 'How do you like it, then? A college professor and that.' He laughed awkwardly. His emotions quickly replaced one another.

'I'm not a professor yet,' Michael said. 'I doubt if I get paid three-quarters of what you do.' He smiled at my uncle. My mother watched us carefully, half smiling.

'Nay, you can come off that.' My uncle turned his hands palms upwards, but still pressed to his knees to keep his balance, his elbows drawn into his sides. 'You don't get hands like that, for a start.' They were big and thick, and scarred. 'Aren't I right, Reg? Thy can ask your dad.'

My father didn't say anything. He nodded absent-mindedly at his brother.

'If thy's got any brains in your body you won't work like us,' Jack said. 'Me and your dad – we were wukking six days a week at fourteen.'

Michael nodded. For the first time he looked tired.

'You like it then, at the university?' Jack asked. He couldn't accustom himself to his nephew being a teacher.

'This is only my first term,' Michael told him.

'Nay, you mu'n only read out on a book at them,' Jack said. 'I don't reckon there's much learning needed for that. What were you doing down south afore you came back up home?'

'Research work in a factory.' He said it clumsily. He hated the conversation.

'He's taking our Margaret to the university's Christmas dance this evening,' my mother said. Jack looked at me, his red, jowelled face unsmiling. 'It's the end of term, you know. I don't think their grandfather'd want them to give that up.... You're looking forward to it, aren't you, Margaret?'

'Well. It's something.'

Jack looked strange now, and unwanted. 'Yon's a sensible lass,' he said, and nodded at me. 'Not wed or ought. That's the road to live. Are you still typing, Margaret?'

'She's a secretary now,' my mother said. 'At the N.C.B.'

'At the coal-hole! If that isn't something.' Jack laughed. 'Well, you couldn't drop on a better number than that. There can't be much rushing about up yonder, thy can bet. I don't know, Reg. What with thy Michael, and Margaret. They more brains a piece than any four on us put together. If I had my time o'er again I know damn well where I'd mek a start ... I'd be at school till I could grow a beard to begin wi'.'

'You've to have the brains first,' my mother said.

'A'd find the brains all right.'

He looked at my father. He wanted badly for him to talk. 'He was a good un to all on us,' he said, trying to read his thoughts.

'We never knew where he wa',' my father said, 'not for these last five years. We didn't even know he'd gone into the Home.'

'Well ... you know how it is when you get to that age,' Jack told him. 'When we had him living wi' *us* he could only mope about the place, saying how he wished he were on his own. You know what it's like.'

The car went on softly through the wet streets. A glass partition divided us from the driver and my cousin – I'd even forgotten his name. The taxi had become separated from the others. The streets were full of traffic, then as we turned round Albert Square we could see the tall Victorian tower of the university.

'They're a couple o' quiet uns,' Jack said, looking at

Michael and me. 'What d'you do wi' both on 'em at home?'

'They can be noisy enough when they get arguing,' my mother said contentedly, as if we were children again. She looked at me as if to warn me against showing any resentment.

When we reached the Golden Dragon the other three taxis had already arrived and some of the relatives were waiting for us outside.

'Come on, Reg !' someone shouted.

'I'll gev you two guesses where all the rest on 'em are,' Jack said. 'I' the bar. Knocking it back. A never saw a family like'n ours for funerals. . . . Dos't remember when Mother died, Reg?'

My father didn't answer. He was looking at Michael.

'I'm not feeling too well,' Michael said. 'I think I'll go on home.'

'Nay, you'll feel better, lad, when you've had a drop to warm you,' Jack said. He clapped his hands together and rubbed them against the cold.

'Aren't you staying to the lunch, then?' my father said.

'No. I don't think I will. I tell you, I couldn't face a meal.'

'All right, then.' He avoided Michael's eyes.

'You're coming in, Margaret? Aren't you?' my mother said. She'd put her arm in mine.

'Oh, I'll come,' I told her. She watched Michael.

'I'll be going then,' he said.

He shook hands with my uncle. He'd flushed. For a moment we watched him as he walked down the hill towards the bus station, his figure seemingly folded up against the weather, and everything. My mother held my arm tightly.

'Well, let's be getting in, then,' Jack said. 'I'll tek this branch of the Thorpe family to show 'em how to behave properly, I've no doubt at all.'

My father followed us in. I could hear his heavy breathing close behind me.

*

The broad steps up to the large university entrance arch were crowded with students. Michael guided me through them without actually touching my arm. The road outside the university had been deserted and dark, and the sudden burst of life and light startled me.

Inside the entrance hall decorations had been hung up across the ceiling and on the walls were sheets of paper with clowns and pierrots roughly painted on them. Michael waited while I took my hat and coat to the cloakroom. It was very crowded.

'We'll go up to the Prof's room, first,' he said.

He led the way up a flight of steps from the main assembly hall. The noisy dancing seemed to follow us up to the first floor. At the end of a dark, panelled corridor a door was open, and from its beam of light came the sound of conversation and glasses. Michael stepped behind me. 'Go on. Straight ahead, Margaret.'

Although he was behind me I knew how aggressively he entered. The room was like a large and well-kept sitting-room: its dull blue haze was lit only by reading lamps and curtains in a contemporary design covered the windows. For a while no one spoke to Michael. We went to a table in the corner where a girl in a black dress and white apron gave us our drinks. He stood close beside me while we looked round the room. The people were packed in the large central space between three long bookcases, and were busily talking.

His Professor saw him and, excusing himself, came across. He was scarcely middle-aged. He greeted Michael without feeling. 'You've got drinks, Thorpe?' he asked, looking at our glasses. He smiled unseeingly at me.

'This is my sister, sir,' Michael said.

'It's very good of you to come.' He looked round the room to see where he could attach us. 'You've met Jenkins, from Physics. Physicist . . .' he said. He had a slight stammer.

'Yes. I know him.' Michael nodded at a thin man, with a

narrow, consumptive face, who came over almost immediately.

'I'll leave you to it, then,' the Professor said, smiling at us again, and touched Michael's back before he went away.

'Why didn't you introduce him to me?' I asked. He looked blank, then surprised.

Jenkins came. He held his glass in both hands, his fingers tightly interlocked. He spoke quickly and eagerly to Michael, and swilled the red drink round in his glass. Across the room a man with fair hair watched me.

Michael talked about the Professor. A young man in a corduroy coat joined us. His collar-button was undone behind his tie, and there was a thin sweat on his forehead. His eyes could only turn slowly. He and Michael started laughing. Then Jenkins.

The fair-haired man lit a cigarette, watching it intently as he took his first puffs. He'd been talking to someone but now he stood alone by a long cabinet. On it were a skull and two pieces of sculpture. He saw me looking at him.

'Do you want another drink, Margaret?' Michael asked. I was unused to him using my name. I smiled at him.

'Just stay there,' the man in the corduroy coat said. 'I'll get you one. What're you having?'

'It's a gin and it,' Michael said, and looked at Jenkins. 'She wouldn't know.' They laughed and I protested. Michael was happy.

'I'll tell him it isn't one and see what he says,' I said.

'I shouldn't do that,' Jenkins answered. He didn't look closely at me. 'It would be just the thing he wanted. He'll spend all night having it analysed.'

The man came back with the drink. Jenkins watched me taste it, then repeated what he'd said. Soon they were laughing again, Michael almost with his back to me.

At home were my Uncle Jack, my Aunty Dot, and Uncle Phil, talking about the funeral.

The fair-haired man stood in a space now. He was broad shouldered; but it might have been the effect of his Harris tweed jacket. His trousers were unpressed. He'd picked up one of the pieces of sculpture and was looking at it. But not intently. He held it in both hands, sceptical, with his cigarette; and the smoke curled round it. The light behind him glowed through the fringe of his hair. It was luminous. Behind him was the skull, white and yellow.

I went and stood by the cabinet.

'Who's it by?' I asked.

He looked up, but not in surprise. It was as though he'd been interrupted.

'Moore,' he said. Then he went on, 'It's a maquette by a sculptor called Henry Moore – he was born in this area. Do you like it? He's very famous.' He watched me cautiously.

'What's it supposed to be?'

'It's a reclining figure. A woman lying down.' He ran his finger carefully over the green undulations. 'It's the idea of a figure lying down. The physical excitement.'

'It's very small.'

'It's just an idea,' he said. He stubbed out his cigarette, grinding it into the tray. He seemed to disapprove of his own criticism. 'It's not the real thing. Are you Thorpe's wife?'

'I'm his sister.'

He raised his eyebrows. His skin was fair too, pale, and must have been freckled when he was a boy. He had grey-blue eyes, which were almost colourless when he moved into the light. But they were bright, and sharp. Almost as if they'd been stroked into his face, and fine. They were full of energy, and careless.

'I didn't think he was married,' he said. He looked at me intently. 'How do you like it here?'

'What? The university?'

'No. Just this room.'

'I like it. It's very cosy and warm-looking.'

'I'll just put this down,' he said.

He leaned over and replaced the piece of sculpture beside the similar one on the cabinet. His hair was thinning round the crown. He must have been thirty-five, or -eight, perhaps.

'Have you been here before?' he asked.

'No. This is the first time. My brother's only been here this term.'

'Yes, I know.' He looked across at Michael. 'I think he'll be a success.'

Some people left the room, going down the corridor chatting. There was suddenly more space and I felt more relaxed. I was tired. 'Are you a lecturer?' I asked him.

'No.' He shook his head, and smiled. He looked pleased. 'I'm across the road. At the Art College – I teach Industrial Design.' His pale eyes intermittently relaxed in a glazed fashion, as if suddenly frozen, then thawed. 'I know a few of the people over here.'

'You're the odd man out.'

'Aren't we all?'

He looked as though he could have amused himself with me. I'd felt that when he was showing me the sculpture; it was the way he held it, as if deliberately exaggerating its preciousness.

'What do you do for a living?' he asked.

'I work for the Coal Board.'

'Oh . . . The Director of mineral research.'

'I'm a secretary in the accounts department.'

He bowed his head very slightly, his eyes on mine. 'Do you dance?'

'Here?'

'No. But *that* would be amusing. I mean downstairs.'

I looked across at Michael. He was in a large group now and talking so intensely that I could hear his voice above the others in the room. Not his words, but the eager, bursting impetuosity, and his aggressive northern accent.

'I think he'll manage on his own,' he said.

'I thought I'd better tell him.'

'He'll know where to find you. In any case he only brought you for support, isn't that right?'

'How d'you mean?'

'Why does a man take his sister to the Prof's party? It's one step below bringing your wife. Have you heard Sinatra's "Chicago"?'

I moved towards the door with him. 'In Chicago a man danced with his wife,' I said.

He laughed.

'Is that why *you* haven't brought your wife?' I asked.

'No.' But he was still smiling. 'You're looking tired already,' he told me.

'We've been to a funeral today. My grandfather died at the week-end.'

He let me go before him into the corridor. I waited while he tried to catch the eye of the Professor, but he must have failed. He followed me to the stairs.

'Are you still feeling upset?' he said.

'No. I didn't know him at all. I only went for my parents' sake. We had a terrible lunch after the funeral. That's what really wearied me.'

'You're still living at home?'

'Yes. You sound very interested in my affairs.'

He walked beside me down to the dance floor. The hall was comparatively quiet: a spot dance was being judged. 'Well, I know a little about your brother. I've spoken to him once or twice. Your father's a miner. Mine was a down-and-out. It doesn't matter, does it?'

'No.'

'Then there's no cause for resentment, I suppose.'

He held my elbow and guided me down the side of the

hall; the band began playing again and a group at the far side were cheering. It was a quickstep.

'Shall we dance this one?' he said.

He held me loosely and neither of us danced well. We passed some students in a corner of the room jiving. He held me at arm's length and made one or two erratic, facetious gestures with his body. 'Can you jive?' he asked.

'No.' I shook my head.

He nodded quickly and said, 'Ah, yes,' as if reproving himself. 'Your brother's living with you at home as well, then?'

'He has been. For the past two months or so.' He held me against him as we turned sharply at the corner of the hall. We were jostled back into the circulating stream. 'He's hoping to get a flat.'

'They're difficult, I know.'

Streamers and rolls of toilet paper were suddenly thrown across the hall, and scuffles broke out on the floor as people tried to disengage themselves. A large yellow balloon was bounced about over the heads of the dancers until it burst and there was loud applause. Some people were in fancy dress.

He looked at my face. 'You don't have to dance, you know.'

Another quickstep tune started, and he held my hand. We came off the floor and pushed our way through the crowd of students. He nodded at several, and called out once, 'All right. All right,' in a tone of deep irritation.

A large notice was painted in dripping red over one of the exits: 'This way for nervous wrecks, dyspeptics, paranoics, and lecturers. Professors only: Gents.'

'There's a rest room somewhere here,' he said, not seeing the notice, and finding the right door, pushed it open.

Students sat about in pairs amongst benches. He sat down on a bench, moving along for me, and nodding quickly and awkwardly at another couple, as if disturbed at his own familiarity. It was fairly quiet. There was a small bar in the corner which was just closing down. He got himself some beer, and a glass of draught cider for me.

'I think I'll be going soon,' I told him.

He set the two glasses on a sloping desk, and we held them upright.

'Do you find it a bit much?' he asked. 'All these bloody students.' He smiled, perhaps at his own irritation as well. 'They're only young once,' he said. 'Thank God.'

'Wouldn't you like to be a student all over again?'

'I don't know ... perhaps I would. But I was in London just after the war. It was different then. Most of us were old soldiers. Being a student in the provinces isn't much to being one in London. You can imagine.' He offered me a cigarette. 'Do you smoke?'

'Yes. But I won't now if you don't mind.'

He lit his cigarette. He smelt of tobacco.

Beyond him was a large wall chart illustrating the circulation of the blood. I was thinking of Michael, and I stared at it as if it were a diagram of my brother himself.

'Where do you live?' he said. But I felt he wanted to talk about himself.

'At Upton. It's a housing estate on the outskirts.'

'You've always lived there?'

'Yes.'

'Have you any other brothers?'

'A younger one who's married. He lives at Maudsley. It's near Doncaster.'

'Have you been married?' He asked it leisurely.

'No.'

'And you think about it?'

'Often.'

'But they don't come up to your standard.' He was looking along the bench, with one eye closed.

'Or I don't come up to theirs.'

'It's not very common,' he said, 'to find somebody like you not married.'

'I must have been unlucky.' Perhaps I was staring reproachfully at him. He flushed. 'You sound as though you know a lot about marriage,' I suggested.

'No.'

'Why do you think people get married, in any case?'

'You should know,' he said, 'if you live on a housing estate. So they can get a room to have sexual intercourse in.' He stubbed out his cigarette only half smoked. 'At least, that's the working class half, isn't it?' He was nearly smiling again, and indulgent.

A group of noisy students bursting into the room gave me a shock. 'The bloody bar's closed in here already!' they shouted. He stood up.

'Are you going to see your brother before you go?' he asked. 'I'll see you to the front steps. I'll most likely be going myself soon.'

'I think I'll tell him I'm going.'

We seemed to be chased from the room. We seemed to have been chased from one place to another since we'd met. We went back through the crowded hall, which was now dimly lit by coloured revolving lights. His hair was blue, then green, then red.

'You didn't drink your beer,' I said, as we went up the staircase.

'No. I'm slimming.' He stopped to pull in his chin and exaggerate the two creases of fat; then he unbuttoned his Harris tweed jacket to show me the premature bulging of his stomach. There was this carelessness about him.

He was holding his stomach in this way as we went into the Professor's room. Michael saw us come in, and raised his head. There was now only one group remaining in the room, of seven or eight people, with the Professor, and they were talking heatedly. Michael came away quietly. 'I'm just going,' I told him as he looked at the man behind me. 'I feel worn out.'

'I'll see her to the door,' the art teacher said.

'You're sure you won't stay?' Michael said to me. He was polite.

'No. I've seen enough for one day, I think.'

He smiled and put his hand on one side derisively. 'O.K.,' he said. 'I'll see you at home. Tell my mother I'll most likely be late. And *not* to wait up for me.'

He was already going back to his group before we reached the door, but he was watching us.

He came back down to the hall again. It was garish with its coloured lights and noisier than ever.

'Did you leave your coat in the cloakroom?' he said, and waited while I fetched it. He looked at my hat, quickly, when I reappeared. The hall was almost empty and many of its decorations torn; the clowns were peeling from the walls. It was cold. A porter stood stamping his feet in the archway.

'We might meet again,' he said.

He held out his hand and I shook it. It was slim, and hard. 'Yes, I hope we do.'

We stood a moment, blankly.

'Do you want me to see you home?' he asked.

'No, of course not. I was just wondering why my brother looked so annoyed.'

He came to the archway. The porter said good night.

Then he followed me to the top of the steps and stood in the open portico. 'Good night, then,' he said, as I went down. There was a burst of noise behind him, of shouting and cheering.

I called back, 'Good night. And thank you.'

When I reached the street and glanced back he was still there. He was lighting a cigarette; then he airily waved with it in his hand, and looked up at the dark sky.

I didn't see Michael until the following evening when I got home from work. But he was waiting, delaying getting ready for another end-of-term celebration, arguing with my mother about his white shirts.

'I see you picked yourself a winner,' he said, the moment I'd taken off my hat and coat. He often resorted to a northern accent or colloquialism when he wanted to deride someone for whom he had an affection. My mother was puzzled, but sensed the usual breaking of animosity in the air.

'Don't go on at our Margaret,' she said. '*She's* been working.'

'What did you think to him?' Michael said.

'Who?'

'That Howarth camel ... the indestructible mentor from across the way.' He was unexpectedly bitter.

'Is that his name? Howarth.'

'He didn't tell you? But then that's typical. He goes everywhere on the assumption that he's "known".'

'I was impressed with him. I've seldom met a more interesting person ...' But it sounded so serious that he was the only one to laugh.

'Who was it you met last night?' my mother asked. 'And you want to be quiet,' she warned Michael. 'Your dad's off to work in two hours and he hasn't had much sleep.'

'Nobody,' I told her. 'If I did it'd be somebody objectionable to our Michaelouse.'

He'd never got used to this suffix to his name – a girlish remnant of anger which somehow I'd kept in spite of his and my parents' long distaste. As a boy he reciprocally used to call me Margarine. When he was ten. But I had clung to my habit.

My mother went into the scullery to get my tea. 'You want to be quiet,' she said. 'Your dad's not sleeping well.'

Michael was impatient. 'What did you think to him?' he asked again. 'I'd like to know.' He was polite now. He began to unbutton his shirt, casually, before going up to shave.

'He didn't tell me much about himself, and I was too tired to bother asking.'

'It didn't look like that from the glimpse I had – he was showing off his belly when he came in the Prof's room with you. It's one of the habits he keeps for his closer friends: to ask them to share his concern over his figure.'

He looked at me openly and determinedly, making sure that he had stamped out this Howarth person for good. 'A few people noticed you with him,' he said. 'You want to be careful who you're seen with. After all, I've got a position to keep.'

'Oh shut up!' I flushed strongly, and grasped the table.

He was looking at me with his strained grimace of victory. 'I'm beginning to think you *were* taken in by him,' he said.

'You can think what you damn well like.'

My mother was bringing in my tea. She wearily repeated her entreaty, but awkward and ashamed at seeing me angry. 'There,' she said.

The springs creaked in the double bed as my father rolled over and pushed his feet into his slippers.

'Here comes the bloody martyr,' Michael said. 'Dragged out of his sleep by his greedy, selfish children. Will there ever be an end to their selfish stinking meanness?'

'You might have shown some consideration for him *yesterday*,' my mother said slowly. 'Walking away like that.'

'But I couldn't have sat down there with all those people,' Michael said, as though he'd only been waiting to give his excuse. 'Having a meal after a funeral. It was just a chance for a bloody gossip and nothing else, Mother. Look at my Uncle Jack in the taxi coming back. Christ . . .'

'You know why Jack's like that. He's on his own. You might have given him a chance. But your dad felt it. Jack's his brother, and it *was* their father.'

'Ah well, I'm going out,' Michael said. 'I couldn't have eaten a meal like that.' He went upstairs to shave.

I heard him wait on the landing while my father used the bathroom. When they passed one another they said nothing.

My father came down in his underclothes, into the living-room. I never knew what he meant by coming down like this: whether to humiliate himself or merely to outrage us with his indiscretion.

He sat down with his bare legs to the flames and his veins stood out in blue relief against the whiteness of his skin. He stared at the fire, his eyes screwed up against the heat, and leaning towards it. My mother rearranged the table, going to the trouble of pouring out my tea. She fetched my father's pot and poured him his tea, setting it down by his bare feet. Then she went quietly into the scullery.

'I didn't see you last night,' he said.

'I came in after you'd gone to work.'

'Your Aunt Dorothy was here, and your uncle.'

He didn't touch his tea. Upstairs, Michael began to sing loudly. 'What was all the noise about?' he asked, tired.

'He's going out soon. He doesn't *have* to sing as loud as that, I know.'

He suddenly felt for his pot and brought it slowly to his mouth. He drank slowly, in long gulps as a man needing it, the muscle surging in his short throat. Then he rested the pot down clumsily in the hearth. Its steam curled into the glow-ing fireplace. 'Aye. We mu'n better wait for his lordship to leave afore we can breathe.'

I wanted to smile at his anger, to torture him out of it.

'Where's he going tonight?' he said. 'It's a right fair job he's dropped on yon – gallivanting off every night.'

'It's only the end of term. You don't want to take so much notice.'

'What were you two shouting about, then?'

25

He didn't expect me to tell him. But I did, about Howarth and how Michael had disapproved.

'What's he expect,' he said, 'taking you out to a place like that then dropping you as soon as he's inside the door. That's just like our Michael. I suppose he reckoned you'd come on straight back home.'

'I don't know.'

'What was this chap, any road?' He looked at me with interest now that I'd given in and sympathized. It had been his idea that I should go with Michael.

'I don't know him at all. We danced a bit and talked, then I came on home.'

'Yes. But what does our Michael say about him?'

'He doesn't like him for some reason. I don't know why.'

'You don't want to mind our Michael.' He leaned down for his pot. He drank more quickly, then rubbed his hand round the pot. 'He left the funeral yest'day. Just like that.'

'You ought to know our Michael by now,' I told him. But I was angry that he was so resigned, and had no advice.

My mother came in, now that she thought he was soothed. 'Are you staying down, or are you going back for an hour?' she said.

'How can I go back with that row on?' He seemed oppressed by the ceiling.

'He'll have gone soon,' she said fiercely.

'You've heard how he's been on at our Mag?'

'It's none of our concern, is it, Margaret?' She began clearing the table, and I stood up to help her.

'Oh no,' he said. 'They only own the house.'

But Michael was quiet now. He'd moved to his bedroom at the front of the house, and no doubt was changing into his evening clothes.

When he came down I was in the scullery washing up with my mother. He stood in the hall to avoid arguing while he pulled on his raincoat.

26

My father called out, 'Aren't you taking Margaret to-night?'

'If she doesn't mind talking about dark adaptation or the learning curve of psychotics. I don't mind.'

'Don't start coming with that,' my father warned.

'No. I'm sorry.' He sounded sincere. 'I won't be too late to-night. If you want to come, Margaret, you come.' He waited for me to refuse. He called cheerfully to us all as he went out.

'There goes a real smart spiv,' my father said.

'Well, I've *told* you,' my mother called through to him in the living-room. 'You shouldn't interfere.'

'I don't like seeing him act the king an' all round here.'

'Well don't say I haven't told you.' She was weary with him. She shrugged her shoulders at me. 'It's just like him never to learn his lesson.' She looked at me hopelessly, aware of his distress.

But we could hear my father still talking loudly. 'When I think what I've sacrificed for him and Alec . . . for *him*, any road. And our Margaret.'

My mother dried her hands. She went through to the room. 'I've *told* you, Reg. What's done is done. We've made them like that, and it's not right to keep bringing it up like this. It's not fair.'

But behind her words were her own misgivings, and her own unspoken questions. Where has Michael's knowledge got him as a person; why does he come back to clutter up the home? Why isn't Margaret married? And why are *you* always humiliating yourself in front of them? And why – why am I so resigned, so controlled about it when it tears the life from me?

But her affection prevented her from doing more than goad him on the surface. In her late middle life her resignation was religious, a love-smothering thing. She struggled to look outwards all the time and wanted my father to do the same.

When she'd finished shouting he said nothing.

She came into the scullery and we worked in silence. We sensed him, as if his feelings burnt like a furnace in the next room.

2

I heard the band for several minutes before it flashed in the sunlight at the top of the hill. Then it was a mass of blue and red as it jerked its way down towards me. The crowd thickened and pressed in towards the road. I saw Howarth.

I recognized his fair hair first, then his sun-flushed face, and those slouched shoulders of his tweed jacket. His clothes were a kind of uniform that seemed never to vary.

He moved slowly through the crowd at the side of the road, waiting for the front of the procession, with its famous Labour leader and large brass band, to draw abreast of him. The long column of miners, their huge embroidered banners unfurled between tall, varnished poles, had crept slowly from the assembly point in the cattle market square and, like two similar groups at the other side of town, was converging on the arena at the City Park.

It was windy, and the stocky miners, in their dark, baggy suits, had great difficulty in keeping the huge sails of their pennants upright. I waited for my father's contingent and its decorated lorry, but I'd only time to glimpse my father clutching a rope attached to his district banner before Howarth saw me and blinked his eyes in recognition.

'Are you all right?' I said. His eyes were damp and glistening.

'Oh, hello.' He shrugged, his hands swinging helplessly at his sides. He shook his head in shy despair. 'It's nice to see you again.' He held my hand lightly to shake it. 'I've never seen anything like this.'

I followed his gaze as he turned towards the coloured floats, packed with fat, grinning wives and children, waving and shouting at everything around them. I was aware of them through his eyes: their amusement and their rude gestures, the miners swaying about the road as they clung to the poles and ropes. I wanted to spoil his spectator's feeling.

But when my father came opposite, clutching the guy line of his crimson and yellow banner, a pleased smile of indulgence on his face, I couldn't help catching Howarth's arm and pointing. 'There's my father!' I shouted.

He nodded stiffly, impulsively. He began to walk abreast of the procession. 'I'm half choked with all this.' He held on to my elbow tightly and guided me through the thickening crowd. He seemed to accept it: that the crowd had united us.

We could follow the trail of the banners now as they turned into the main park gates and became separated amongst the spring foliage and branches. 'All these bloody bands and banners,' he said, laughing at the simplicity of his feelings. 'Have you ever seen so many crude emblems before?' He was tense, excited not only by the scene but by his own scepticism of it.

Inside the park the crowds were so thick, spectators caught up with demonstrators, lorries wandering loose like huge beasts amongst the banners and the flags, that we were carried along helplessly. Ahead, from the direction of the arena, loudspeakers were urging some discipline on the gathering, occasionally interrupted by manic cries as someone encouraged the already assembled crowd to sing.

The noise grated harshly through the trees like a mechanical insect. 'A ... a ... ar ... arbide with me ... ee ...' Howarth pushed me forward more urgently as we neared the arena. 'Look at them,' he said. 'Just look at them all.' It was a boyish wonder, as if, somehow, it might all be found trivial.

Some brass bands had come to a standstill and were depositing their instruments in neat piles under the trees; one band stood in isolation up a deserted footpath, blowing and thumping independently for its own amusement. Others had collapsed on to the grass mound at the side of the path and were drinking beer from bottles which were being unloaded from a lorry. Groups of men were scuttling everywhere with crates of beer. The marquees floated on the black sea of the mass, flapping and swaying in the wind as the banners were slowly lowered around them and disassembled with great shouts, and carefully rolled up. It seemed that the trees swayed and the canvas billowed not with the wind but with the strain of the throbbing agitation below, the flanks of the marquees expanding and contracting like giant animals terrified of their surroundings.

'Whoever's going to control all this?' Howarth shouted behind me. He forced me through a gap, and along with a disintegrating band we overflowed on to the grass. I straightened my coat and took off my hat.

Howarth looked at the hat smilingly. He said something, but it was lost in the crowd. When I bent towards him he said, 'I wonder what makes you wear a hat?' He had no thought for his familiarity.

We began to climb the grass slope overlooking the arena. But by now we were aware of one another.

He was panting in a stifled, flushed way, hiding his fatigue. 'It's just about dry enough here,' he said. We'd climbed almost to the top and found a space. He knelt on one knee and felt the grass with his palm. 'It's all right,' he said, and looked up at me, full of a sudden curiosity. A man just below us was playing softly on a trumpet.

The three columns had coiled and interlocked in the arena. The tails of the procession, interrupted every hundred yards or so by still more brass bands and coloured floats, were dragging themselves through the gates and disgorging their members in every direction. The hillside below us began to fill up as the arena, now black and scarcely moving, was packed to its short terrace boundaries.

On a stage like a boxing ring several ant figures were struggling from the arms of the crowd, brushing down their coats, and dropping on to the wooden chairs and benches. Someone had handed up a bottle of ale, and the Labour leader was ostentatiously applying it to his lips, whether it was full or not, and getting a cheer for his matey gesture. He made one or two comments into the microphone which raised a burst of laughter and a fractured applause from those round the platform; then he sat down. He vigorously dusted the turn-ups of his trousers.

'I seem to be always finding you with a crowd,' I said. Howarth leaned back on his elbow, and screwed his eyes up in the sun. But he was not relaxed: his whole body was tense and alive. 'But it's not often you can see a thing like this,' I told him without thinking, hating to express my feelings to him. He was impatient, wanting to find his own reaction and convince himself about it.

'All these people,' he said. He watched them with a certain helplessness, as if they had a great deal to do with him. He turned to look at me. 'I've seen you about town,' he said.

'Why didn't you say hello?' I asked him.

'I don't know.'

'I've seen *you* once or twice. But you were striding along so fast I thought it best not to interfere.'

'Interfere?' The loudspeakers were beginning to crackle with the first speech and he turned to stare down at the arena. 'There're so many of them,' he said.

'You don't like people coming near you?'

He waited, then said, 'I like them to keep their distance, if that's what you mean.'

'Then you're like me,' I told him, almost vehemently.

'Am I?' He smiled to himself. He was stroking the short

grass with the palm of his hand. 'Yet I don't mean physically. You don't like to be touched. Aren't I right? I noticed down there when I got hold of your arm. You went rigid.'

We both looked at the crowd below. It was quiet, like a dying fire. The voice over the loudspeakers was sharp and strong but from this distance unintelligible.

'It's the *emotional* kind of touching I draw away from,' he said.

'How do you mean?'

'People who drop a little bit of feeling here, a little bit there. Who can never *commit* themselves.'

'There aren't many of those.'

'Aren't there? Then I must meet them all.'

'You never told me your name when I met you,' I said.

'Didn't I?' He looked genuinely surprised.

'Was it because you didn't think it was worth while?'

'No, of course not. I don't know why I didn't. Why didn't you ask?'

'I thought you might have had some reason. Some people are like that.' I wanted to laugh at him, but he ignored it. 'My brother told me in any case. But he didn't tell me your Christian name.'

'It's Gordon. I don't like it – I used to be called "Oh Gord!" at school.'

'Was that because you were stuck-up?'

'No.' He watched me smiling at him. 'Perhaps they thought I was an idealist. Pretentious, therefore.'

'I don't like calling people by their real names if they mean something to me. It makes them sound as if they could easily be somebody else. Do you know what I mean? Somebody strange, that you don't know.'

'Yes.' He nodded. 'What did your brother have to say about me?' he asked a moment later.

'I don't think he likes art, or artists.'

'I can understand that. But I'm no artist.'

33

'He probably counts you as one.'

'Well.' He sighed. 'That *is* a mistake. And I quite liked your brother. He's made a good impression at the university, you know. What does your father think about it all?'

'Him and Michael – they just haven't learned how to get in touch with one another yet. Not since Michael and I went to the grammar school.'

'You went to a grammar school?'

'Edward the Fourth. Then a secretarial college in the evenings.'

'I can see your brother making short work of your father: he's a kind of intellectual gangster.'

'That sounds terrible. It's not like that at all.'

'It's a habit of his class. Your brother always shows he's working class. He has a habit of taking advantage of the disinterested nature of his work to make *personal* claims for it – and other things. It's a workman's habit.'

'You sound as though you don't like him one bit.'

'Oh, but I do. I like him a lot. But don't tell him that.' He laughed, elated. He pulled himself up into a sitting position.

'I think you're very strange,' I told him.

'Yes.' But he didn't smile.

'You sound shut in. Your opinions and things ... as if they're *your* opinions only.'

'How else should I have them?'

'You could have shared opinions, like other people's.'

'Do you really mean that?' He looked at me closely, leaning over his knees, his face turned sideways to me.

'What should I have said, then?'

'I think you're trying to suggest you find me lonely.' I hadn't thought of it, but I said, 'I think you are.'

He turned his head at an exceptionally loud burst of applause; the movement was thoughtless, impulsive like an animal's. 'That sort of thing is bound to spoil them,' he said.

'*Are* you married?'

'No.'

'Why not?'

His eyes lit up with amusement, and he said nothing, looking slowly at me.

'Do your moods usually change so quickly?' I said.

There was something strange about him, as if he might be afraid that he was laughing at me, or at himself. 'It's a middle-age affliction,' he said.

'What sort of people *do* you go about with? Are they from the university?'

'Not as a rule.' He was undecided how much he would tell me. 'I'll introduce you to one or two if you're so interested,' he said.

'Do you like teaching art?'

'I teach Industrial Design. But then, if I really told you what that meant you'd have no respect left for me at all.'

'Why don't you like art?'

'I do. But I don't like all these questions. In any case, I shall have to be going.'

'Why?' I tried not to be offended by his clumsiness. I could only smile and shake my head. 'As soon as we start talking one of us has to go.'

He looked at his wrist watch. 'I *shall* have to go,' he said. 'I was on my way somewhere when I met you.'

'And now I've frightened you off.'

'I'm being damned rude, I know,' he said, offended. He waited for me to accept his half-apologetic stare.

'It's all right,' I told him.

He stood up, and looked down at me, pale now, but uncertain. Beyond him the crowd were cheering at the end of the first speech. 'I'll see you, then,' he said.

For a while I sat and watched the arena. He set off down the hill, then turned to wave quickly, and was soon swallowed up in the crowd. Something had suddenly drained all his interest. It seemed as though he'd been driven away.

It was hopeless even to think of finding my father. Now I didn't want him to know that I'd seen him. I turned away and climbed over the brow of the hill to the opposite exit from the park. A tremendous burst of applause echoed through the trees. Some birds were flung up, cawing, into the air.

'I thought this was a bit much,' Michael said. 'I found it in my rack at the department.' He'd interrupted his evening's conversation with my mother to look suddenly at me. The university had found him a small flat in town, and he visited home now once a week. He put his hand into the inside pocket of his suit and brought out a white envelope. In spite of his resentment it was still clean and smooth.

'Why, who's it from?' my mother said, watching me open it and pull out a slip of bright yellow paper. The handwriting was large, black and mechanical.

'It's from that character she met at Christmas,' he said. My mother couldn't remember. She frowned with curiosity. 'That dance I took her to.'

Her interest turned to me as I looked up from reading the letter. She followed my eyes anxiously.

'I was silly to bring it,' Michael said.

'Why did you, then?'

'I should have given it back to him.'

'He wants to meet me. Is that so very bad?'

'I don't want to talk about it,' he said.

But my mother interrupted him. 'I'd like to know,' she said quietly. 'Is there anything the matter with our Margaret seeing this man?'

'I don't mind who she sees,' he said. 'I resent acting as a post-box and messenger, that's all.'

'He's a lecturer,' she suggested heavily, paining herself with such open curiosity.

'He teaches in the Art College and he comes over to our

common room occasionally. Though he's no right there at all. He's made a habit of it, and he's got one or two friends there.'

'And you don't want to help Margaret, then?' she said. Her calmness irritated Michael. 'She's got few enough friends as it is.'

'All right then – I don't like the man. But that's all there is to it.'

'Is he a clean man, Margaret?' she asked, stressing the adjective which she used to inquire about all my men friends. But she added quickly, 'I mean – is he decent?'

'I hardly know him. But he's as decent as anyone else I know.'

'How old is he?'

'I don't know. In his middle thirties, I suppose.' I tried to control my impatience with her, but she was affected by Michael's attitude, and also by the letter's unusual delivery.

'It seems, you know, very personal, sending a message to you like that,' she suggested.

'I don't think it's very good either,' I told her.

'And he's not ever been married,' she stated clumsily.

'You don't have to be like this, Mother. He's not married and I hardly know him.'

'Did he tell you that?' Michael said. He looked at me slowly.

'Yes.' I stared demandingly at him.

'All right,' he said, raising his hands in apology.

I couldn't identify his tone. When he went, my mother, as always, saw him to the front door, and stood waving into the darkness until the sound of his footsteps had faded. When she came back in she sat knitting and didn't talk.

I saw him some time before he saw me. He was going into a phone booth the other side of the island in Albert Square. I crossed over and sat on one of the seats beneath the two royal statues. The little crescent-shaped garden between the statues was full of tulips, colourless in the early street lights, arranged symmetrically around a dry fountain.

Howarth had propped his head on his hand, his body leaning across the narrow width of the box, and he was speaking slowly and patiently into the phone, as if tediously explaining something. He listened for long stretches, then gave several brief replies, nodding vigorously, in assurance. He put the phone down and rubbed his face, and came out.

Although I was only ten yards away, he was so intent on searching the pavements that he didn't catch sight of me. He seemed to look through me. He stepped one way, then another, as the circulating traffic interrupted his view. I was frightened he would not see me.

When he eventually recognized me I walked stiffly towards him, aware of some sort of deceit.

'You got my letter, then. I hope you didn't mind too much.'

'No.'

'I couldn't think of any other way, not knowing your address. I tried to catch your brother but he wasn't in the building.' He was looking at me with the same offended stare as when he'd left me at the Miners' Gala.

'I've come, haven't I?'

'That's the main thing,' he said.

We walked across the square – the main square of the city. He held his hand against my back as we crossed the roads.

Prince Regent Road was empty. 'This is where I used to make some friends,' he said as though he wanted to provoke me. He pointed to the Victorian mansion of Youth House up the road, opposite the Education Offices. 'I haven't been here for some time, as I told you in the letter. So it all might be a bit rusty.' The road was off the bus route, and in the evening it was very quiet and empty, the wooden blocks of its surface streaked with oil and grease from the daytime parking.

The rivet-studded door was open and Howarth led the way up a short flight of stone steps to the small assembly hall.

Seven or eight people stood about. A slim man with a crew cut and a clerical collar was pushing tubular steel chairs into a rough circle below the stage at the far end of the room. They all looked up as we entered, and nodded briefly. But apart from the clergyman they carried on talking.

The young parson stared at Howarth and myself with a curious open frankness, not in the least ashamed. Then suddenly aware of his own interest he broke into a pleasant smile and said, 'Hello, Howarth. You're a stranger these days. We're just waiting for Ben.'

Howarth nodded. He didn't reply. It was as if he wanted me to notice the distance he kept between himself and these people. Aware of this as an intrusion, the group of talkers glanced up occasionally to the corner of the room where Howarth had taken me to sit. He leaned forward, his elbows on his knees, looking up to smile at me. He made them uneasy.

They each had at least one book. The young clergyman went round the circle of chairs, straightening them unnecessarily, examining one or two as if they were in doubtful repair, standing up to push his hand through his short wiry hair as if the sensation both delighted and bewildered him. When he glanced at me it was with the same unaffected curiosity, as if he felt a sincere right to know why I was there. Howarth was relaxed by it.

'Did you used to come here often?' I said.

'Fairly often. There used to be more people here then ...' He almost stood up, but instead leaned back in his chair as a tall, heavily-built man with a bright pink face and thick blond hair strode into the room. A large off-white macintosh flapped about his muscular body.

His arrival caused the group to split up. He shook someone's hand: several people took their places in the neat circle of chairs.

As if the arrival of the leader were enough to dispel his own shyness, the young clergyman came across to us. 'Aren't you coming to sit over here with us?' he asked. 'My name's Johnnie Fawcett.' He held out his hand to me. Howarth introduced me as Margaret as we shook hands.

'Oh, yes,' Fawcett said, as though it were something he'd expected.

We followed him across the room and Howarth whispered clumsily in my ear, 'He takes all this seriously, so don't offend him. . . .'

Fawcett had reddened. He sat stiffly in his chair on the other side of Howarth.

It was the meeting of a literary group that I remembered having seen advertised just outside the bus station. I already sensed Howarth's motive in bringing me here, and Ben, as if sensing the same, was staring at Howarth with a look of resentment. His macintosh, thrown over a chair, spoke of a rural leisure, a military tradition, a squirearchy in fact, rather than the council house, his mother's stall on the market, and his father's shunting engine, which were, Howarth afterwards insisted, the actual background from which he'd come. I, too, resented Howarth for bringing me here. It was as if he wanted to ridicule me as one of them.

Howarth's loneliness had this degree of destructiveness in it. I felt anxious about how deep it went. He had turned it on this group of conscience-stricken artisans unnecessarily, wanting me to applaud. He was careless with it, and small.

I ignored him. I listened intently to the poems that were being read and discussed, the work of a famous writer of the Midlands. I shared a copy with a small, large-eyed woman, whose nicotined forefinger traced the lines as they were being read. She grunted agreements. Her eyes were strained and bulbous with effort.

Yet Howarth was not prepared to allow me to escape.

He shared Fawcett's book. He listened patiently as Fawcett himself read out one of the poems with a moving intonation and intensity. It was like a prayer. His voice was full of redness and flowering, the subject of the poem. Then a middle-aged man was reading a poem about a woman's breasts and the pleasure of sleeping between them, when Howarth, as if to deride the earnestness with which they accepted this as a type of repose befitting the intelligent, laughed.

The reader looked up. He was hesitant: he'd been reading in a dull monotonous voice. They all looked at Howarth. There was some sort of snobbery involved. He told them briefly of a reference that this poet had made to sleeping with his mother. I watched the page. The woman's finger had slurred the lines. One or two people laughed.

Then a young black-haired man, thick-set like Ben himself, read several of his own poems. They discussed them. They were about factory chimneys and slag heaps and collieries.

When we came out it was into one of the nights that had been described in the last poems: the darkening buildings, the bulging shape of the city and its bastion housing estates, outlining every hill and curve for miles around with a battlemented crescent.

Ben and John Fawcett came together in the street and joined Howarth. They apologized for the brevity of the meeting and wondered why he'd come. Ben had his macintosh over his arm, and looked at me brazenly.

'In the summer we tend to keep it short,' Fawcett said. We walked down to the end of the street and Ben invited us into the snack bar at the corner. He held the door very wide as I walked in.

We sat at a table away from four other members of the group, but one of them came over, the dark, thick-set man, and he grinned at Howarth. He nodded at Ben's face and said to Howarth, 'How can I criticize a world that doesn't put in an appearance? Isn't that just it?'

'Get lost,' Ben said. They laughed together.

Over the street the sky still held a haze of colour, the sun faintly illuminating the topmost clouds, and giving the street lamps an emptier, vaguer look. The atmosphere was filled with a damp luminosity.

The clergyman, Fawcett, was smiling consolingly at me, drawing himself apart from the others to catch my attention. He had ordered the coffee, and was holding out a cup to me, sweating slightly, and looking cruelly incongruous beneath the half-nude women painted on the walls.

I stared round at the water dripping from the windows, at the people eating and drinking, the gritty coffee, the thin soup, fascinated and consoled by the peculiar destitution that Howarth had crudely brought to my notice. The Miners' Gala had saddened him. But this he hated. In the middle of the clergyman saying something I stood up and said I must go.

Howarth followed me willingly. He felt now that he'd betrayed my confidence and interest.

But he was still displeased that Ben hadn't put on some characteristic show. The first thing he said when I joined the bus queue to go home was, 'Ben – he's a sort of industrial Don Quixote, don't you think? It took me some time to realize – seven whole weeks in fact. I used to go there regularly. Physically he's the Sancho Panza of his intentions. Perhaps that disguised it.'

'I only wish you hadn't taken me there.'

He didn't answer for a while. He waited patiently beside me in the queue, then lit me a cigarette.

'I wanted to correct any impression your brother might have given you,' he said eventually.

'I don't see.'

'All that stuff tonight – it blows back on me. It's exactly

the sort of bathetic farcing – and the same at the Art School – that makes my position look small.'

'I don't see how it does at all.'

'No. But your brother and people like him think so.'

'It only makes you look small when you go there and when you laughed like you did. You don't have to do that.'

We stood in silence until the bus came, and when the queue started to move up he said, 'Ah well, I don't suppose it'll stop me seeing you again.' He watched me while I took my seat. We gazed bitterly at one another through the glass.

'You don't really mean that,' Michael said. He looked at Alec intently, accusingly. My mother and father were silent at his sudden outburst. Alec's wife, Nora, glanced up from feeding their youngest child, who was strapped with a scarf on to a chair. Alec stopped eating.

His small, stocky body, not unlike my father's, was set stiffly in his seat. He leaned on the table. ''Course I do,' he said.

'You can't,' Michael said. 'It'll be the end of everything for you.'

Alec's eldest son, Norman, stared up at his father with alert, adult eyes. He was four.

'A father who sacrifices everything for his children does them a disservice: that's even a proverb, Alec. I'm not just making this up.'

But Alec was unimpressed by Michael. 'When you get some kids of your own you'll see different,' he said. He smiled and didn't care. He knew his thoughtless, instinctive view of life crazed Michael.

My mother stood up. She went to help Nora feed the baby. For a moment the two women's voices chatted amiably, condemning any interference in their essential task. Alec's broad, easy back hid them.

'When you've endured your own domesticity a bit longer,'

Michael said, 'you might begin to think you *have* lost something.'

'I wasn't making it that personal,' Alec said. 'But I don't mind. Look at my dad. He seems to have managed all right. Where would you be, or me, if he hadn't put us first?'

Michael was pained. He looked at me.

'Nay, don't bring me into it,' my father said, content until now since he was no longer drawn by family abuse. 'I've done what I thought right, and I don't want ought mentioned on it.' He made to stand up, but sat down again at the tea table, and drained his pot. His foot tapped under the table.

Alec was quiet. His eyes were fixed on Michael. 'What do you think, Margaret?' he said. 'What's he driving at?'

My mother, bending over the baby, Leslie, was looking up at me. She said, 'Aren't you off out this evening, Margaret?'

'No. I haven't planned anything.'

'Well don't you be drawn into arguing with them.' She was afraid. She hated seeing me like this, with Nora and her children and her deadening motherly concern.

Nora hadn't noticed the threat of my brothers. She went on feeding the baby from a little saucer, blind to us. It had roused Michael. And Alec enjoyed antagonizing Michael.

'We mu'nt get personal,' my father said, preparing to sacrifice himself to Michael's agitation yet wanting a peaceful Sunday tea and family formalities.

'No, no,' Michael said. 'But our Alec ought to see what he's letting himself in for. A man should be a man not a father. "Working for your children",' he quoted Alec. 'You want to give that idea up right away.'

'But listen at him,' Alec said. 'You'll be saying next my dad's been wasting his time educating us, giving us a start. He could have shoved us down the pit at sixteen.'

'He nearly did.'

'Well you've a lot to thank God for that he didn't.'

'That's what he wants you to think, anyway,' Michael

said. 'But I can still be as miserable and as unhappy now as I could have been if I'd left school at fourteen.'

'Like I did,' Alec said. He hated Michael now.

'You're like my dad,' Michael said. 'You think education's a substitute for people, that it makes them different and better.'

'And doesn't it?' Alec threatened him.

'No. It's the big fallacy of our time.'

'It's not nice hearing you speak like that, Michael,' my mother said. 'It's not right after all that your dad's done.'

'Let them get on with it,' my father said, standing up and going to sit in an easy chair, away from the table. 'Let 'em carry on, Mother. It's nothing to do with us. Our Michael only says these things to be different.' His right foot tapped soundlessly on the hearth-rug.

'So my dad could have been living it up all these years,' Alec said. 'You must think him a bit of a flop or something.'

'No ...' Michael said in a hollow, nearly frightened voice.

'You shouldn't be speaking about your dad like this,' my mother pleaded. She stood by the table, watching us.

'It's our Michael,' Alec said. 'He talks about my dad as if he didn't owe him a thing.'

'That's just it,' Michael said. 'I feel I do owe him something. He's *made* us feel that. He needn't have given us an education ... and you don't want to laugh, Alec. Because you're going to do exactly the same thing with your family. It's because, fundamentally, my dad felt it was a guilty thing to have children. And you do as well.'

'Oh, now.' Alec was laughing. He'd no doubt that Michael was jealous of his family. 'You're forgetting,' he said to Michael, 'you're forgetting the most important thing. A father *feels* he owes something to his children. He breeds them. They're *his*.'

'So you feel guilty about having children,' Michael said.

'I didn't say that . . .' Alec turned to me, but Michael insisted quietly:

'You've got to see, Alec. My dad didn't educate us for *our* sakes. It was very largely to relieve his own anxiety. He's made us feel all along that we owe him something, that it's our *obligation* to accept his so-called sacrifice.'

'What's up with him, our Margaret?' Alec said, as I began collecting the plates to clear away. 'All this family stuff – he's not thinking of getting wed or something, is he?'

Michael was satisfied. His intentness vanished. 'You mustn't bring her into it,' he said. 'She's enough on her plate as it is.'

Alec looked at the plates in my hand. He laughed at the allusion. 'Why, Mag, you're not after a chap?' he said. 'I was beginning to think you were like our Michael here – a frustrated bachelor through and through.'

'You should ask our Michael. He seems to know it all,' I said, and suddenly felt too weak to take the tea things into the scullery.

'You all ought to be helping with the table instead of this silly talk,' my mother said. She came to pick up the cake dishes and carry them through.

'Nay, come on, Mag. Tell us about him,' Alec said, relieved at the shift in conversation, and benevolent.

'I don't know what you're getting so fetched up about,' I told him.

'Me fetched up?' He pointed dismally at his chest. 'But I'm only asking. Why, if you'd rather not say . . .'

'She's got tangled up with a right load of trouble,' Michael said in a broad accent. 'Only she won't take my word for it.'

'Who bloody would?' Alec said. 'What sort of chap is he, Margaret? Has he got dark hair like me?'

'He doesn't exist,' I said.

Alec sensed the family's coldness. 'What's it all about?' he asked. He put his arm casually round his small son's shoulders.

My mother came back into the room and started piling the cups and saucers. 'We want to get this cleared,' she said. 'Then we can sit round the fire.' When she saw me hesitating, she said, 'Come on! I don't want to do it all on my own.' Her anger started the baby crying. I got my pile of plates and carried them into the scullery.

'Take no notice of our Michael,' my mother said firmly, once we were behind the door. 'D'you hear, love? Take no notice at all. He's just like that at times.' She reluctantly allowed me back into the room.

'She's got caught up with an artist of all people,' Michael was saying.

I piled the remaining dishes, and folded the cloth up. 'You want to leave well alone what you don't know about,' I told him.

'Oh, then he does exist, this fatal charmer,' Alec said.

'That's what he reckons to be himself,' Michael said, still looking at me. 'But then that's only half the problem.'

Alec looked at me demandingly. My mother came back in. 'I've told you, Margaret,' she said.

Michael watched her. 'What's that? What have you been telling her?'

'I've told her not to listen to any of your nonsense.'

'You shouldn't try and protect her like that,' he told her. 'It's not fair to her.'

'Not fair! And I suppose your sly digs at her *are*. You can just shut up about it. Both of you.' Worn out, she glared at them, despairing of her sons.

I took the crockery and the cloth into the scullery. I went into the back yard to shake the cloth. It was sunny. Starlings flew up off the lawn in a cloud. The garden was covered in weeds; though at one time it had been well-kept. But my father had got tired, and the garden itself seemed to have sunk with him.

When I went in I heard Michael still talking in the living-room. 'You've done that all along,' he said. 'She's not sensitive or anything.'

'I don't mind you talking or arguing about anything, but that.'

'What's that?'

'Her men.'

'She hasn't got any men,' Michael said.

'And that's all thanks to you.'

'To me!'

She lowered her voice so that I shouldn't hear. 'You take to pieces any man she goes with. Well, leave her alone with this one.' Her voice was guttural.

'But this is crazy!' I heard Michael crash his fist on the table.

'Ay, now,' my father shouted. 'You don't go talking to your mother like that.' The baby's crying became insistent, and Nora's sing-song murmur of easing it. A moment later she brought the baby out, and glanced at me quickly, half-afraid, before she hurried upstairs. I went quietly into the hall, behind the room door, and lifted my coat off the peg.

'You don't understand it, at all,' Michael was saying. 'This bloody chap's married!'

3

Even before we reached the top of the rise we could feel the coolness of the Ponds seeping into the woods, and could hear the cries of children. The path swung round the stone ruins of Lindley Mill, and climbing to the top of the bank we looked down on the three steps of the pools, the lowest one hidden by close foliage.

We walked round the upper pool, past several families. In the middle a flat-bottomed boat shimmered in the heat, and two men crouched in it like rocks, their fishing rods motionless, the surface unruffled, smooth as ice. At the far side a group of boys were swimming. Their voices echoed in the hollow of the pools, but their splashing was remote and distant in the hot stillness.

We followed the path down to the second of the Ponds. It was deserted except for one family; the children were trailing nets through the shallow water and paddling amongst the reeds.

'We'll go right to the end,' Howarth said. 'You never know, we might get the place to ourselves.'

'I like seeing people here,' I said.

'Yes. But just for this once – I'd like to get away.'

He climbed down the third bank to the smallest of the pools. A rotted boat rested on the pebbly shore, and a small boy looked up in surprise from the shadow of the hull. He watched us until we'd reached the water's edge, then kicked the rotted timber savagely. Climbing hurriedly up the bank, he disappeared.

'We've disturbed a flea,' Howarth said, laughing at me. He pushed his way along an overgrown path leading round the opposite side. Here he discovered a grassy shelf by the water, and taking his coat off, lay down with a long sigh of relief.

The light was glaringly reflected from the surface of the water, and hid the other bank. 'We've found our little bolt hole at last,' he said. His eyes were closed; his mouth was open in a snarl at the warmth and the penetrating light.

He lay there a while on his back, but moved restlessly. 'Why don't you take your stockings off?' Rolling on to his side, he pushed himself slowly into a sitting position, and un-buttoned his shirt; then pulled it over his head and folded it into a pillow. His body was white.

He lay down on his stomach. 'You want to get brown while you've the chance,' he said. 'We don't often get a sun like this.' He spoke with his eyes closed, his jaw moving against the ground. 'It's the moisture in the air like today that makes it so browning.'

I felt through my dress and slid my stockings down. I put them in my handbag. The grass was short and fine, and fresh on my legs. I went to the side of the pool and sat down, my feet and ankles in the water. The whole pool was warm and luxurious, then the water was cold to the touch.

When I glanced back Howarth was apparently asleep. My eyes ached with the glare from the water. The hawthorn around the side of the pool was peculiarly lifeless too, the small leaves shrivelled in shape, still and absorbent. The whole place hung limp and silent.

He was completely still, dead, his breathing imperceptible. There were three large scars on his back.

I stood up in the water and accustomed myself to the cold-ness in sharp breaths. The bottom of the pool was very soft, so soft I could hardly feel it. I felt the mat of weeds sliding up between my toes, and the soft mud was just like air.

He lay stiffly. The marks on his back had reddened, and stood out, stark, against the dead whiteness of his skin. It gave his back a strange expression of its own, as if that too had emotions, of which he was unaware. Beneath the surface of the water shoals of tiny minnows weaved, like interminable threads, like flaws in glass.

I sat down on the bank and rinsed my feet, then walked over the warm grass to where he was lying. His eyes were closed. A breeze had lifted the haze, and across the pool the boy had returned to the rotten hulk, and was playing in it alone. I could hear the drone of his voice as he talked to himself.

I felt Howarth move. He was staring up at me. He didn't say anything.

'What are those marks on your back?' I asked.

He seemed to have forgotten. He moved his body, then turned on his side. 'They're shrapnel wounds.'

'You were in the war?'

He sat up. 'Yes.'

I wanted intensely to know if he'd suffered.

I could feel the heat of his body. He stroked away the grass that had clung to his chest, and looked at my legs and feet.

'You've had a paddle then.'

'It's cold. And the water smells.'

'I used to come here when I was a boy. Sometimes we went swimming. God knows how long ago that was.'

'Did you live near here?'

'Four miles away, about. We used to walk here, by the fields. It took us all day, there and back. I remember carrying a frog all the way back home in my hand, spitting on it to keep it alive.'

He looked at me restlessly, as if suddenly wearied. Then he felt for his shirt. 'I think we'll go on,' he said.

Shaking out his shirt, he stood up. 'We'll have to be going back soon, for the train. What do you think?'

He looked closely at me, then wiped his hand across his face.

'Yes,' I said.

I waited for him, and he walked close behind me, almost beside me, ducking his head to avoid the twigs.

The path rose up from the Ponds and wound between small steep hills. They gave way to low mounds of grey-blue slag, partly overgrown with silver birch and thin grass. In a large hollow beside the track were four concrete posts round a wooden platform raised on bricks. 'This is where the pit used to be, before the war,' he said.

He climbed up on to the wooden platform, like a stage. 'Listen!' He stamped his foot.

A muffled echo boomed inside the platform; and boomed again as his foot beat on it.

'It's the old shaft.' He pulled me up beside him, and then knelt down. There was a crack between the timbers and he searched round for a small stone. He pushed it through the hole, pressing it in with his finger, and we listened to the silence. Then came a faint splash echoing up.

'That's the other shaft there,' he said, and pointed to a large, overgrown hole in the bank of the hollow. 'It's the diagonal shaft. It goes right down, under the Ponds. That's why it's abandoned – it's all flooded.'

We stood at the lip of the open shaft and looked down into the blackness. There was just the steady drip of water from the crumbling brickwork.

Suddenly he cried out and held his hand up for me to listen. His voice boomed and reverberated, then was muffled as if by clay. He shouted again into the hole, and sent cry after cry thundering into one another. They crashed and boomed and seemed real. Then he made me shout into it.

We listened to our cries going down and down, returning, then disappearing, looking at one another as they fought in the hole.

He searched round for a stick. 'I'm going to have a look,' he said. 'Do you want to come?'

'No, don't go.'

'I won't be long. It's quite safe. Are you sure you won't come? Just a bit of the way.'

'No . . . and don't go.'

'Oh, it's all right.' He tried to reassure me, and waved his stick at me.

He walked slowly into the huge burrow, feeling the slope with his stick, and leaning back with one arm to keep his balance on the clay. He went down a few yards, then vanished in the blackness. I could hear his scuffling and the scraping of his stick. Then he called up with a deep booming voice that he could still see me.

I climbed up to the fencing at the top of the hollow. Beyond it was a railway cutting with a single track, half wild; a faint haze of greenery showed through the fine ash of the track itself and the rails were brown with rust and wear. A thin band of bright steel ran down the centre of each rail.

Occasionally I could hear fragments of the rotted brickwork fall and roll echoingly down the floor of the shaft. It was liquid. It was as if the inside of the shaft had absorbed him, and it made no sound except the deep liquid gurgling of the crumbled bricks.

He seemed gone a long time. I went back into the hollow and stood outside the mouth of the shaft. There was just the darkness; I couldn't hear the noise of his feet or his stick; but the liquid gurgled, as if deep down it was boiling.

I sat and waited. The rain had worn the slag mounds into steps and rifts and along the edge of each step clumps of grey wiry grass were growing, drooping down with their own weight. It overhung the mouth of the shaft and had set itself in the mortar between the bricks. In the shaft I could hear something tumbling and falling.

He came out quietly, unexpectedly. His eyes were shining and blinded. He blinked them, smiling strongly in the fierce light. His shoes were covered with thick, black mud. 'You can't get down far,' he said. 'The thing levels off, then it's all water. Look at this.'

He held out a stone and a piece of wood: they were scaled with grey crustations. He ran his finger over them as he had over the piece of sculpture. When I gave them back to him he went to the mouth of the shaft and threw them in again.

I sat on the fence while he cleaned his shoes. He stared down at the track, as though dazed by the seclusion, by the emptiness and the lack of use. The single line cut cleanly through the untidiness of the wood and the mine, its curve disappearing slowly and neatly round the shoulders of the cutting. It was the uselessness that excited him, like the wet and disintegrating darkness of the mine. He gazed through the fence at the cutting while he bent down scraping his shoes.

Beyond the railway the wood looked thicker and less disturbed. It rose gradually from the cutting and the silver birch gave way to oak and beech. Howarth stared across, his hands grasping the fence. We could still hear cries from the Ponds, and from beyond the woods the occasional guttural roar of a lorry on the road.

Howarth's fascination with the place was real. It meant a great deal to him: the crumbled mine, then the wood growing over it, and the ordered emptiness of the cutting. It was bound up with his restlessness.

'We'll go over there next time,' he said, and nodded across the cutting. I turned back down into the hollow.

The heat was going out of the afternoon. The sun was low and bronzed the silver birches. Howarth was tired, suddenly. He didn't speak as we walked down towards the Ponds, then found the path round. The air was heavy with the heat and the musty smell of ferns.

He sat beside me in the train. I felt the shape of his body. Black trees lined the track, and the sky was red, and deepening. We moved in a shallow loop towards town, and could see the smoky ridges, like a huge dark castle, with interminable battlements and turrets. Howarth looked at it silently, his nostrils taut and the skin shadowed round his nose as if he were in pain. He pressed against me as the track straightened and we passed over the junction of the old canal and the river, and drew away from the widening meanders. Across the valley the birch woods were dark and smouldering on the ridge.

'You know one of the reasons why you never went to college,' my mother said. Her ironing filled the living-room; the table was covered with old sheets and the straight-backed chairs were draped with ironed clothes. The fireplace was hidden by the clothes-horse, leaning over on its leather hinges with the weight of clothes, glowing with the fire. She pushed the electric iron searchingly over the sheets, fastidious. The table creaked and groaned. She never expected replies to her spoken thoughts; sometimes she couldn't tolerate being answered. The habit of her daytime solitude in the house overflowed more and more into those moments when she was no longer alone.

'One of the reasons,' she said, 'was our Michael saying it'd be a waste of time and money educating a woman. At least beyond the grammar school. And your dad agreed with him.'

'Why do you start bringing these things up now?' I said loudly, hoping to startle her out of her dreams. 'You know I've never grumbled about my work. I enjoy it in its way.'

'I sometimes reckon it'd been better if you'd gone to college.' She searched mechanically for creases and folds, staring at her ironing. 'At least you might have found yourself, if you know ... and gone into something where you weren't shut in so much.' She hated me in the house when she was working.

She disliked having two women contending for the housework. At times she was unwillingly malicious, her small round figure emanating an impotent rage, like a child's, in her own household. She would be ill with it; with the dilemma of having me in the home, and for half a day she would go to bed, pale and shivering with her imagined exhaustion, while I took over the house. She wanted me to, but couldn't release herself; and I would try to preserve her domestic mannerisms about the place so that afterwards she wouldn't dwell moodily on her absence.

One day my father would be saying wearily, after she'd gone to bed, 'Your mother's old. You don't realize. She'll be in her grave afore you'll do ought about it. You want to give her more of a hand about the house.' But the next day she'd be up beating the carpets in the back, shaking rugs, and becoming so busy and intense in her housework that I knew she was wishing violently to banish and exclude me. Like all experienced housewives, she'd learnt how to humiliate or make guilty any one of her family by the direction and intensity of her work. She exhausted herself in order to reproach me. I stayed on at home as if this were the only battle left for me to fight; as if our love were only there to drive us to greater and more outrageous tests of its strength.

She'd tired of her ironing, and sat down in front of the clothes-horse with her arms resting on those of the chair. Her limbs wearied her so much now: whenever she was tired, each one seemed to have an existence of its own. As soon as she lay back in a chair, they splayed themselves out with her weariness of them.

This evening tiredness had dulled her, and she glanced at me with awkward, demanding looks. 'Do you see much of that art teacher?' she asked, vaguely, yet accenting the last two words with Michael's own pointed searching.

'Sometimes once a week.'

'And our Michael says how he's married, and that.'

'You don't *have* to believe everything he says.'

'He seems to know.'

'*You* sound as though you wanted him to be married.'

She looked at me guardedly, with no sympathy and no hardness. 'I wouldn't want you to make a mess of things, Margaret. But it's not my business, I know.'

'Well, there's no need to worry, then.'

'You like him,' she said.

'Yes.'

'If he's an artist and that . . .'

'He's not an artist. You listen to our Michael too much at times. *Everything* he says in this house is God's truth.'

I stood up and folded the sheets on the table and unplugged the iron, then put them away in the cupboard.

She watched me at the table; then she shook her head, wanting to smile. 'You used to be glued to that blessed table every night about now,' she said. 'Scribbling away in that diary. I never could think what you could find to put in it.'

I pushed the table back against the wall and pulled out the carpet. 'Oh, I'm still keeping it.' I couldn't find anything else to do, so I sat down.

She stared vacantly at the red glow on the sheets round the fire. The smell of airing clothes filled the room. 'You write it upstairs, then, i' bed.'

'I'm not like that with it, Mum. I don't write in it every night. Sometimes I don't write anything all week.'

'But what do you put in it, love?'

'Things I've done. And how I feel about things.'

'I see.' She glanced at me sulkily. 'I remember once your Aunt Joan showing me her diary. It'd be no more'n a month after Jack left her. She was still right upset. It was plain to see in everything she did. She had a way of feeling things with the tips of her fingers as she was talking to you. That absent-minded. She always was.'

'Why did they split up?'

'I don't know. Your dad's mother was ever so fond of Joan. She used to call them Jack and Joan – like the rhyme. When Jack took her home, "Jack and Joan flit up the hill, and fetch us a pail of water," she'd say.' She patted the arm of the chair and smoothed her hand over it. 'Anyway ... you can't go carrying other people's worries on your back all the time. And you can never be sure about things like that: husband and wife. It's best not to interfere. It doesn't bear to think about other folk at times.'

'And yet you have to. Or you fade away.'

She swung her gaze round to me. She'd longed for me to be like her. 'You don't have to be that way, Margaret.'

'No, but what's the choice? To live like this, here, or to live like Alec's wife, blooming with health and children ... and as empty as a tin can.'

'Oh, Margaret.' She was shaken. 'Nora's a fine mother. They couldn't have a better mother.'

'But *I* don't want to be a mother.'

'Love ... it's not like you ...' She struggled to find her words.

'It's *just* like me! Why have I stayed like this, like I am? Being a mother – it's just the end of everything. Just to go on like that ... like any dog or cat. It makes *nothing* of me.'

She was afraid of her own anger. Her hands lay flat on the arms of the chair and she didn't look at me. It was too much. 'You're a woman, Margaret,' she said. 'What d'you reckon you're talking about?'

'Of course I'm a woman. I'm a woman, not a mother.'

'Don't you feel.... Don't you *ever* want to have children?'

'Yes. But I'm not so silly as to think that means I *have* to have them. Children ... they just ruin a woman. She becomes just a mother. Just *look* at a mother when her family have grown up and left her – groping about, wondering why she isn't a person any more, how she can fill in the day with nothing to do. Oh, Mum! I'm not trying to hurt you. But being a mother, to me, it all seems so hopeless and useless.'

'Nay, I want to hear what you think,' she said, labouring, rigid in the chair. 'I'd like to know.'

'I've said it. I don't want to say any more.'

She was aching as she sat there. 'I've felt all along, somehow, that you've resented Nora in some way. There've been times ...'

'I haven't. She couldn't be anything else. Most women have to be mothers: there's nothing else in them. She's got her children and she talks and talks. I couldn't ever face that sort of life. It's just nothing. Useless. She's just going on and on, doing nothing.'

'She's bringing up two grand kiddies.'

'What for?'

'Oh, but you're talking such nonsense, love,' she sighed. 'What d'you think I've spent all my life doing in bringing you up? You're a woman. It's what you *are*. It's like saying you don't believe you've two arms and legs. You *are* a mother, even before you have children. Your body's enough to tell you that.'

'I don't have to be a mother.'

'Then you're stunting half your life. You can't be like a man ... not caring.'

'Then I'll have the bit of life, and do without the rest.'

'Margaret.' She shook her head from side to side. 'It's such a great silly thing.'

'I know, I know.'

She pulled herself to her feet, and lifted the sheets off the clothes-horse. She refolded them, turning the insides to the fire, feeling them with her cheek. The leather thongs on the horse creaked and strained as they took her weight a moment. 'You mustn't come to me, then,' she said, 'when you find out how you've cheated yourself.'

4

When he rolled away he lay back and said nothing. The sky was grey and it was drizzling.

There was an awful sound. It was a train in the cutting. The hoarse panting echoed across the rise of the hill, through the trees, mounting up to me in successive waves of nauseous liberation. It shattered the wood with its steady reverberation, gasping and wheezing in its hidden trough. It seemed as if the monster would never reveal itself, but simply menace with its struggle. Then a white plume of smoke rose above the trees, slowly lengthened, boiling gradually in the sky, and filtering away.

Howarth appeared to be asleep. His eyes were closed, and his forehead glistened with the fine rain. A dribble of water escaped from the corner of his mouth, like colourless blood. His smell was in the heavy dampness of the dead undergrowth and leaves around us.

'Are you all right?' he asked, and opened his eyes as if measuring the disappearance of the train in his mind. The noise, after its slow accumulation, was sustained; then it began to drain slowly and we heard the heavy clacking of loaded trucks over the rails. The echoing faded into itself; there was the steely slur of the last wheels on the rails, then that too disappeared and the final exhausted panting of the engine gave way to the faint hiss of the drizzle on leaves. 'Are you all right?' He turned his head towards me.

'Yes.' I sounded irritated, and condemning.

I stared up at the wet leaves and the low scudding

greyness. There was a silence and stillness through the wood, which the strange hissing of the rain only intensified. It was an atmosphere of watching and waiting. The water slid off the drooping, still leaves, and dripped slowly into the ground.

'Aren't you going to speak?' he said.

He waited, then went on, 'You feel independent now. Is that what it's done for you?'

'If I'm like that, why did you bother?'

'You're a sort of prisoner in your body,' he said. 'You don't seem to recognize your own feelings.'

'It must be entirely in your own mind. I only feel wet.'

I stood up and buttoned my coat. The sense of physical strangeness vanished, and my body relaxed. The lining of the coat was damp; the dampness was in my hair and on my face.

Howarth pulled himself wearily and clumsily into a sitting position, uncaring.

'Are you coming?' I asked.

'I'm in no hurry.' He waited a moment, staring round at the foliage, then he slowly stood up.

Globules of rain clung to the fine hairs of his tweed jacket and made it shiny and luminous. He felt the dampness, and took off the coat and shook it violently. A thin spray fell from it. He put it on again and picked up his raincoat from where I'd been lying. Shaking out the creases impassively, he pulled it on.

I led the way towards the cutting, pulling the thin brambles aside, startled by the cold dampness of the ferns and leaves on my bare legs. Howarth trudged sullenly behind, breaking through the undergrowth indifferently. When I reached the side of the cutting and started to climb the fence a man, cycling on the cinders beside the track, looked up in astonishment. Then he turned his head away compulsively, objecting to seeing me in the wood. He was fixed in his task of pedalling. The cycle moved slowly, with a slight rasp of the tyres on the roughness of the ash. He disappeared round the curve of the track, his private momentum unchanged.

Howarth went quickly down the banking, sideways to the slope, dropping on the insides of his feet. The marks of our previous crossing were in the grass, the tufts loosened or pulled from the soil, the long tears of heelmarks.

He waited on the rails while I slowly clambered down. My feet were lost in the immensity of the rails. Climbing ahead again up the opposite side, he stood at the top and watched me hurry the last few yards as the noise of an approaching train intruded into the wood. We stood on the fence and waited nervously.

The black cylinder of the engine nosed round the bend of the cutting, pushing its way into the neat valley on feet of vivid steam. It stalked through the cutting, filling it with a heavy shuddering. The driver didn't see us. He stared intently through the glass flange at the side of the cab, his shiny hat angled to protect his eyes from the drizzle. The train dragged wearily through, embarrassing in its noise, ignorantly excessive. Each wagon had a heavy, wearied dependence as it rolled by, glistening with wet coal, graded in huge chunks or fine dusty mounds. The guard's van hissed by on the steel.

Howarth took my arm, and helped me from the fence and down into the hollow of the colliery site. He suggested we shelter in the mouth of the diagonal shaft, and for a moment we stood there, his arm round my waist, looking out at the dismal weather. But I was soon aware of the blackness behind us. At first there was no sound from the darkness. Then the faint, empty running of water echoed in the shaft, of a stream breaking through the decomposed roof and draining into the flooded depths. 'I'd prefer to walk,' I said.

He peered behind us at the water running down the side of the shaft floor, and the little debris that it took with it;

then he reluctantly led the way out of the hollow on to the path towards the Ponds. 'Do you think it's true?' he said. 'You acted so coldly up there.' But he disliked the complaint in his own voice. 'Do you feel frightened of showing your feelings?'

'I don't give myself as easily as most people, that's all.'

'You don't seem to care about it,' he said.

'I wasn't meaning so much making love. I'm slow to place any emotion – even friendliness.'

'It amounts to the same thing.' Stopping, he tore a twig from a willow clump; shook it like a whip, and began to pull the leaves off. 'It goes deeper, too, when it's like this. There doesn't seem to be any *bodily* response in your nature. It's all closed up inside, and you won't let anyone in.'

'I'm sorry if I seem like that.' But the complacency in my voice made him swish his cleaned stick at the grass and the birches.

'Why did you come this afternoon?' he said.

'I don't think there's any point in asking, is there?'

I myself felt disillusioned by my own slowness and lack of response. I'd never been so astonishingly aware of it before, and yet I was unashamed: I'd taken something from him, and now he rebelled at not being able to take it back. He rubbed his head fiercely. Then he flung his stick away. The waters of the Ponds gleamed feebly through the foliage, until the path curved round the lower pool and we ascended again, towards the mill. The place was deserted, with a week-day emptiness. The rain drizzled emptily on the ruffled surface.

'You must feel that you've come for nothing,' he said. 'It beats me. You must be disappointed.'

'No – I think it's you who's disappointed in yourself.'

'I didn't expect you to be so cold. I can't understand you coming like that. When you knew it was going to be nothing.'

'I've not been cold about it,' I told him.

'Indifferent, then. I wish now that we'd never come.'

He saw that he'd probably hurt me, and looked at me with greater irony. 'What is it, then? What's wrong?' he asked, mystified.

'I'm sorry that you feel like that.'

He thought I might be crying, and put his arm round my shoulders. I winced at his touch, and he pulled his arm away. 'What is it?' he said, angered now. 'You're not the same two minutes running.'

'I don't know. I'm so frightened . . .'

'I can't see why.'

'I don't like showing affection, like that.'

'You don't have to show how you feel ostentatiously. You can show it privately. Up there in the wood – we were alone.'

'It didn't feel like that. It felt . . . communal. Just like an assault, as if none of it mattered.'

'No,' he said sullenly. 'It's not like that. You're wrong.'

'It's degrading somehow – showing strong feeling.'

We reached the summit of the upper pool and started down the sandy track to Four Lanes station. 'We ought to have found a room in town,' he said. 'Yet – it feels better, coming out here. Less deliberate.'

'That's because you're married,' I said with an inexplicably smothered wildness.

He went on walking, and said, 'Yes. That might be a reason.' He had curled up into himself, instantly removed and distant.

'And you told me you weren't,' I said, drained by the speed of his submission.

'You've known all along I was married.' His eyes flared; they were vicious and glistening. 'What do you think this has been about, for God's sake?' He wanted to condemn any distress I might show. 'Everything . . . you're not that blind.'

'You *can't* blame me like that. I've relied on you.'

'Oh no. I can't accept that. You've seen all along, you've

felt it too. You've known all the time I was married. I've been wanting to break up my marriage.'

'And children?' I said.

'And children. And children,' he repeated almost deliriously. We were scarcely moving down the track. Howarth walked very slowly, just taking the edge from his distress. 'You *must* have known. Your brother's told you.' He looked at me to see if it were true. 'Why did you come with me today?'

'I don't know.'

He quietened. He cut the edge of his shoe through the sand. 'It must seem to you that I've dragged you into my private mess, and now I'm trying to make you sound responsible. And you've no idea at all what it means to me.'

'I can guess what it means. I have *some* idea of you.'

He sighed disbelievingly. 'I could cry at the way I've behaved. I never imagined I could be so weak.'

'I don't want you to go on,' I said.

The trees began to thin as the track broadened and joined the tarmac lane leading to the station. A tractor was coming down the lane to the right, its exhaust sticking above the hedge and leaving a film of light blue smoke in the thick air. The driver's head followed it, watching us. He nodded as he came abreast of the track, and Howarth slowed his pace to a bare crawl. We walked between the broad muddy trails of the tractor's wheels, down towards the station. The rain had slackened and the air was warmer, as if the evening were accumulating heat and drying the ground. When we reached the station yard the tractor was standing in front of a trailer loaded with a tarpaulined farm machine, its spindly red limbs protruding awkwardly over the low roof of the booking office. The driver with the aid of the stationmaster was hooking the trailer's shaft on to the tractor. 'Will you give us a hand, cock?' the labourer called to Howarth.

The sudden demand hardened him. He strode across and,

at the labourer's instruction, lifted the trailer's heavy arm as the tractor was backed under it. The stationmaster dropped the link and stood back. The farmhand called out and waved his arm. The tractor stuttered rapidly, emitting a dense blue smoke, and the trailer was slowly hauled across the yard towards the lane. Its soft rubber tyres bulged through the pools, and splayed mud behind in two even paths.

Howarth came to the booking hall and we watched the machine towed out of sight. His eyes were glowing and he rubbed his hands together slowly. 'I'll take the mud off your shoes,' he said, looking down at our feet. We went on to the platform and sat down, away from the entrance. He hunted around for a piece of wood, suddenly absorbed and forgetful of the afternoon. He came back with three or four pieces and I took my left shoe off. He cleaned it methodically, round the sole and heel, wiping out the instep on a metal strut of the seat. He did the same with the other shoe, then took them to the far end of the platform and wiped them on clumps of grass on the railway embankment. He held my legs to put them back on. Then he sat down on the seat beside me to clean his own. He was pleased to do it, to make it unnecessary to speak. No sooner had he finished than he went away to find the time of the train.

I went into the waiting room and shivered in front of the empty stove. It felt colder than outside. I took my coat off, straightened my skirt and blouse, combed my hair, and wiped the back of my calves clean of mud. I was remaking my face when Howarth came back. 'We've only twenty minutes to wait,' he said. 'Are you cold?'

I let him kiss me and rub my back. 'What are you going to do now?' I asked. He looked out of the little dark room at the unprotected platform the other side of the track.

'That's what I've got to decide now, isn't it? But I'm glad it's happened like this.' He sat down and stared at the yellow-brown wall opposite with its picture of the Lake District.

'What do you want me to do?' I said.

He shook his head. Then stared up at me. 'Do you think I've been deceitful?' he asked.

'I've tried not to think about it. It's all like doing the actions to the words of another play.'

He smiled strangely at me. 'I've not been very brave at all,' he decided.

'How many *children* have you?'

'Two.' He was suddenly indifferent now to my knowing. 'It used to be three. The eldest died of diphtheria when it was a year old. She was very fragile. Like glass.' He laughed at the commonplaceness. 'It makes it all sound insuperable, doesn't it? I'm not somebody who can just jump in and out of these things. I suppose you were beginning to think I was.'

'Why have you been wanting to leave your wife?'

'That's only part of it.' His hands fidgeted together. 'I'm past the stage of making new compromises. If I wanted I could stay with her, and everything would go on as usual. It'd be a terrible business, but we both could manage it. We came to a tentative sort of agreement a couple of years ago. But at that time I thought we were doing it for the sake of the children. Now, they're old enough to sense what it's all about. I reckon they must have known all along. They even tend to be derisive about it at times. Even cynical. And Sheila's only thirteen. Brian's nine.' He looked up at me. 'It's foul, isn't it? It's unbelievable.' His hands brushed cleansingly against his thighs.

The rain dripped from the canopy of the station, but the sky had lightened, and the landscape beyond the station had a watered brilliance. 'I don't think you should leave her,' I said. 'I don't think you can.'

He looked at me helplessly, demanding some consideration. 'I always think of your family life as being too successful,' he said. 'Too shut-in on itself and secure. Families to me are just like vicious animals, radiant with solicitude, and affection until you touch them. Then they rear up like crazed beasts. They seem to be the worst parasites of the lot, living off everything around them that they can: neighbours, jobs, friends, anything. I know ... I'm not the best authority on family matters. In my experience they've destroyed far more than they ever created.'

'That's something more than bitterness ...' I said, my feelings tumbling down in front of him.

'This afternoon's meant a lot to me, Margaret. I thought I was all lost. Washed-up.'

'How does it make it any better? Everything's far worse now.'

'I can have a *sort* of self-respect about it. Can't I?' He approved of himself nervously, his hands still clasped together. 'It can't have been easy for you to come with me today ... You've got a peculiar sense of loyalty.'

'But ... I don't know....' I covered my face with my hands.

'Margaret, I've to start being real somewhere. I feel relieved by it all.... It's made me feel I might get something back, even yet. However little it is.'

'But I *can't* go on seeing you when you're like this at home. Your children – you can't just cut them off, like that. It's cowardly.'

He looked at me cruelly, draining his whole face with his breath. 'I'm not a coward. If I stay with them I am.'

'I can't believe that,' I told him, ignoring his feelings, not wanting to be lost with him.

'Perhaps if you saw Sheila and Brian you'd understand. It wouldn't do them much good to be without a father, but in my case it'll do them less harm. You've got to believe that *that's* true, if nothing else.'

'But I can't believe it. How can I just take your word for it, as easily as that?'

'No,' he said.

He went to the door and pulled it open. The dry shadow of the platform still bore the trail of our wet feet. Howarth dropped on the seat outside the door, resting his hands on his knees. I followed him out slowly and sat on the seat, away from him.

'I can't go on seeing you,' I told him.

'Why *did* you come with me this afternoon?'

'I never realized how much you were meaning to destroy. I didn't want to give myself like that.'

'You wanted us holding hands and talking about art?'

'You forced that sort of thing on me. I wanted a decent friendship . . . not anything like this, like you've made it.'

'All right. All right. You don't have to cry.' He looked away.

'All the same,' he warned. 'You mustn't give me that sort of stuff. It makes it sound worse than ever. I'm not a "friendly" character.'

'The way you talked about your children – the way you said their names – it didn't sound as though you hated *them*.'

'I don't understand you at all. What do you want me to say? Don't you see – I'm giving things up now. I'm not building them up. I'm not going to make do with things as they are any longer. Whatever you might believe in that happy-home mind of yours, I'm leaving *my* home as soon as I can. I've decided that already.'

'You make it all so terrible. You make me the sole cause of it all. Even if it isn't true, it'll look like that to other people.'

'No one's going to blame you,' he said patiently. 'I haven't made much concealment of going out with you, but I've made even less about my married life. The students at college know more about it than you do. And they don't even know of your existence.' He shook his head scornfully at me. 'It's the first time I've thought realistically of leaving her. It's the decision that shocks. And I've made that now. For some reason I made it when I was hooking that trailer on to the tractor. There it is ... you can sacrifice the wrong things for people.'

'If you do this ... you've got to see I can't go on seeing you.'

'Are you sorry you ever met me?' he asked.

'No.'

'Why did you come with me this afternoon?'

'I don't know. ... Because I wanted a friendship.' He looked at me contemptuously. 'I don't know why,' I repeated.

He tried to deny his feelings and look at me with some tenderness. For a moment I watched his conflict, then turned away.

'You don't love me?' he said.

'You don't believe in love. Any longer, you can't. How can you go from one parasitic thing to another?'

'It doesn't have to be like that.'

'No?'

'Do you have that sort of thing in you?'

'I don't know. I've never wanted to.'

We sat in silence. At the other end of the platform the stationmaster was piling some crates on to a trolley. A bell rang in his office, and a few minutes later the sound of a train came down the track.

'I seem to have gone on aimlessly and not cared,' he said.

The train was already slowing when it came into sight. The stationmaster waved as the engine blasted down the platform. The carriages were virtually empty. As I climbed in Howarth said, 'If you like I'll wait for the next train.'

'It's a bit late for that sort of thing now. You'd better come with me, I feel too awful to be alone.' He got in and banged the door. He sat opposite, looking first at me and then abstractedly out of the window. The stationmaster walked past carrying a green flag, glancing at Howarth, who was close to the window. He must have been watching our quiet quarrel.

A moment later we could hear his brief conversation with the driver; then the engine's whistle screamed and the train lurched into a smooth glide.

'What time is it?' I asked him, resenting his silence.

'It was due to leave at a quarter to five. We should get into City station before half past.'

'Then it'll seem I've come straight home from the office.'

'It will, won't it?' he said emptily.

The landscape on either side of the track was dampened down, hanging low and murky as an evening heat spread out from the city. The greyness had lightened and was almost transparent, with the hidden sun. The wet trees and foliage collected shadows, holding together in simple, stark clumps, which slowly converged on the track, then disappeared to be replaced by isolated trees, and finally the gradually ascending walls of the city. We were like rabbits hurtling back into the warren.

Howarth sat crouched close to the window, his arms folded determinedly, deep in thought. He wanted to be alone. He himself would have preferred to have travelled on a later train. His brooding gave him a clownish air of independence. It emphasized the strangeness of his physique; the odd way he held his hands. His eyes were an abstracted blueness, and the fairness of his hair was no longer exaggerated by his flushed skin – his face was white, with small patches of colour on the cheekbones. He was older and more sullen, intently self-possessed.

The city was limitless in the rain. It was raining more heavily as the train rumbled over the arches, and the hard, angled shapes appeared and disappeared with an unending sameness. It was infinite: there was no fringe to each bricky vista, but line after line of successively fainter summits, disappearing uncertainly into the low greyness of cloud. The buildings were a part of the rain; and, as if such an identity had to be confirmed, the sky opened as we left the train and a sudden torrential spasm filled the yard. We sheltered under the archway by a row of taxis. I was shivering. The warmth of the carriage had brought out the dampness in my clothes. Howarth had his hands deep in his raincoat pockets, his elbows clutching his sides.

'This is really something.' he said bitterly, as if it were both unexpected and yet indicative of the whole mood of the day.

'What are you going to do?' I asked tonelessly.

'It's all over and decided, isn't it?' he said. 'And I'm going now.'

Like a boy longing to escape from some persecution, he darted out from the archway and ran quickly across the yard. I shouted after him, but he didn't pause in the rain. The taxi-drivers watched. His feet splashed and exploded through the rivulets: then all I could see was his head over the wall, as he ran out to the street. In a moment he'd gone, and I hired a taxi to take me home.

Michael announced his engagement out of the blue. He came especially on a Tuesday to tell us, then brought Gwen home the following evening. He was shy yet dogmatic about it, almost impersonal, and secretly pleased. His sudden politeness was all part of his satisfied reserve. My mother was shocked, alarmed, then nervously elated; serious with herself all day, she set about preparing the home for Gwen's visit with her usual slow thoroughness. Between the Tuesday and the Wednesday evenings she'd scrubbed and polished the living-room, scrubbed the stone floor of the scullery, vacuumed and polished the three upstairs bedrooms, and carefully washed out the bathroom. She was desperate to wash the living-room curtains, but daren't in case they wouldn't be dry and ironed in time. My father became extraordinarily amusing, with his swift intuitive humour that had scarcely shown itself since we were children. He joked all the time about Gwen's coming, and was very serious when she entered the house, extending his hand like a Victorian father and introducing my mother and me without waiting for Michael. He took the initiative deliberately, showing Gwen where to sit. Michael was pleased to let his father succeed in these formalities.

She was a surprise to all of us: seven or eight years younger than Michael, Welsh, and a teacher in an infants school. She seemed completely at home the moment she came in the door. She had the confidence of someone who is prepared to trust at first sight: a compassionate, unthinking girl, who made me feel harsh and resentful. Her already plumpish but not fat, body seemed ready to accommodate any number of emotional responsibilities. Michael had picked himself a little mother. It wasn't what anyone had imagined, ever; but now that it had happened it seemed to have been inevitable. My mother was tremendously taken with her, more than she had been with Alec's wife, Nora. Gwen looked much more assured, and full of common sense.

'And what's a Welsh lass doing up in these parts?' my father said, laughing, and chewing his false teeth. 'I never thought we were a tourist attraction or ought.'

'I was at the training college here, and I thought I'd stop,' Gwen said. Her accent amused my father. He grinned shyly at its novelty, and looked at her wonderingly.

'She means she was taken up with a teacher she met here,' Michael said with his heavy humour. Gwen laughed and poked her hand at him.

'Go on,' she said, shyly provocative. She evidently took Michael's instinct for destroying illusions as a sign of honesty.

'Well, don't tell me I'm wrong,' he said. 'It was only last week that he threatened to flatten my face if I even spoke to you again.'

'He's very bad-tempered, you know,' Gwen entrusted this schoolteacher to us. 'You know how girls are at college. They go out on school practice and meet some mature teacher ... well, he wasn't really mature,' she naïvely anticipated Michael's criticism.

'Oh, aye,' my father agreed.

'Anyway,' Michael said, 'I've to look out whenever I'm in town with Gwen. This chap's warned me I mustn't speak to her again.'

'Oh, he's not like *that*,' she told him seriously, and Michael laughed, with my father.

'Ah well, you're engaged,' my mother said, sighing with satisfaction that something at last was resolved for her eldest son. Gwen glanced at her ring with nervous pleasure. We'd all been pretending to ignore it, but now my mother felt assured and stared at it invitingly.

'Would you like to have a look?' Gwen said, and went across to show my mother. 'It's three diamonds in a gold setting.' My mother examined it with great interest and delight.

'Oh, it's *very* nice, love,' she said, and added with great emotion and deliberateness, 'Can I give you a kiss?'

She strained up to Gwen and the two of them embraced. My father smiled awkwardly. And Michael didn't look.

Then Gwen came to show it to me. She was consoling.

'It's very nice,' I said, and deliberately held her wrist. There was a sudden hardness between us, as if we'd physically collided.

'I never knew you'd afford such a thing,' my mother said to Michael in triumph.

'Nay, when we're married,' he said, assuming an accent, 'it'll be pawned. It's only the bait on the hook is that, you know.'

He and Gwen laughed. They already had a deep confidence between them, and an unspoken pride.

'Yes, there comes a time when you have to face up to things,' my father said seriously. He moved his false teeth around inside his mouth, unaware of Gwen's sympathetic scrutiny.

'We're getting married in a month,' Michael suddenly stated, and gave the date. He laughed at my father's surprise. 'You've got to face up to things some time, Dad,' he said.

Gwen's eyes darkened at my parents' change in concern.

'It's a *bit* soon,' my mother said, her doubts and elation swiftly concealed. My father stared at Michael inquiringly.

'I think it's all right,' Michael said. 'We want to get married. I don't see any reason why we shouldn't.'

'It's a serious business is marriage,' my father said. 'You don't want to go rushing into it without thinking, you know. And I'm talking from Gwen's point of view as well as yours. She doesn't want to take up with a man straight off when she hardly knows him.'

Gwen didn't say anything. She glanced consolingly at Michael, and he said, 'Oh, we've settled it all. We're sure about it. And literally, there's nothing to stop us. So why should we wait?'

'But you want to be sure,' my mother pleaded. 'As your dad says, it's not a thing you can go charging into.'

'We're old enough to see that, Mother, I'd 'a thought,' Michael reassured her colloquially. 'It's not a thing I want to rush into, any road. I've waited long enough to mek sure.'

He looked at us all confidently, smiling at our concern. We avoided him.

'Well, you want to wary on him, lass,' my father said. 'Don't go letting him rush you into things you haven't first thought about yourself. He's like that is our Michael. Just you be careful on him.'

'Oh, I'm able to watch him, Mr Thorpe,' she said. 'I've got forty worse than him at school to watch all day.'

My father liked her humour. His eyes shone, and he

laughed. 'Ah well, you might know about it then, after all,' he said.

'I'm not so slow, Mr Thorpe,' she said directly. The family laughed at her matronly assurance.

'I'll go and put on a cup of tea,' my mother said, and when Gwen stood up to go and help her in the scullery, she said, 'No, you sit down, love. I've got it all laid out ready. It only needs me to carry it through.'

But Michael went through with her. She was glad, and pleased that he did.

'Michael's told me you work for the Coal Board,' Gwen said to me. 'What's it like there?'

'Oh, it's straightforward. There's not much hard work attached to it. It's just routine.'

'I've often thought of going into an office myself,' she said. 'It's so exhausting teaching nippers, and you never seem to get anywhere even when you make a special effort.'

'I don't think you'd like the routine of an office, not after the liveliness of a school. But if you're getting married, will you carry on with teaching?'

'Michael wants me to. Then we could save all I earn towards a house, and that sort of thing. It's a nuisance being tied down like that, to saving, and so on. But . . .' She patted her thighs and looked down at her blouse, then smiled at me. Her confidence hardened me. She was aware of my uneasiness with her: her benevolent nature gave her a patronizing attitude. But she was not hard. She was frightened of Michael, and she instinctively leant towards us for protection. She had already sensed my parents' uncertainty with him, and allied it to her own.

'By the way,' she said. 'We met a man who Michael says you know – at a social at the university last week. I can't remember his name, but Michael said that he'd left his wife. Or there was a rumour going around about it.'

We could hear Michael talking to my mother in the scullery,

an assured monotone, explanatory, and perhaps tendentious. 'There's a lot of that going on today,' my father said, indifferent, absorbed in his thoughts and gazing at the fire. 'People don't seem to have any backbone these days. There ne'er used to be all this divorcing when me and your mother was young. You'd to get stuck into marriage if you wanted to make a go on it. But now, it doesn't seem to count,' he said mildly, afraid of being fierce with a stranger in the house.

'I think you've got to leave people to themselves,' Gwen said uneasily.

I resented her, wondering how much Michael had told her about me, and if she was only being polite about Howarth. I hated her idea of a well-brought-up marriage. But I struggled to create a fondness for her. I was fond of her, already. And she was trying to encourage it.

When Michael came back carrying the tea tray, she said to him, 'Who was that man you showed me at the university, the one you said Margaret knew?'

'Oh yes.' He looked at me with sudden interest. He held a cup of tea in either hand, and gave one to Gwen and the other to me. 'It was that Howarth character. He seems to have had a wife after all, our Margaret. There's a rumour that he's left her, and applied for a job, down south probably.'

'He's left town, then?' I said.

'No. He'll have a couple of months notice to work off. He mayn't leave the college until Christmas. How long is it since you've seen him?' he added deliberately.

'Two or three weeks.'

My mother looked at me uneasily. She was still flushed from her joyful talk with Michael, like a young girl.

'The common room will be a different place without him,' Michael said. 'No dark brooding, or lurking suspicion that we should all be artists.' He laughed pleasantly, and handed my father his pot of tea. 'What do you think of these artists, then, Dad? I bet they'd be less sickening after a couple of shifts down the pit.'

'Nay, everybody's got their place,' my father said defensively, but with no conviction.

'You see that I've got you your pot,' Michael told him, overlooking his father's feelings. 'Your wife wanted you to have a cup like the rest on us. But I stuck out for you. Gwen ain't impressed with formalities.'

'Oh, Michael,' my mother said. 'At least Gwen likes to see a decent cup, not a great thing like that, I'm sure.'

'We ought to have something in, you know,' my father said. 'To toast the happy pair, and that. It's nowt exciting supping it i' tea.'

'I thought of bringing something with us,' Michael said. 'But then I thought you might be offended, presenting you with all the plans *and* the stuff to celebrate them with. . . .'

'Where are you getting married?' my mother said acceptingly. She had obviously heard about it from Michael. She looked at Gwen.

'I'd like it to be in church,' Gwen said. 'And my mother wants me to wait until Christmas, at least, and to go home for it to Cardiff. But Michael say's he'll only get married in a Registry Office.'

'Yes, he's been telling me,' my mother said. 'And I've told him he ought to go along with you, Gwen, in a thing like this. It's the biggest thing in a woman's life. I think you'd be wrong to be married in a Registry Office if Gwen's set on church.'

'Anyway,' Michael said. 'She's chapel, not church.'

'Even if you don't believe in God, getting married in a church makes it a different thing again,' my mother said. 'It makes it lasting and more important. You can ask your dad. He wasn't going to get married in a church, but he's glad now that he did.'

'You mean he tells *you* he's glad,' Michael said. He sat on the arm of the chair beside Gwen; he enjoyed his novel situation more than anything else.

'It's nowt to joke about,' my father said. 'Getting wed in a church does mek a big difference.'

'If you've that sort of mind,' Michael said. 'But don't let's spend the night arguing about getting married. Let's talk about something pleasant.' He and Gwen laughed. They imprisoned us.

'I know what that means,' my mother said. 'Michael'll have his own way in the end.'

When they'd gone the house was quiet, as if a great deal of life had suddenly been taken out. My mother cleared up the cups and saucers, and my father went upstairs to bed. He'd been pleased and tired by the visit and, as if yet another responsibility had been taken from his shoulders, he went to rest.

'Do you want another cup of tea before I finish?' my mother asked.

I went into the scullery and made it while we washed up. We worked mechanically, separated from one another, without speaking. When the tea was mashed we put the pots away and took our cups into the living-room.

'What do you think of her, then?' my mother said, finding it intolerable that I should say nothing about Gwen.

'She's just the woman Michael needs,' I told her. 'But I'd always imagined he'd picked somebody different.'

'Yes,' she said, relieved. 'I never thought I'd see our Michael walk in the door with a girl like that. But I'm right glad that he has. She'll do wonders for him, I'm sure.'

'What sort of wonders do you want seen done to our Michael?' I asked, laughing at her.

'Nay, but she'll take the hard corners off,' she said deeply. 'I can't tell you how glad I am that he hasn't picked on some

. . . you know, high-up young woman. It's a right nice ring he's picked, don't you think?' She was happy to talk of Michael: she'd been longing intensely for a Gwen to come into his life and bring him, through such a warm personality, back to her own maternal feelings. Even back to her class. Gwen was one of us. 'I do hope he makes a proper go of it,' she went on passionately. 'I couldn't bear him to play up with a girl like that. Not now. You can tell she relies on him.'

'You seem to have sized it all up, Mum. She was only here an hour or so and you've got it all neatly tied up.'

'But a mother sees these things, Margaret,' she said indulgently. 'I haven't watched my own son for thirty years without realizing what he needs and what he doesn't. The only difficulty I can see is the wedding. If she was my daughter I'd want her married at home, and at church, whoever the chap was. But our Michael – he's so headstrong. I can quite see him getting his own way.'

'Yet you wouldn't be so bothered if they did get married up here, and not in Wales.'

'Oh, I wouldn't say anything about that . . . I might prefer it, for myself.' She stroked the arm of her chair, trying not to smile possessively. 'But it'd be wrong for me to say anything about that. Yet our Michael always was one for getting his own way. Even as a baby. His mouth was everlastingly open. He bawled and bawled until he got exactly what he wanted. Even as a baby. It was strange that – knowing just what he did want all the time. I can't see it stopping now.' She drank her tea quickly, excitedly. Michael's independence and power often stimulated her when it was directed away from her and the family. 'It's a great load off my mind,' she said.

'Yes. I'm glad it's worked out like this. It's the best in every way,' I said.

'We might even get a bit of peace at home, Margaret,' she

went on, laughing; and pulling out a handkerchief from her skirt she began to dry her tears of relief.

'Oh, I'm so glad about it,' she said, and hurried out to cry quietly in the hall.

5

I went up to the pit on the Friday. During the week I'd been ill, and this was the first time I'd been allowed out. Michael had been engaged two weeks, and seemed to have been in and out of the house all the time. Gwen liked to see my father and mother. They'd formed a sudden and profound attachment. I was glad to get out.

My father was on the afternoon shift and I offered to go up to the pit and collect his wage from him before he went down. I walked up through the estate, along the winding roads bounded by privet hedges and heavily-pruned syca-mores. The houses, usually so dead in the sameness, were fresh. Each house had its own identity for me, particularly if I knew the occupants by sight. The fronts of the houses, in spite of their regularity, bore the expressions of frowning walls or smiling windows that were outward signs of the family inside. The houses of my childhood friends still possessed the heavy expressiveness of their remembered faces; the houses used to look at me, their fronts the familiar masks of friends or dislikeable neighbours.

Soon I was away from the boundary of my childhood games, the estate rising over former moorland to Moorfield Road. I came out by the newly-built private houses. The road was broader, and the hedges and trees were more varied in the larger gardens, with thick banks of rhododendrons blazing from the dull green. On the road itself the colliery traffic was relieved only occasionally by a bus or a car. Between the houses, with their cosy, sometimes leaded windows, I could see across the broad dip to the other side of the city; the university tower stood up clear.

I soon lost interest: the heavy moan of the colliery and the sulphurous smell began to dominate the road, and the new headgear came into sight over the lowered slag heap of the older, renovated pit.

My father was not to be seen on the road outside. I stood at the yard gate and waited. The lorries came in at regular intervals, bouncing and crashing over the deep ruts and pools, and parking at the side of the coal shutes. As each full lorry drew out, coal spilling over its tail boards, it ran up to where I was standing, and parked on the steel platform of the weighing office. A moment later it drew away. Its place under the shute was taken by another lorry, the driver clambering up into the darkness of the loader to hurry the coal down with his shovel. The yard was filled with dust, rising in tight, blinding eddies in the wind. Through the blackness gleamed the red lip of the dynamo fan, revolving invisibly at speed, like a tight red mouth grimacing.

The men worked near it, absorbed, occasionally shouting to one another, or staring and pointing at me. Across the far side of the yard the rails curved into the pit, two rows of trucks standing under the new shutes of the renovated section. A small colliery engine, black and red, stood fussing steam, waiting for the lane the other side of the pit yard to be cleared of traffic before it could cross.

I didn't recognize my father at first. He came across the harsh, dirty yard of men, a tiny figure against the inanimate scale of the workings. He'd just changed into his pit clothes. I was nervous at his strangeness. He was shy and cold. His knees were padded, and his trousers tucked into bright football stockings. His too-large boots gave him a heavier, staggered walk. He looked cold. He was already holding out the wage packet before he reached me, wishing that I should be gone immediately. His face was straight, and serious, squashed up, without its teeth, below the beetle hardness of his black helmet. His coat was the only thing I recognized about him: he'd brought it home once for my mother to sew on doubly large pockets. They hung on him like a clown's heavy pouches.

'I thought your mother said she'd be coming up,' he told me.

We were both shocked.

'I thought I'd come up for a breath of air and a walk,' I said.

'Ah well,' he said uneasily, hurt. 'You shouldn't come up here. It's not a place for you.' His unhappiness was a hard, protective one. 'Go on, then,' he said. 'You get off. Tell her I'll be home as usual.' His hard-worked, nugget-like shape made me helpless and monstrous. He'd been hiding this from me all my life: his work and his fear of it. I said good-bye, and walked away. I turned round to watch him cross the yard to the pit-head. He joined the disordered queue of miners standing silently under the corrugated iron roof. Two or three of the men were talking; the rest waited dumbly and still.

The pit was hostile to my back. There was the whine of the dynamos and the fan, then the sudden gasping of the winding engine as the men were lowered. I imagined my father moving through the earth below me.

I walked quickly. There was a tremendous urgency. I no longer felt protected. I'd never considered the pit, nor my father in it. I'd forgotten it. I'd given him to the pit, and taken everything that was left over. It was only a small part of him. Behind him was a great deadness, as if I'd only been grasping his shadow.

The familiarity of the estate was transparent as I wound into it. A council housing estate with its one bombed house still a vacant site, and its endless interlocking rows of houses bound up in one tormented shape of winding roads and twisting crescents, its one long avenue pushed through the middle like a spear. The huge knot of houses was bolted to the city by this single straight avenue. The traffic fled through it into town.

When I got in the house was empty. I sat in front of the fire, staring at it, my hands pushed to my mouth, as if I'd never see my father again.

Michael and Gwen visited the house frequently. They were patronizing. I hated to see the ring on Gwen's finger, as if she insisted on displaying their feelings, and they couldn't exist without this blatant memento. I found it unbearable to be in the house with them. I wanted to deride my mother's concern, but chose only to ignore it, assuring her that I wasn't miserable and that I hadn't a mood. 'What is it, love? ... I don't know, there's something wrong, and you just won't say.' Time seemed endless. I had never been so alone before. I clung round my mother helplessly, silent and resenting, holding to her.

Then Howarth came to the house. I could hardly contain myself. He was stiff and formal. He knew I'd been waiting for him. He looked as if he'd been chased to the door, as if he'd come to the house for protection. My mother went into the scullery and shut the door after she had been introduced.

'Is she offended?' Howarth said.

'No. She thinks we want to talk on our own.'

'Does she know about me?'

'A little. What I've told her, and what Michael's said ... that you'd left your wife.'

'Did you expect me to come?' He was strange and oddly threatening in the living-room. The juxtaposition of Howarth and the familiar was always threatening.

'I thought you might come,' I told him.

'I was hoping I might have seen you in town somewhere.'

'I preferred you to come.'

He looked at me uncertainly, not sure what I meant.

'Michael said you'd taken a job elsewhere, and that you'd be leaving by Christmas.'

'I've given in my notice. Nothing more than that ... I haven't taken on another job, or anything.'

'Are you going away?'

'I think so.'

He stared round at the room, noting its details carefully as if they oppressed him. 'I've seen quite a bit of Ben these last few days,' he said. 'He wants me to take a job with him. As a scaffolder! He works for his uncle somewhere in town.'

'Do you want to do that?'

'I thought I'd feel free after leaving her,' he said inconsequentially. He moved restlessly about the room.

'How are you feeling about it?'

'I don't know.' He rubbed his face as he looked at me. 'Destroyed more than anything else. I feel let down, for some reason.'

'Where are you living?'

'Well, I'm staying at the Studio – it's a room some painting students have over a plumber's in town. They use it for their little bohemian excesses. They were very sympathetic at first – as though leaving your wife condoned their sort of licentiousness. Instead – my staying there seems to have stopped it. I think they're just beginning to resent my being there now. I've been trying to get a room of my own.'

'You seem to have gone back on your tracks – the last time you mentioned Ben, or students, you sounded as though they were God's last creatures.'

'Yes,' he said.

'Are you going to divorce your wife?'

'We've talked it over.' He stared dumbly at me, then went across to the window and peered into the bareness of the road. 'We've talked it over. But she's not sure about it. She thinks there's another woman at the root of it all. I suppose that's her pride.'

'Is she altogether wrong?'

'I don't know . . .' He lifted the curtain, for no reason, and looked up and down the length of the road. He turned round biting his lips, yet trying to appear indifferent. 'I can't untangle all the threads yet.'

'Why did you come here, today?'

He gazed round the room at its cosy furniture. He made it seem small and too precious. 'You've changed,' he said. 'You sound as if you're more definite about things.'

'That's what you'd like me to be, isn't it? But I'm still the discriminating spinster you first thought I was.'

'Yes. You must be right discriminating to have tangled with me.'

'You're going to take me out,' I told him. 'Just wait there until I get my coat.'

He sat on the arm of a chair, smiling. 'All right,' he said.

I went into the hall. 'We're going out, Mother,' I called to her.

She didn't answer for a while. Then she said distantly, 'Oh, all right.'

I opened the scullery door. She was busying herself in the sink and didn't look up. 'Is that all right?' I asked.

'Yes,' she insisted.

Howarth was pained by her coldness. He came into the hall while I pulled on my coat. He wanted to explain to my mother, but I touched his arm and shook my head.

'I won't be late, Mum.'

'Good night, Mrs Thorpe,' Howarth said.

'Good night, Mr . . .' she answered emptily, forgetful.

I knew she wouldn't watch us from the window. She didn't want Howarth to exist.

'I don't think she did like me coming,' Howarth said, smiling, as we waited in the avenue for a bus.

'She's always peculiar with strangers. Don't mind her.' He knew I was happy with him.

He stared around him knowingly. It was dusk and the evening was settling, with red strips across the clouds, glowing through them, and not moving. The road was emptying of traffic.

'The vicar, from home, came to the college to see me this week,' he said. 'Asked me if I realized what I was doing.'

'What did you say?'

'I told him some rubbish . . . I don't know. I tried to point out to him the difference between someone who made a profession of their convictions, like him, and those who merely lived them. He didn't believe that I'd tried to reconcile myself to the situation – as *he* saw it. Even that parson pal of Ben's came to see me. Fawcett. Told me to give it another try. You see how they're ganging up. So your mother's not the only one.'

The bus came and we sat at the front downstairs. I was relieved to be on it, away from home.

'Ben's got the notion that this is the great turning point in my life. I ought to renounce everything now and devote the rest of my life to painting pictures in an attic he knows about . . . collieries, factories, and working people. He's lent me a book on Gauguin.'

'So you were bored and came to see me.'

'No,' he said seriously. 'I've done what I said I'd do, and now I feel *free* to see you. . . . But then, I am a bit stuffed with Ben.' He laughed, looking into my eyes, and wanting me to forget his tone. 'I can't say I wasn't glad for some chronic distraction, Ben or otherwise. He just gravitated towards me: the cultural philanthropist. He's even offered to buy me brushes and paints and a few canvases. It'd have been heavy going without somebody like him.'

'You really would have liked to have been able to paint, wouldn't you?'

'No.' He stood up and we got off the bus.

We turned up a street at the side of the Education Offices:

the buildings were a mixture of Victorian terraces and shops, the brickwork purpled with soot and caked yellow with old posters. He unlocked the rickety door at the side of a shop and I followed him up a narrow flight of steep wooden stairs on to a small landing. It was stacked with hardboard and paintings and an old black oil stove. The place smelt impregnated with paint and turps.

A student was reading inside the small white room. He offered to go when he saw me, and Howarth said it would be good of him. He clambered down the stairs like a disturbed animal. Howarth had this strange power of disturbing small things, and causing their flight. He seemed to be ignorant of it.

He switched on a cream portable wireless without thinking. I sat down carefully on a chair that pulled out as a short bed, and he lowered himself into a bucket seat of red canvas. The walls were plain and white, creaming with dirt, and several dark paintings hung on them, all in monochrome and of fruit and jars, and of empty roads and large empty fields. The place was moderately clean, as if it were being subjected to only a cautious and not a wholesale dissolution. A series of sports results were being given on the wireless. Howarth listened to them while he gazed at me. The announcer gave the winners of several athletic events, and the times of the runners. Howarth was laughing to himself, as if this record of useless effort bitterly amused him.

'Don't you know of a better room than this?' I said.

'It's indescribable, I know. But even then it's better than any of the places I've been to see so far.'

'You don't sound really bothered.'

'I don't think I am.' He fingered a spot on his forehead, inflaming it with his nervous fingers.

'You don't want to let yourself go ... just because you're like this. You've got to take trouble with yourself.'

'It's nice to hear somebody cares.' But he was no longer pleased.

'We're going away next week-end. My brother's getting married. She's Welsh ... and we're all going down to Cardiff.'

'Yes. I heard something about that. Your brother, you know, is really a reasonable man. He came up to me the other day and said he was sorry about what had happened. Do you realize, he's the only person who's actually *commiserated*.'

'I suppose it's like him, in a way. He's like that ... once he knows he's on top and can patronize.'

'Has he been getting at you or something?'

'No.'

'He'll be different when he gets married.'

'I *don't* think. We're going down on Friday afternoon, and coming back Sunday. They're getting married in a Registry Office, so it won't be very splendid.'

'You should have quite a party when you meet. The Thorpes and the ...'

'Morrises.'

'Well, you couldn't get two much commoner than that.'

The programme changed to light music. Howarth looked perfectly at home. He leaned his head back and draped his arms grotesquely over the sides. It was a conscious relaxation, disguising his loss and indecision.

'How have your children taken it – Brian and Sheila?'

'Sheila cried a bit. Partly because she thought I wanted her to. I told them I was going away but that I'd come to see them now and again ... I don't know. I keep expecting somebody, or something, to come along and tell me I've done right, that it's all right.'

'I only wish you hadn't suddenly run off like that ... on that Wednesday. That was the worst part: leaving me like that. Just running off, as if you were running away, as if you didn't care a bit how I felt.'

'It's been something I've had to do on my own. I wasn't going to have you mixed up in it at all.'

'What did your wife say?'

'Joyce? She was frightened, I reckon, more than anything else. So was I. I couldn't believe that it was true, that I was really doing what I said I was. But she was relieved in her peculiar way, as well. I've always avoided threatening her with leaving, or anything of that sort. Yet it was still there. Perhaps she *was* more relieved than anything.'

'Really . . . you'll expect me to share the blame, in the end. Won't you?' I resented the quick way he could sum up his wife: his knowledge of her was arrogant. He had this arrogance towards me, unknown to himself.

'You sound hardened to it all already,' he said, distrustful. 'Almost unscrupulous, if I didn't know you better.'

'I've come to see *some* things differently. . . .'

'And you're so complacent about it too. You still have that working class complacency, in spite of yourself. You'll never admit to being wrong.'

'And you do.'

'I've been tamed just that bit. I'm even sentimental about the working class, so I always treat them suspiciously. Like your brother – he's got the split feelings of the class he's left behind. On the one hand extremely sentimental and on the other incorrigibly hard.'

'And you're not like that.'

'With me the hardness is a bit blunted. The sort of work I've been doing – it's made me too soft. It's one of the reasons my marriage is a failure.'

'So in a way you resent my brother.'

'Yes.' His eyes dulled, as if suddenly tired. 'He's got a purpose in life. I've just got nothing.'

Even now his sudden changes of mood could surprise me. They seemed to have no underlying pattern, no reason – unless it was a deep and virtually implacable pessimism. His fair hair and complexion gave his moodiness a clownlike helplessness, uncomplaining and unrealized. It gave him the superficial characteristics of someone who could not be approached.

'Why did you give in your notice?' I asked him. 'There was no need to do that.'

He stared at me, then leaned over lazily and pulled out a packet of cigarettes. He lit my cigarette for me, and dropped the packet and the matches loudly on the floor. 'Do you still respect me for what I've done?'

'I respect it, if I don't admire it.'

'I wondered.' He was half-satisfied. He smoked seriously for a few minutes.

'Why did you give in your notice?'

'I've a vague idea of going away.'

'And starting afresh?'

'If I can.' He looked at me, wanting to laugh.

'Doesn't the job you've got now mean much to you?'

'No. But I'm not blaming that for anything. They're charming people and all that. But teaching art, and worst of all teaching art to people who couldn't get into a university – you can't sink much lower than that, can you? Not even if you try.'

'You're not going to give yourself much chance.'

He stood up and gave me a wondering look. I couldn't catch the depth and the real meaning of it. 'I've got you. Haven't I?' he said.

As the train roared across the raw, desolated plain of buildings towards Manchester, my mind was slowly made up. The desolation was endless, extending beyond the denuded escarpments of rubbish dumps to the concertina ridges of the factories and the short stern ligaments of streets: it was a pleasant desolation, with an unsuspected warmth. A heat that increased as my determination grew.

Michael and my father sat opposite, both quiet and alien in

their best suits. Gwen had gone on ahead two days before to soothe her parents. If anything, Michael resented us accompanying him. It diminished in an amusing way the independence of his marriage-intention. My mother sat beside me, small and precise, nursing her silence with the strangeness of travelling. It was the first time that she'd come west in a train, or even left the county. Lancashire, in spite of its industrial similarity, was less secure, less intimate. Its greyness was everlasting, an unending battle.

My father was ready to be amused, and ready to be found amusing. He liked seeing Michael in this nervous situation, and was warm to him. He smiled at all of us in turn, and kept a conversation going between himself, Michael, and me. In his best suit and with his red, scrupulously shaved face, he looked inescapably a man of intimate good humour; a figure of reliability. He wanted to draw my mother from her silence and its foreboding of a strained, argumentative week-end.

I had to leave them. They were unsuspecting. When I told them, between changing trains at Manchester, that I was going back, they were more hurt than I had anticipated. My father was suddenly quiet and indifferent, and my mother frightened. She wanted my support over the week-end even more than my father's. She hated any disrespect for her feelings.

'We've got our tickets and everything, Margaret,' she said quietly, suddenly small and lost in the station's immensity. 'What with our Alec not being able to get away, and now you ...'

'I'm not doing it to be awkward,' I tried to explain. 'But I've made up my mind.'

She was close to tears, her eyes wide and inwardly blazing. I'd derided her family pride. We'd set off that morning pleased to be together, warm and big in the family union, and dominant. Now the whole thing was empty. 'I don't know what Gwen'll think ...' she said. Michael stared at me bitterly, although he must have partly understood. 'Aren't you feeling well or something?' my mother persisted. 'We needn't rush to change trains. We've half an hour or so. We can get a cup of tea.'

'No, Mum. I'm going back.'

Her eyes were wide with tears. She'd sensed my feeling, but wouldn't recognize it. 'You might have said something before we all left,' she said.

'What do you want to prove by it?' Michael said. He was angry, and resentfully jealous.

'I'd like to come to your wedding. And I wanted to. But I can't carry on with it, that's all. I don't want to argue about it.'

'How does she mean: carry on with it?' Michael said.

'Nay, you've got to tell us summat.' My father rubbed his face.

'I don't mind you going back,' Michael decided. 'But you want to give my mother some sort of explanation.'

'You just *accepted* that I'd come.' I was almost in tears at my mother's distress, angered at her. 'You took it for granted – you never asked me. It makes it all so petty arguing about it like this. And *that's* what you're trying to do, Michael. I'm going back, and that's an end of it.'

'What's got into the lass?' my father said shyly.

My mother stared fiercely at me. Michael said something, but neither of us heard. My father answered close to my ear, but his head was turned away towards the barrier. 'Still, we mu'nt grumble. It'll be a bit more stuff to sup and eat.'

My mother trembled at his will to soothe us. 'Why are you going home, Margaret?' she asked quietly.

I shook my head, looking at her. 'I've a feeling you've planned this all along,' she decided.

'I haven't planned it, Mother.' I struggled to impress her with my seriousness. But I felt that her suggestion was true, that I'd deliberately deceived her. 'It's awful of you to say so.'

95

She listened disbelievingly. 'Now she's going to get on her old self-righteous pinnacle,' Michael said. 'Come on, Dad. We'll go for a drink while these two argue it out. We'll be on platform three waiting for you.'

She wiped her eyes when they were gone, and she lost her intensity. 'There's nothing else for me to say, Mum. I'll see you on to your train, then I'll catch the next one back home. I'm really sorry.' I examined her distress, but I was afraid to touch her. 'It's just unfortunate that I've chosen a time like this. But I can't help it.'

'It's not fair on us, Margaret. Michael was looking forward to having you there as his sister. It's not going to be a big wedding or ought. You might've just put your pride in your pocket for once. It's not much to ask of you.'

'I've always been pushing my pride away.'

'Have you,' she said with quiet scorn. It was unlike her. She was pained and surprised at the extent of her upset.

'I know it seems meaningless me acting like this,' I told her, 'but it's the only way I've got left. Can't you see my side of it a bit?'

'I don't think you're being honest with yourself,' she said, white with dread.

'Why?'

'Aren't you a bit jealous of Gwen? But I don't mind,' she added quickly. 'It's only natural, isn't it? But you shouldn't let a thing like that take a hold on you. You ought to come just to show them you're as good as they are, any day.'

'I thought you might have understood,' I told her.

She was silent, afraid to go any further with the suspicion she might have had. She stared distractedly at me, then swung away. I walked hurriedly beside her towards the platform. 'Do you want a cup of tea?' I asked her as we passed a stall.

She shook her head. But she followed me when I went to order two teas. She stood and waited beside me, almost as if she'd suddenly forgotten me. But she disliked eating or drinking in public, and she didn't drink her tea.

She waited beside me while I drank mine, and I took her full cup back. We waited for the men by the ticket barrier. The train was in. 'You'll bring me some cake back?' I said.

'Yes. We'll bring you some.'

'Shouldn't you get something to read? It'll be late before you get into Cardiff.'

She shook her head. 'No. I don't like reading on trains.'

We watched the other passengers filing through the barrier. 'Has she changed her mind, then?' my father said cheerfully when he came up.

'No. It's all right. We'll leave her here,' my mother said, lifeless.

I held out my hand and shook hands with Michael. 'Good luck and best wishes. And give my love to Gwen.'

'Yes. Thanks,' he said, and they joined the queue through the barrier.

I wanted to be with them. I waved to them and waited until they'd climbed into the train before I went away. I walked across the forecourt of the station: it was deserted now. Then I could hear their train pulling out.

6

He'd been expecting me. His surprise hardly lasted a breath, then he sat down, after standing up at my entry. 'Why, what's all this?' he said. The room was tidier and he looked as if he'd been asleep, and dozing. He was in his shirt sleeves. 'Is the wedding off or something?'

'I left them at Manchester and came back.'

He looked at me carefully. For a moment we were both aware of some sort of intrusion, then I sat down and took my hat off. 'What have you been doing with yourself this evening,' I asked.

He shrugged. 'I've been on my own.'

There was an air of independence about him, as if an evening's solitude had fortuitously produced it. I mistook it for resentment at first, and felt like going. But he suddenly stood up, almost dutifully, and came to sit on the broad wooden arm of my chair. 'I'm glad you came back,' he said. He was stretched across the back of the chair, and I leant against him.

'I couldn't have gone off like that. Not now. It meant a nasty argument. But I can't tell you how relieved I am.'

'I think I know.'

'Coming back in the train I felt really exhilarated.'

'It must be like leaving your wife,' he said lightly, and laughed. 'Now you know how it feels.'

He was assured and still patient; all this had been expected. He leaned over and turned my head with his fingers so that I could see him. His head rested against my cheek. He watched me closely as he lowered his head, and we kissed each other with our eyes open, watching one another, drinking our looks in. 'I'm glad you came,' he said.

He felt my breasts reassuringly, then my shoulders. 'What would you have done over the week-end if I hadn't been here?' I asked.

'I don't know. I was wondering what I *could* do with you away.'

'I don't believe you at all. You're too independent to worry about a thing like that.'

'Am I? It shows how much you know.' His hands searched my body and I turned up to him, needing him. 'I'm never sure it is you until I can feel you like this,' he said.

'Aren't I cold and unfeeling?'

'But this *is* you. At times you're just not there. And then it's not you.'

'Let's go out of here.'

'Don't you like it?'

'I don't like seeing you here. It makes me feel you're in a kind of prison. It's as though you've been put here.'

'Where do you want to go?'

'Let's go up home.'

'Your place – at Upton?'

'Yes.'

He thought about it, then said, 'On one condition.'

'What's that?'

'You let me pay your bus fare.'

The house was empty and strange. Its emptiness seemed right. I had to realize that it wasn't my house, no longer really my home. Its familiarity was worn and insipid. It was a stranger's house. There was nothing about it that belonged to me now. 'Don't put the light on,' he said.

'Why not?' We stood in the living-room, a faint street light glowing in through the curtains.

'Let me take your coat off.'

He unbuttoned my coat slowly, kissing me, then slid it off my shoulders and embraced me. 'It's cold,' he said.

'There's no fire.'

'There's no need.'

I rested in his arms while he unfastened my dress. I was terrified of hurting him; he was lifeless in his touch. His mouth was in my hair, bringing it to life with a prickling sensitivity. Then his hands stroked my back, feeling my clothes; then my breasts were free.

We trembled against one another, breathless and searching. 'Let me take my dress off.'

'No.'

'Please.'

'Stand still and let me.'

He felt down round my thighs and pulled the dress up, and turned me against him. 'Lie down. Lie down, Margaret.' He was quivering and pleading. I took his hands. 'Not down here.'

I was exultant that he followed me, that I could lead him. I held his hand as he followed up the stairs. The house was in darkness with the light faint, coming in through the curtains.

It was such a tiny room: when he came in he filled it. 'This is my bedroom. It's at the back.' For a moment we stood and said nothing. Then I lay on the bed and waited for him.

He looked down at me in the pale light, silhouetted against the curtains. Then he began to undress.

I touched him as he undressed. His legs, his back, feeling his body when he came to the bed.

He knelt by the bed feeling me.

'Margaret,' he said quietly, so that I raised myself to him. My hands gripped the soft skin of his scars. His back was patched with them. Their softness collapsed beneath my fingers, penetrating him. But he didn't feel it. He took my clothes off slowly, needing to excite me, until we were seething.

His body was warm against mine. We lay still and the furnace seemed to accumulate between us. Then we were burning. He moved his body slowly, then his hands, until I was completely surrounded by him. He held me hard to ease the trembling. Then in a moment he rolled me on my back, folding his arms round my thighs, and lay deeply between my legs.

He was slow, full of a strange consideration. Even when it was over he was still searching and demanding. The weight and feel of his body was still on mine. He collapsed beside me, one arm in my hair, the other across my breasts. I'd felt no climax: his satiation had been enough. I felt full of him, loved with him in me. His identity had gone. We were together.

He slept briefly, bound to me for warmth, then he was suddenly awake. He got off the bed and stood up. He began to feel for his clothes.

'You're not going?'

'Yes.' He was quiet, and dressed quickly.

'But you can't.'

'I think it'd be better to go. I'll see you tomorrow, don't worry.'

'I'm not. . . . But you mustn't go.'

'Why do you want me to stay?'

'I don't . . . but the neighbours will hear you. It's nearly twelve. They know we're away for the week-end.'

I still lay on the bed. He ran his hand over my body, and made a sound when I flinched.

He stroked my body. 'I think I'd better go,' he said. 'I'll do it quietly, and nobody will know.'

'Why *are* you going?'

'I'd feel uneasy sleeping here. I want to leave you in bed.'

'You'll have to walk all the way back into town.'

'Never mind.'

He sat on the bed, looking towards me, then bent down to pull on his shoes. I got up and felt for my dressing-gown behind the door and put it on. 'Why do you want me to stay, really?' he asked, the whiteness of his face still turned towards me.

'It's all right.'

'It's much wiser for me to go,' he insisted.

'Yes . . . You go.'

He was uncertain. I went downstairs with him and unlocked the front door quietly. He made an arrangement to meet me the next day, standing in the dark a moment. Then he touched my breasts again, wanting to kiss them. I held him away.

He felt his way down the steps and across the narrow front garden. He walked on the grass verge until he was down the road, then he stepped on to the roadway itself. I shut the door. I could hear his feet thudding between the houses, beating back up the street. I listened for some time, standing perfectly still in the darkness of the hall, afraid of the house. His sounds echoed towards me as if he were returning, then retreated slowly, fading away so slowly that I felt I could still hear them long after they must have disappeared.

He was confident the next day. He seemed physically larger.

During the morning he had found a room, and moved his few belongings in. He was pleased with himself, and shy. He took me on the bus to see the place, tucked away at the far end of town, lower down the river. I loved being with him when other people could see us. I held his arm, proud of him and of what we were.

But his room, in a street of detached houses turned into flats, was depressing; it had a dampness and darkness that clung like an inherent thing, never leaving and always accumulating. He was unaware of it, just as if its dull smell and the darkness, the dirty embossed wallpaper and the metal bed were exactly what he needed.

'I can see you're annoyed with me,' he said. 'Why is it?'

He sat on the edge of the bed, the door wide open for the landlady who moved about on the stairs.

'It's an awful place.'

He sighed, but not disappointed. 'You're always full of "awful" things. One thing then another.'

'I didn't think you'd come to a place like this. I prefer that Studio place to this, and that's degrading enough.'

'Degrading?' He lifted his eyebrows in mock surprise. 'Is that how seriously you take it? You think it affects my pride?'

'Yes.'

He bounced up and down on the bed complacently, making it creak and groan; then leaned forward to listen to the landlady's movements. 'I don't think my pride's concerned at all,' he said lightly, almost laughing at my seriousness.

'You're letting yourself go,' I told him.

He stood by the bed, resting one knee on it, his hands in his pockets. He looked contemptuous in his anxiety, then he smiled. 'You daft thing, Margaret. What're you taking it so seriously for?'

'It's where you're going to live.'

'It's only a room. You're not going to judge me by appearances, surely?'

'I think so. Somehow you've encouraged me to do that. I don't always, of course.'

'No, of course not.'

'When you think how you promenaded Fawcett and that Ben in front of me . . . you judged them harshly, from appearances. You wanted me to do the same.'

'Ah, but not with me though.'

'Well that's where you get some of it back.'

'I'm satisfied with it, and that's all that matters,' he said brightly. 'Come on, we'll go back to town, and I'll never bring you here again.'

He seemed sure of where he would take me. We hurried through the thick Saturday afternoon crowds without speaking. He was remote and intent, and large with my feeling for him. 'Where are we going?'

He shook his head. 'You'll see.' And took my hand.

We joined a long bus queue in the street behind the bus station. 'We're not going to the football match?' I said.

'Oh, now, show a bit of life. It's something I like, so try and smile a bit. In any case, why don't you like it? There're plenty of women in the queue. One or two anyway. And we can get seats.'

'It's so crude,' I told him, and he laughed.

'That's very good,' he said. 'I only wish you'd come out with more things like that. It's much more like you if you only knew. What's so crude about it, then? I'm not crude, you know.'

'You are in some ways.'

He was amused and delighted with me. He still held my hand, and was elated as he always was by the presence of a crowd. 'In what ways am I crude?' he asked indulgently.

'In ways you're not aware of.'

'Oh, is that it?' He laughed, squeezing my hand and resting his cheek against mine a moment. 'I love you, Margaret.'

'You're not conscious of a lot of things about yourself. I suppose it's that which makes our Michael think of you as an artist rather than just a person. You're helpless with it. Artists are helpless people to our Michael.'

'When am I so crude like this?'

'Whenever you're doing things instinctively, or out of feeling. Then you begin to be crude.'

'Now isn't that just the root of everything with you,' he said, darkening. 'You're *afraid* of feeling, of letting yourself go. You call it crude. And the rest of your family, I should imagine. You're such a bloody puritan. *Only* an out and out puritan could think and act like you do. Aren't you ever aware of this little strait-jacket you carry around?'

'I don't call it that. It's order, it's discipline. A real person needs it.'

'To be respectable.'

'To be a *person*, not just a selfish lout.'

'Am I as much as that?'

'At times you're a lout.'

'What's got into you today? You've got this so sane attitude to everything – that it mustn't impose iself, it mustn't show what it feels. It makes everything lifeless and undistinguished. It destroys everything. We're asked to be like this. But it doesn't mean you've got to obey.'

We were walking aimlessly, holding hands. As if we'd been joined together in spite of our feelings.

'What do *you* do with your feelings?' I asked. 'You've destroyed far more than I could ever do. I can't destroy any-thing.'

'You destroy what's in you. Where *are your* feelings? You only call *me* helpless because I care for myself. I can't stick this ever-so-nice respect you have for other people. Not with you, I can't.'

'Except you make love to me.'

'Isn't it just like a woman to say that? Yet even then, a thing like that, it's an obligation to you. An act of pity or benediction or some such lousy thing. Haven't you got any respect left for yourself? You let yourself escape in well ordered little dribbles. You're just like everybody else.... Like a mother feeding a baby, giving it milk when *she* feels like it, not when the baby wants it. Don't you realize? – I've got something to *give* you, Margaret. I'm not just grabbing what I can get like everybody else. I've *got* something, and I want you to have it.'

'But why did you want to go to the football match if it's

just that sort of discipline that hurts you? Won't you find the crowd a pack of trained animals?'

'I like to see it,' he stated simply. 'But I don't like seeing you a well-trained puppy, obeying all the demands of your family, shuddering at anybody who might show themselves in public.'

'I love my family.'

'I know. But this is the first sign of life that you've given, to my knowledge. I can just imagine how they must have shouted at Manchester when you told them you were coming back ... the little pup cocks its leg up in the wrong place at last.'

'They didn't shout, and they didn't fight back. I never want to hurt them again.'

'Why ever not? Your family's a rotten family, although you can't do anything about it. It's *dead*. You should all have been pigs like my parents. Your house is like a mausoleum.'

But unaware, we'd been walking towards it, along Petersgate towards the rising mound of the estate. Howarth was lost in the traffic and the violent business around him. The old brick factories enclosed the road.

'You want me to despise myself, that's really what you're asking.' He walked stubbornly beside me, clutching my hand tightly.

'Then you'll want me to turn to you,' I said. 'You're like an evangelist in that. You want to destroy everything around me so that I've got to turn to you.'

'Isn't that something *you* want?' He smiled ironically at me. 'You've been wanting a saviour all your life. It was the first thing that struck me when I met you. And now that you've got one you're more afraid than ever, and want him to be condemned after all like you. Rather than have one person saved, you'd prefer all the lot of us to go.'

'And *you* want to save me from my family.'

'No. I don't want any of that. It's you who's crying out for salvation.'

'I am a princess, after all, to you. You think you've seen me wave my handkerchief from the window and you come dashing up in all this emotional armour.'

'It'd be pretty silly. Only I've got no armour. I've no protection at all against someone like you. That's something you've never understood at all.'

'You're not as weak as all that,' I said. 'It pleases you to think you're helpless. The poor orphan. You're always talking in that sick way about the working class and your awful parents. I can *see* the implication all right.'

'It was you who told me I was helpless.'

'Yes, and you are. But my God, you know how to take advantage of it. Don't ever tell me you don't.'

'I don't know . . . I must seem very artful to you.'

'There's nothing babyish about you, Howarth. You're clever and smart, I can tell. And you know how to destroy.'

'How am I helpless and crude, then?' he said, knowing now that he had triumphed.

'Because other people make you helpless. They're prepared to deny themselves so that you can be as you are. It's really *them* who've given everything to you. You're like a lost person to other people, but you irritate them by insisting that you know exactly where you are. It's so obvious that you're wrong.'

He laughed at his incomprehension. We walked up the avenue between the rows of houses without speaking. He glanced up occasionally at the blank fronts as if they vaguely amused him.

A neighbour was raking in her front garden when we got near the house. She looked up in surprise and called out, 'Isn't your Michael getting wed today, Margaret?' She stared at Howarth with a vibrant curiosity. 'Aren't you going to be there to see them off?' she added.

'No,' I told her.

She was satisfied at my awkwardness. She watched us go round the back of the house. Howarth stood on the steps while I unlocked the door, gazing at the backs, nervous and contemptuous of the place.

'What sort of house is it ... that you have?' I asked him.

He followed me into the scullery and shut the door. 'I suppose you think it's a lot, giving up all I've done. But now ... it doesn't seem to have had any importance at all – the family, responsibilities ...' He watched me taking my coat off.

'I wish you wouldn't try and mislead me all the time,' I said.

'That's a nasty tone,' he said. 'And just because that woman annoyed you out there.'

He took off his coat and knelt down in front of the fireplace and with a small shovel began scooping out the ashes from under the grate. He wafted the dust carefully up the chimney with slow, steady motions of his hand. 'No, leave this to me,' he said when he thought I might interfere. 'I'll find everything myself.'

As he worked in the small neatness of the room he looked strangely in sympathy with it: the care and the concern he had. My mother had left the room, with the glowing, polished table, the white, smooth, embroidered dust covers on the backs of the easy chairs, as if it would be minutely inspected during every second of her absence. He seemed to work with consideration for her.

He went to the back porch and came back with the bucket. He shovelled the ashes in with the same care for the dust. When he returned from emptying them in the yard he brought a collection of wood refuse, and the bucket was full of coal. His hands were black. He worked now with a careless preoccupation and absorption, as if he knew I was aware of him. I wondered how he had been with his family, how he had reacted to their warmth and their early affection.

He crumpled the newspapers up in the grate and arranged the pieces of wood on top. 'We use some proper wood to light the fire,' I told him. 'It's out at the back. Pit props that my father chops up.'

'It's all right,' he said. 'You can leave your father out of this one. I'm lighting the fire. All you've got to do is be ready to laugh: I'm exposing myself.'

He was freshly confident. He lit the paper and waited for the wood to crackle, then began laying on small pieces of coal, dropping them into place with a delicacy for their weight. The flame curled round the coal, and there was hardly any smoke. He propped the shovel across the opening and draped a newspaper in front. The fire began to roar.

He stood back, pleased, his black hands clasped together, watching the redness expand behind the paper. He waited until the paper was singed brown, then pulled it away to reveal the coal well ablaze and roaring strongly, the flames darting up the chimney. He looked at me gladly. 'You never thought I could do it.'

'Of course I did.'

He laughed to himself, and went into the scullery to wash his hands. He came back conscious of my resentment.

He pulled the easy chair up to the fire and sat over it, greedily. The flames had subsided after the force of the draught. 'You haven't much sense of humour,' he said. 'I reckon that must be a big disability.'

'Why?' I said, cynical about him.

'It might be better if you laughed at me sometimes.'

'Perhaps I do – when you least expect it.'

'Oh no. I just don't think you know what laughter is. You've got to be *concerned* to laugh.'

He sat for a while crouched over the fire, gazing at its slow brilliance. The room grew warm, and less strange. The fire had seemed strange, just because he had lit it. But he was at last absorbed by the familiarity of the room. I accepted him there. He held his hands together, near the flames, his fingers clenched together. 'You try and see too much in me, Margaret. I'm a very simple man.' He looked at me meaningfully, then suddenly came across and sat on the hearth rug. He leaned his back against the arm of the chair, and pressed his head against my legs. 'You're like some inarticulate woman who hires herself a preacher. Are you that sort of patroness?'

'No.'

I touched his head and held it beneath my hand. His hair was thick and luxurious. He stroked my legs as if he were ignorant of all my feelings.

'Don't you see what it means, to love somebody?' he said sombrely.

His touch was urgent. He turned his head to look up at me.

'I've tried to be what you wanted, Howarth.'

'It's not a sacrifice,' he rebuked me.

'It's something I couldn't do, to sort of rely on somebody ... as if there were nothing else. It'd make me helpless like you, and I couldn't bear that.'

'You'll have to accept me in the long run if you want any life at all. You can't hide away and hope it won't notice at all. Is it *me* that stops you? Is there something in me that puts you off?'

'No.'

'What if I wasn't married? What if I was a strapping young prince and not a doddering old king who already had a wife?'

'No.' I kissed him impulsively. His head rose stubbornly, straining to reach me.

'It goes deeper, then,' he said, looking closely at me. 'I *am* a sort of conscience to you. You want me to experience all your feelings for you, while you stay tucked up safely in your castle.'

'No, I don't want that,' I said miserably.

'Shall we go upstairs, Margaret?'

'If you like.'

'If I like! Won't you show any feeling for it?' he said, flushing with anger. 'Why do you make *me* do all the giving? You make me feel an intruder, as if I had no rights. You make it so furtive.'

'I'll go up, then. I'll go up! What else do you want?'

'No.'

He stood up and went to sit at the table. He sat stiffly, his elbows on the table and his hands clenched to his mouth.

'I'm going up,' I said, and went upstairs.

I undressed and waited in the bed for him. He was a long time in coming up. Then he came in and shut the door. The room seemed oppressed with both of us. The curtains billowed inwards, the daylight glowing in patterns on them. He pulled me up and held my shoulders. 'Is this how you always want me? You on some altar and me pillaging it?'

'I *can't* do any more, Howarth.'

He sat on the side of the bed. I wanted to touch him, but he was remote, as if his scars, his mood, his dilemma gave him that immunity.

'I *want* you to love me, Howarth. I want it. But I can't bear the thinking.'

'Yet you do nothing but think about it.'

'Don't you see what you're doing? You're putting all your uncertainty into me. As though I were the cause of it all.'

But I lay back and waited for him. He undressed, tired and resigned.

'It's like an obligation to you,' he went on. 'A sense of duty or something. This is what you feel you should be ready to do. . . . But it's nothing at all, really. It's nothing.'

He came under the sheets beside me, aching with his passion and resentment. I felt his body for him. He was steeled, withdrawing himself. But he submitted, tortured by his remoteness, and with no faith in him.

It was darker when I woke, though there was still daylight behind the curtains. I could tell by the loudness of the voices across the backs that it was early evening. I looked at Howarth: his eyes were closed, his face peculiarly expressionless in sleep.

There was something lifeless about the way his body rose and fell in breathing, as if it were automatic, sustained without him. But I was still afraid of him in the house. I listened for noises downstairs, imagining the unexpected return of my parents. The house was quiet; I liked the intimacy of the voices outside: the recognition of them so close, and yet both of us hidden.

He stirred but didn't wake when I slid out of bed and took my clothes into the bathroom to get dressed. The fire was almost out when I got down. Howarth might want to light the fire, but he wouldn't want the trouble of keeping it in. There was something reckless about his sudden passions and wants and amusements. I built the fire up, and drew it with the shovel and newspaper.

By the time the fire was roaring I had made some tea in the scullery. I filled my father's pot and took it upstairs. Howarth was still sleeping. He had moved into the middle of the bed, his arms splayed out either side. I suddenly realized how he must have done without a great deal of sleep.

But when I touched his shoulder he was instantly awake, staring up at me with a moment's hesitation that frightened me, then smiling.

'I've brought you some tea.'

His eyes glowed. 'That's lovely,' he said in a deep northern accent. 'What can I give you in return?' He took the pot and placed it carefully on the chair beside the bed and caught hold of my arms. 'It was worth everything,' he said.

'I hope you won't forget.'

He stroked my back as he felt me shaking. 'I'll never forget anything like that.' He drew himself away, watching me, confident and smiling. He lifted up the pot. 'I look a real workman with this. You have a drink, then I'll drink it.'

I dipped my head over the huge pot. When my father let me drink out of it as a girl he used to laugh. He held the pot between his two thick hands and I stood between his thighs and folded my hands over his, drinking from the enormous interior while he leaned over me, laughing and holding me tightly, and heavy with his smell of coal and tobacco.

Howarth laughed. Then he took the pot and drank, holding it in his right hand, his thumb slotted through the handle. 'It's lovely, here,' he said, crouched up in the bed.

'I'll go down and cook something. It's getting late.'

'There's no hurry for you.' He stroked the pot between his hands, looking up at me. 'That's the first rest I've had for weeks,' he said.

'At least you'll have a proper bed in that room of yours. You shouldn't be looking so exhausted from now on.'

'I wish you'd come back into bed.'

'I'm going to cook something.'

'You're always rushing after things.' He set the pot down as I stood up. 'For a minute ... just a minute. Won't you come back?'

'No. I've got things to do, even if you've only got to lie in bed.'

'A minute ...' He stroked the bed beside him.

'It's no good you asking.'

'Ah well.' He settled down in the sheets. His body was big and brave in the small bed. 'I'll have to lie here and wait for you, then. I know you'll come.'

But soon after I'd started cooking I heard him moving about the bedroom. He didn't like to be alone now. He came into the scullery and stood behind me, his arms round me, watching me cook.

'I can't do it when you're like that,' I told him.

'Don't then. I want you again.'

'You spoil it.'

He was wearied by the idea. He sat down on a wooden chair near the stove. 'I'm feeling very hungry,' he said.

We stoked up the fire after the meal so that it would be bright and blazing when we came back in. We went out to the pictures. The air was cold. There were a few people about on the estate, and children played noisily in the small fields and wastegrounds between the rows of houses. It was a children's landscape, the square houses set on the hillside like plain wooden blocks, everything reduced to a uniform size. As a child the estate had seemed infinite to me, but as I grew up it had gradually reduced itself, until when I was returning from holidays and absences I was surprised to see how really small and cut-off the whole thing was. But with Howarth it was large again, and warm and reassuring.

He was at ease. I held my arm in his and he walked down the road with a careless rolling gait like a workman, calling good night to strangers with a calm politeness that made them turn their heads knowingly, in respect, when we'd gone.

I felt at home in the local picture house, although it was full of people I knew. I met their amused curiosity with a smile or a nod. In the darkness we sat close together, yet with great propriety.

When we got back we could see, from the road outside the house, the glow of the fire flickering on the curtains and the ceiling of the living-room. The whole front of the house seemed to glow, and spread its deep light on to the gardens and the road.

Howarth locked the door, then shut the door of the living-room behind us.

He watched me undressing, and watched again to see if I was ashamed and frightened. Then he came to hold me, standing in the blaze, red and glowing, with the room full of shaking lights and flickerings.

'Do you mind it – undressing?' he said.

'No. I want to do it for you.'

He felt my body bravely, running his hands over it lightly, full of curiosity and queer wisdom. 'Let me undress you,' I asked him.

'If you will.'

I ran my hands round him, feeling his chest and shoulders move. He stood close to me, his hands on my hips, watching my body and the way I looked at him. His shirt was small for him, and stretched in tight folds, clinging to him, and his tie hung limp. I kissed him, but he held my body away. 'I'm waiting,' he said, wanting to laugh and smile.

'I don't know whether I can.'

'Are you frightened of it? Here – I'll take my tie off for you.'

'No. . . .' I pulled his hand away and began undoing his tie, then the buttons of his shirt. He held me to him when my hands found his body. The shadows raced and danced about the room, climbing the walls and folding and unfolding on the ceiling. The fire crackled and fell, and a new burst of flames shot up. I pulled off his shirt and vest. His hands raced over my body, pressing hard and searchingly.

He folded me in his arms and we knelt down together, the full heat of the fire burning close. He found my mouth and we clung together, and he lay back, taking me with him, until I was lying on top and he was pressing me down, into him.

I pulled away and crouched over him. He reached up to my breasts with his mouth, his hands caught on my thighs. But he was wild. He writhed and called to me, on his back, and looking up with his eyes full of the firelight and the shadows.

I felt for his trousers and unfastened the buttons, and pulled them down. Then he was reaching forward for me and pulling me into him with his wild intimacy. He locked me with him, and rolled from side to side, kissing me, clutching my thighs, and murmuring.

He was sleepy and tired, exhausted with himself. We went upstairs when the fire faded. He laughed when I covered myself to walk up the stairs. He walked nakedly, showing himself to ridicule me.

I locked the bedroom latch, shutting everything out. He lay in the bed turned on his side, and I pressed to him, resting against his back, my arms wrapped round him. He was soon asleep. The house was quiet now, only the wood in the skirting board creaking, and the shallow whisper of his breathing.

The estate had a religious silence about it at night, with the distant panting of trains beyond the town, and the close, harsh coughing of a consumptive, carried across the houses and the intervening patches of bare ground like an anonymous signal. But the stillness was strange. As I fell asleep I could still hear the wood creaking and the gurgling of the water in the pipes, and the weary rattle of coughing, dreary and subsiding to a whimpered exhaustion.

Sunday was a bright day. The sunlight came coldly through the green curtain. I was warm, my hands tight and warm between his thighs. I didn't want to be awake. I curled up to him in the narrow bed. I tried to force myself to sleep.

But the brightness of the day and the thought of my parents' return frightened me. Howarth was awake. He tried to grip my hands with his thighs when I slid away, then he watched me dressing, as he always did, minutely, as if continually surprised.

Then he leaned out of bed and pulled me back, holding me so madly and strongly I couldn't move and I almost cried out in pain. He made love to me coldly. I was glad of it. I wanted it never ending, with the warmth and the feeling and the forgetting. It was the end of everything, yet everything still went on. It was the going-on and the ending that I wanted always there, feeling him in me, the moving and the thoughtlessness.

I lay beneath him miserable that he was spent, but glad to feel him struggling for his sensation. When he was finished he was really exhausted. I touched him but he wouldn't revive. He lay back, his eyes closed, with no power in him; as if I had fought him and beaten him.

I got up and pulled the bedclothes from him. He lay there naked and limp, watching me through half-closed eyes. 'Well. What do you know?' he asked.

I knelt on the bed beside him and felt his stomach and his chest and his shoulders. I rubbed my cheek against him, and kissed his stomach and his hips, looking up at him and smiling knowingly. 'Yes, yes, I know,' he said, as though I'd been telling him. I stroked his legs and his sides, to his arms.

'Now you've got me,' he said, smiling down at me. I crouched by his stomach holding him. 'Just like a cat.' He stroked my hair, pressing his fingers into my scalp reprovingly. I kissed his body, laying my head against it, and he stretching out. 'I'm not asking too much,' I told him, looking up to his face, then putting out my hand and stroking the bristle round his cheeks.

He caught my hand and held it and kissed it, folded the fingers and gave it back to me, laughing. 'Now you can keep it,' he said. He crouched up in the bed, turning against me.

I got up and dressed properly, and washed. I made the fire and cooked our breakfasts. The house was our own. I loved him away in the bedroom, waiting while I cooked. My parents could never come back at all. They were intruders. I couldn't imagine them ever again in the house. We'd taken it away, and it no longer was theirs.

When the meal was laid out I went back to wake Howarth. He was lying with his hands clasped behind his head, staring at the cracked ceiling.

'I shall get a divorce,' he said, turning to look at me. 'I'll go and see her on my day off this week and tell her.'

'You never told me you had a day off in the week,' I said, strangely, as if he'd hidden something of importance from me.

'Didn't I? But then I haven't told you a lot of things. It's hardly important, is it?'

'No.' He thought I was sulking; he tapped me under the chin and said, 'Smile, Margaret. . . .'

I smiled at his earnestness and he laughed too. 'Why don't you laugh at me more often?' he said.

'You'd better be getting up,' I told him. 'I want the house straight before my parents come back.'

'Oh yes. We must cover up all the evidence.'

'That's a petty sort of bravado.'

'No . . . you mustn't say anything. I'll help you. Just tell me what to do.'

'You can get dressed and have your breakfast. I'll clean up everything in here. Then we'll go out somewhere.'

'Somewhere.' He looked up at the curtains filtering the light. 'It suddenly sounds very empty.'

He'd tidied up the living-room before I got down from making the bed, and had kept the breakfasts hot on the gas ring. I could see where he'd neatly replaced the chair covers, straightened the rugs, shaken the cushions. But nevertheless I knew my mother would recognize the minute difference. She could even tell, coming into the room, which one of her family had last touched the cushions or sat in a chair.

When we walked down the road to catch the bus I knew it would be too obvious to the neighbours, but I didn't care. Howarth was aloof. He was so preoccupied I threatened to leave him, pulling my arm from his and beating his shoulder.

'I feel it's going to be ages before I can get a divorce,' he said.

'I don't want you to talk about it.'

'Aren't you interested?' he said in deep surprise, and flushing.

'No. You won't understand, but I don't care what you do.'

'What if I go back to her?'

'You won't. And I don't care.'

'Aye. You're too damn sure,' he said, wanting to laugh. 'You've been too sure all the time ... underneath. Right from the start.'

'Does it hurt you?'

'No. I don't mind.'

We caught a bus up to Fleeingwood Park. It was crowded with Sunday strollers in spite of the cool wind. They walked along by the lake, and gathered round the aviary. I liked to be with him in the crowd, to hold his arm and people to see us.

He was worried, and listened to me talking without interrupting. When we stopped to sit down by the lake he went to the water's edge. I sat back and watched his still figure like a giant, contemplative bird, his raincoat hanging loosely from his shoulders, his hands sunk in his pockets. Beyond him, across the lake, rose a thick bank of trees, their branches almost bare, and heavy against the water, leaning down. In their summits were the remnants of rooks' nests, and some of the birds glided over the trees, but never near the water. The surface of the lake was brown with rotted leaves, floating on top or submerging. Along the bank children were throwing bread to the ducks, and to a tall, dignified swan, sulking and swimming to and fro. The reflections of the trees were like wrecks in the water.

The children didn't disturb Howarth. They moved round him and past him but he didn't raise his head. He came back very tired. He wanted to tell me, but he sat silent, looking across the lake to the bony barricade of trees.

'Do you think you love me?' he said.

We looked at one another swiftly, almost contemptuous. 'You think I shouldn't ask you.' The blood ran into his face.

'I don't know what *you* mean by love. You must take me as I am, that's all there is to it.'

'Will you go away with me, then?'

'Where to?'

'London.'

His eyes were almost indifferent. I avoided their expression: the concealing and carelessness. 'Why should I go there?'

'We can be together.'

'I don't know whether I want to be alone with you ... with no one else there, to turn to.'

'Not until the divorce is through,' he suggested.

'That's nothing to do with it, Howarth. And you know it.'

'Why *don't* you ever call me by my name?' he said with a pained seriousness.

'I don't know.' I looked away from him.

'It's strange, is that.'

'I don't like calling people by their names if they mean something to me.'

'How *do* you think of me, then? What name do you connect me with?'

'Just Howarth. But it's not odd ... I've done it before. As it is, you don't like your Christian name.'

'Will you think of going away with me? I shall have to go. I couldn't stay on up here, it'd be like carrying on a left-over life.' There was a certain weakness in his tone. He resented it, and tried to garble his words, twisting the pitch of his voice. I despised him for making me see something abject in him. I wanted nothing to do with his situation, only him.

'I might come away with you,' I said. 'But if you rely on me then I won't. If you expected me to go then I couldn't do it. I'd feel as though I'd owed it to you. You'll not have to press me.'

'All right,' he said, standing up alertly and very quietly. 'I'm going to London just before the term ends. If you want to come I'll look for you.'

'But aren't you going to see me . . .?'

'I can't, can I?' He was angry, the colour mounting in his face. 'It's only three weeks and I'll find something to do. I'll let you know when I'm leaving. I'm not going to beg you.'

He walked away quickly, moving so hurriedly through the crowd that people looked after him, then back at me, furtively. I didn't move, but went on watching the brown stillness of the lake, assuring myself that I hadn't been deserted.

7

'Is that why you came back, then?' my mother said quietly. 'Just so you could have that man in here.'

'It wouldn't have mattered to me if I had. I don't care what the neighbours think.'

'Oh, that's a very old one indeed,' she said, her anger rising. 'But I do care. We've to go on living here, woman, long after you've gone gallivanting off.'

I sat at the tea table, unable to eat; wondering why my father should stay in bed. It was only two days since the Sunday, and I hadn't got used to them in the house, and I was missing Howarth.

'Why did you do it, Margaret?' she pleaded, softening, and sitting down at the table. 'You know you can't bring a man back here when you're in by yourself. You can't do it without everybody knowing. And yet you do it so brazenly, when everybody knew we were away.'

'I can't blame you not liking Howarth, Mother. But you've got to allow me my own discretion.'

'I've a mind that Mrs Tunnicliffe was reckoning to suggest he stayed here all Saturday night. I'm almost sure that's what she was trying to say. I could have cracked her face for her.'

'What's the use? If you go on like this I shall have to leave home.'

'Are you going on seeing this man, then?' she said aimlessly.

'Yes.'

'But what do you see in him, pray? A married man, living

122

away from his wife and family. Just to think of it, Margaret. And if he's an artist – well, he doesn't care. He can't care, letting you bring him here like that. It's a terrible thing.'

'He's not an artist. And you're making it sound so crude that I won't talk about it any more.'

'Our Michael says he's an artist, an art teacher or something, it makes no difference. And he knows him. He doesn't like him either, and you can't say our Michael's an unfair judge of character.'

'I don't care what Michael says ... I don't know why either you or him should push yourselves in.'

'We're not pushing in,' she said hopelessly, dismayed by my lack of feeling. 'I don't want to interfere like that. But I can't go clapping my hands when I see you with a chap like that. There's nothing right with it, and it's not decent.'

'I'm not going to argue. It's one of those things you can't do anything about.'

'I suppose I could go and see his wife and see what she thinks of it all. She must be able to do something.'

'I don't think you'd do that.'

'No, I wouldn't,' she said, standing up, small and fierce with her emotion. 'I didn't mean to get het up about it like this, either. But that Mrs Tunnicliffe fair enraged me, she was so sly ... I feel like going now and having it out with her.'

'You'd only degrade everything. And I'm not going to be dragged about amongst the neighbours like this. I'd rather leave home than see that happen.'

'I don't want you to do that,' she said slowly, suddenly afraid now that it seemed possible.

When my father came down he was quiet. He was going to the pit in two hours, but he must have been listening for me to come in from work, and to my mother's arguing. He was tired, his eyes were red and inflamed, and his cheeks sunken and dark with fatigue. His whole appearance was one unspoken reproach. I would have bled rather than hurt him, rather than have him condemn me. It wearied both of us, this worn appearance of his. He sat by the fire without speaking. I sat at the table too numb and sick to eat. When I stood up he said, almost indifferent to me, 'You know you've hurt your mother a lot doing this.' His head turned and his eyes flared at me with hate and disgust. I felt myself colouring and burning. His punishment was no longer physical, but when it appeared it was more implacable than his occasional blows. I was terrified with fear and love of him; of when he had hit my brothers and I had screamed at their helplessness, at the break in their dignity, tearing at my chair while he beat them. I hated his physicality, and the way it could destroy that dignity. He had a miner's uncouthness about him, and a miner's silence in pain, retributive, embracing all those who watched it. He had a miner's indifference to the physical, a savage complacency, that turned his silent reproach on me with a long association of childhood meanings.

He had nothing to say or advise; his helplessness sustained his desire to hurt me. Yet if I didn't respond to him he would think I despised him, that not only had I betrayed him by bringing someone to the house in his absence, but was unrepentant about it.

He watched me pile my few tea things, but as I moved to the door he couldn't restrain himself any longer. He staggered in his chair, as if attacked, then jumped to his feet and in spite of his tiredness rushed across the room and threw the tea things out of my hands with his fist.

'Aren't you going to say anything to me, you sly bitch!'

The crash and my cry brought my mother into the room. We stared unbelievingly at one another, my father's mouth wide and vacant, trembling with rage and frustration. I burst into tears and ran upstairs.

I beat the bed with my fists. But I didn't know whom I loved. Howarth or my father. I wanted to love one of them above everything. To love one of them with everything. I lay sobbing on the bed terrified of my father's helplessness and his rage.

The door opened, and I could hear his breathing. He watched me, his breath roaring through his nose. 'I'm sorry, lass. I'd give ought not to have done that.'

He waited dumbly. I stopped crying, and lay with my face hidden in the blankets. They still smelt of Howarth, almost of his warmth. I waited for my father to go, but I sensed him standing helpless in the door. 'It's all right,' I said.

'I shouldn't have done that.'

'It's all right. Let me be.'

'Are you sure?' he said, with an unnatural, masculine tenderness. His pain weakened me. I didn't look up.

'Yes.

I heard the door shut, and his slow steps downstairs. I couldn't restrain my pity for him, and I fell asleep sobbing, yearning to give him peace and some sort of absolution.

The process of tearing myself away had already begun, at Manchester and now back at home, and my father's remorse grew during the next few days. He lived in a silence which nothing would disturb: a miner's silence of emotional entombment, of justified fears and helplessness. Nothing I could do or say relieved him. He came back from work lifeless, staggering with exhaustion and with hate of the pit, but he couldn't sleep. I began to doubt that I was responsible at all; that I had merely brought to a climax a long and terrible despair. It seemed that it was something that moved in him, independent of all of us. Whenever he ate he brought his food up, in great, agonized retchings that filled the house until the building itself seemed convulsed. When Michael and Gwen came he made a token response, pulling out a tired humour, with none of his amiable invective and disinterest. He had the curious, inquiring humour of a miner; but now it staggered out half-torn by its own amusement. Michael stared at him sullenly, unaware of the cause. In a way, neither did my mother understand. My father sensed something, and failed to recognize it or sympathize. He was aware only of himself.

But whenever we were alone, and I sat sewing by the fire or reading, I would catch his eyes on me with their terrifying look.

I couldn't understand. I longed for him. I wanted him. I wanted him to talk to me, and to laugh and to show his rough affection. He turned his look away quickly and I was sure I was responsible for his unhappiness. Whatever he sensed, it exhausted him completely, and drove away any instinct to combat it. I wanted to touch him. But I was afraid of feeling him. It was the lack of touch that was implicit in both of us: he was careless of it, yet conscious of my fear of it. His bewilderment grew inwardly, destroying and wrapping itself round everything until all his recognizable traits were hidden. There was still his need to protect me, but that too was helpless in the flame that tormented his mind.

I couldn't help feeling angry, even enraged, with Michael, and resentful of Gwen. It was a bad thing. But in a way I couldn't forgive him for marrying Gwen. Everything that he had reproached and derided in me was embodied in her. My femininity, my original wish for education, my domesticity, my concern with my clothes and appearance: he had ridiculed these in his youth, then more subtly and implicitly in his maturity; only to resurrect them in Gwen. In his way he had embittered me and encouraged me to destroy much that was wholesome and necessary in a woman for the sake of some unintelligible and sexless rivalry. My distrust of domesticity and the fatefulness of motherhood were largely his doing. He had insisted on the subservience of women, and as a youth had bullied me into the weaker role. He had painted a picture of woman for me that was denuded and full of his natural destructiveness. He had been contemptuous of motherhood and the breeding animality of women, yet in *Gwen* it abounded luxuriously. She was fully a woman, companionable, sexed, motherful. He seemed to have produced her at my expense, as if her appearance were a direct result of my defeat.

I frightened her. She was puzzled by me. Whenever our eyes met we looked nervously at each other and smiled, a world of misunderstanding revolving between us. She wanted to be kind, but felt that I would rebuff her, perhaps humiliate her, at the first opportunity. I wasn't to be trusted. She only approached me through Michael.

Neither my mother nor my father mentioned to Michael Howarth's visit to the house. Having found out, I would have thought that their first reaction would have been to tell him, to secure him on their side. But they said nothing, not even to me. It was as if Howarth's coming to the house had suddenly separated the family into its components, isolating each one, and fragmenting the domesticity into its final pattern of disruption and decay. At times it still seemed to me that Howarth was in the house: I seemed to smell him and feel his warmth in the bed.

Michael was easily aware of the disruption, but couldn't identify the cause. He even suspected his marriage was to blame, that there was some bitterness amongst us all directed at Gwen. But there was no evidence: my parents had got on well at Cardiff and everyone was pleased with the marriage. He must have mentioned his concern to Gwen: she changed visibly, too, after her first visits, becoming quiet and uncertain in the family atmosphere, and relieved whenever Michael said it was time for them to go.

One evening, when Michael was explaining their plans to take their honeymoon in London at the end of term, and regretting that they'd miss Christmas at home, my father suddenly said, out of his deep inattention, 'I wish I'd never educated our Michael, nor our Margaret.' He spoke loudly, irrelevantly to what Michael had been saying.

At first Michael thought there must be some connection, then he said, half amused, 'Why not, Dad?'

'If I'd known then what I know now I'd never have let you go to that grammar school, nor you to university. I'd rather have had you working with your bare hands at twelve years old than you stay a day longer at school. I regret nothing more in my life than having educated you.'

'Oh, Dad,' my mother said, distressed at his seriousness and simplicity.

'What are you getting at?' Michael said, impressed, yet not far from being amused.

'I was a fool to have educated you. I should have known. I should have known.' His quiet, determined remorse numbed us. He beat his fist against the arm of the chair, slowly, almost with the frustration of a young man. He was far from us, deliberately withdrawn and disowning. I felt I would never come near him again. My mother stared at his loss with empty, in-turned eyes. She looked blinded.

'It's no use regretting a thing like that now,' Michael said, as if he understood what my father meant. 'You can't stop something of that sort.'

'But I could have. I could have,' he said. 'I should have put you to work when you were young.'

'What is it that makes you say things like that?' Michael asked. He was hurt, and wretched at my father's wilfulness.

'What is it?' my father said. 'Why, it's your emptiness. Your great and everlasting emptiness.' He looked at Michael narrowly, his eyes blazing and wet. 'It's your great educated emptiness. And I never saw it. Me, a bloody *man*.'

Yet Michael was not as hurt as I was. He seemed to absorb my father's words as if, deeply, he'd been expecting them all his life. He was just beyond the reach of my father now, but not so far that he wasn't wounded. He looked at my mother with open pain and humiliation. 'What's made him like this?' he asked her bitterly.

She shook her head, clasping her hands together, unable to speak.

'It's because you *are* empty, Michael,' I said, unable to control my anger.

He stared at me without offence, then said to me, 'Yes. But I feel that he really means you, not me.'

8

Howarth accepted my silence. I boarded the train with him and waited while he found two seats and lifted the suitcases, pushing them on to the racks and pressing my bag in on top. He'd deliberately chosen an empty slow train in the middle of the afternoon. Sitting opposite me in the tabled carriage, he watched me carefully as we pulled out of the station. The city was bright in winter sunlight, a light blue sky flooded with small ochre clouds. I sat still as the familiar buildings slipped below and disappeared. The train passed over the town on a series of arches; then a broad metal span took us over the river, and the track buried itself in a thick forest of chimneys and tall banks of crusted brickwork. The walls ran by in yellow and red streams, streaked with blackness.

We turned south in a long shallow sweep, away from the peninsula of arches, mounting slowly towards the low ridges and the black brickwork of the Shawcliffe tunnel. The train was very long. As the track curved I could see the inside length of the brown carriages, heavily splayed out before and behind us, the engine toiling away, soundlessly at this distance, and the purple ridge seemingly impenetrable a mile away. It was cold, the heating had only just been turned on. The faint hissing of the steam in the pipes muffled the conversation from the other end of the carriage.

'You look the epitome of a Happy Christmas,' Howarth said. He looked determined and calm. 'I had a job stopping Ben coming to see me off,' he added. 'I gave him the wrong time of the train. It's not the sort of thing you like to do.'

I shook my head. He stared inquisitively at me, then, finding it painful, turned his gaze to the slow disappearance of the fields and grey stone farms. Out of the opposite window I had a distant view of my father's pit, with its stubborn white smoke and the long, broken-backed slag heap. It looked senselessly powerful and remote on its ridge top.

'There's been an awful coincidence,' I told him. 'Michael and Gwen are taking their honeymoon in London this next fortnight.'

He looked at me blankly. 'A postponed one, you mean.'

'They couldn't get away until now.'

It was irrelevant.

'They're not on the train,' he said.

'No. I'm not sure when they're going down. The end of next week sometime, when Gwen finishes at school. My parents will be alone at Christmas for the first time. Unless Alec comes over.'

'Did you tell them everything about this?'

'Yes.'

The train rose into the tunnel. We stared at one another across the table, then Howarth leaned over and took my hand. He gripped it tightly. His eyes were wet. The train burst out amongst the dark, open fields. 'I'm sorry,' he said.

'It's all been settled now,' I said. 'And I'm glad of that.'

I pulled my hand away and lay back in the seat. He looked at me with a new affection, disbelieving, and full of doubt.

'Have you always chosen the most difficult way of doing things?' I asked.

He smiled earnestly. 'It *used* to be characteristic of me. I was always awkward, according to my mother. What did your parents say when you left?'

'We had a bad scene.'

'I can imagine it.' He shook his head, wonderingly. 'I

shouldn't have let you do it on your own. I should have been with you.'

'I didn't want it like that, did I?'

'You're making it very hard for yourself. In the future . . .' He stared at me reproachfully.

'I don't think my mother's sure you *are* with me. In a way, I didn't handle it properly. I made it seem I was leaving in a temper.' I half-laughed and half-cried.

Howarth leaned heavily on the table towards me, frowning, his hands clasped together tightly. 'What makes us do things like this?' he said. 'All this – and I still don't know. It all seems to have gone on outside us.'

'We're not really going away at all, are we?' I said. 'We're carrying it all with us.'

He gazed at the window. In a moment I realized he was looking at his own reflection; then furtively at mine. The unfamiliarity of the landscape and the increasing speed of the train relieved me.

I'd never experienced the long approach to London. Howarth had relaxed, and sat back smoking after four hours in the train. But the continual surging through tunnels, the brief glimpses of worn brick embankments and the dirty rear windows of houses, the stopping and starting, wearied me more and more. It was a deliberate lingering. The jarring and battering of passing trains entombed us further in the dark brickiness. But Howarth knew the line well. At a certain point he gave a start, smiled at the familiarity of some gasometers, and began to pull the cases from the rack. 'Well, this is it,' he said. I was sick and retching with the fumes and the continual delay in tunnels. It was too noisy and foreign. We seemed to have been chased the whole of the journey.

Howarth went and called a porter. The four cases were wheeled down the platform; we followed them through the barrier and joined the taxi queue. Howarth had told me the arrangements already: but Camden Town, where he had found us a flat with a landlord he had had as a student, was only a name to me. I resented submitting to him as early as this. He was pleased to be back in London. He hardly sensed my strangeness, and for his own peace of mind ignored my feeling of loss. His sudden indulgence repelled me. I could only feel reassured by going to the time-table board and examining with great care the times of the trains back north. Then Howarth called me to the taxi.

'It's great to be back,' he said, his enthusiasm lost amongst the crowded streets. I tried to ignore the scene, just as he ignored me: I had a vague impression of streets narrower and buildings dirtier than I had ever expected; of row after row of sordid houses, filthier than anything I had seen at home. The area we went through was one of disintegration and decay, infected with a parasitic disease that fed on the buildings, the brick and the stone. It was its desolation and the persistence of its life that wearied me: the streets were full of eager, rushing people.

I was relieved at the sight of the room. From the outside it seemed that the building might have been falling down. But inside all this decay was concealed behind neat wallpaper and good second-hand furniture. It had neither the cosiness nor the cleanliness of home: it was crying out for some female hand. On the mantelpiece was a letter addressed to me.

Howarth was smiling. He put the suitcases down and watched me open the envelope. There was a simple message inside, in his large mechanical handwriting. *Thank you, Margaret, for coming. You've made it all worth while. 'Howarth'.* We smiled at one another. It was clumsy.

'I came down a week ago to tidy the place and see the landlord. We're lucky to get a place like this.' He was like a boy offering a present and wondering whether it would be genuinely pleasing or only tokenly accepted. I went and put my arms round him, needing him. 'It's all right, then,' he said. 'And it's not going to be half as bad as you think.'

There was a newness about him, and a freshness: he seemed younger and more certain. 'I'm not really frightened. It's the strangeness,' I told him.

'Do you want to talk about it?'

'I don't think so.'

'I want to tell you about the divorce arrangements. You'll have to hear them.'

'I don't want to hear anything yet. Please, I'd just like some quiet and some peace.'

'Just as you like,' he said, and went into the kitchen of the little flat. There was just the one room and the kitchen.

I sat on the divan in the corner of the room and looked at the four suitcases and my bag in the middle of the floor, and at the old furniture. It was a shock, its coldness and the absence of any familiarity. Howarth was now as strange as the flat. The stains on the wallpaper round the gas fire, the marks of former pictures, seemed to represent the blankness of the journey itself. Yet I had longed for it, to be alone. But it was too sudden and shattering, and uncertain.

When he came back in, quietly, he expected me to be asleep. He had a cup of tea in either hand, in little yellow cups, and he lifted his head in surprise. 'I thought you'd be resting,' he said, and put the tea on the small cupboard beside the bed. He sat on a chair, facing me. 'You want to drink it,' he said.

We were looking at one another, waiting for our first impression of the place to reveal itself. 'What do you think? Rather neat,' he added quickly, in case I should show any disappointment. 'I used to have a room at the top of the house when I was a student here.'

'It looks better than the outside,' I told him.

'London's not so bad once you get *into* it. I'll take you round and you'll see how different it is . . . how different each street is, really . . .' When I didn't answer, he said tonelessly, 'There's only one thing to talk about immediately, Margaret. And that's money. Do you mind?'

'I didn't want to.' I lay back, finishing the tea, and listened to him insist on the arrangements he had already made – leaving everything to his wife except the fifty pounds he had brought with him. He'd already paid a month in advance on this place. His wife was preparing to sell the house and move into a flat.

'There's so much disturbance about it,' I said hopelessly. 'Don't go on.'

He didn't say anything for a while. People chatted in the street below, with foreign voices: the city throbbed beyond. 'I can guess why you don't want to talk about it,' he said. 'Are you afraid that all this is only temporary, or something? That I'll go back to her in the end?'

'I haven't thought about it,' I told him, exhausted and numb. 'But it all seems so unnecessary – all this change. All the argument. Selling your house. . . . It's so simple to me. It doesn't have to have all this restlessness. . . .'

'It's not as neat and tidy as you think,' he said. 'It's no good carrying on with your face turned away from what your hands are doing. I've ended my marriage, I've given up my job . . . You can't expect all the people we've involved to go on as if nothing had happened. You can't enter into other people's lives like that and hope to come away unnoticed.'

'But I don't want to know your wife. Nor your children. I just want our life here, and nothing else. That's what I came for. That's why I came away. I want nothing more than that. Nothing whatsoever.'

'This is a fine start,' he said dismally. 'You can't cut things off like that, Margaret. If we've to have any chance at all we've got to look at what's there.'

'This is how I want my chance: no different from this.

That's the reason I came away. The only reason I came away was so that I could be alone with you.'

'It's made you hard,' he suggested softly, thinly. I despised him for his consideration.

'I hope it has.'

'It doesn't have to be like that.'

'It won't be hard for you. You're a man. But it's going to be hard for me. You don't understand my position at all.'

'You're wrong to treat it as a battle even before we've begun.'

He let me sleep it off. I dreamed of the distant shattering of trains.

It was dark when I woke. He was stretched out in an armchair. The gas fire gave a low, intense light round him, but its heat scarcely reached the bed. He'd been dozing. He started, and looked round when I moved.

'Hello,' I said, as if I'd been a long way away.

He came over and sat on the bed, peering intently at me to see if, in the darkness, he could detect any change. 'Do you feel any better, now?' he asked. He ran his hand cautiously through my hair.

'I'd like to take you out,' he added, and quickly went over to fetch my coat as though he'd been waiting a long time.

The street down to the tube station was piled high with mounds of rubbish from a market. It smelt strongly of fruit and vegetables. Howarth liked the sight and the smell. The stalls were being dismantled, but were still alight with glaring yellow gas lamps. He wanted to take me on the tube to show it to me, but I refused. Instead we caught a bus down to Tottenham Court Road. He wanted to show me everything at once, wanting to soothe me. I insisted on a meal, and he took me into Soho.

At once there was a difference, a lively, superficial, rotting difference, a surface thing that didn't reflect but hid the emptiness around. I enjoyed the oily difference of the food, the warmth of the wine, the faked atmosphere. The whole city seemed an embellishment with no inside, and in Soho was this last finial at the very top. Howarth was pleased that I was thrilled. He was almost uncouth, touching me provocatively, bubbling over with himself. I wanted to shelter him from his disappointment. He was coming back to himself, but doubtfully and frightened.

The evening and the morning were hardly connected. There was a dragged-out peacefulness about the evening, an ease of anticipation. He showed me round the West End with the suspicion that I would inevitably dislike it, that my provincial insecurity would after all identify the place with Sheffield or Manchester. But we'd brought the difference with us. In a way I wanted it the same, yet I clung to the strangeness and the emptiness. They hid us.

We crossed the river over Hungerford Bridge. The lights trailed in the water; they were dragged and dribbled away. The Festival Hall's molten image in the Thames was like a luminous rock, submerged and glowing. We climbed up from the gardens and caught a bus back to Camden.

It was late. The bus moved slowly over the bridge. The road was deserted. Below, the river glistened like black metal, the boats moulded on its surface like deceptive toys and growths. The buildings slowly narrowed and drew close to the road. As the bus moved northwards the decay moved closer, until once more we seemed to be tucked under that rotting façade, creeping under, walking up the street in the still darkness and climbing wearily up the narrow stone steps to the door.

There was the frozen strangeness as we undressed, suddenly ashamed of our nakedness, as if it mustn't be confused with our reasons for coming here. When I went down to the bathroom and found it locked and the noise of someone busy inside, I rushed back up the stairs as if I'd been molested. Howarth went down himself and tried the door noisily, exchanging a few words with the person inside. When he came up he said it was empty. I was afraid of using the lavatory. It had a communal dirt.

Howarth was already in bed. He'd pulled the divan slightly away from the wall, making it look bigger. He kept to the side nearest the wall, and encouraged me to get in by appearing to be drowsy. He didn't touch me, and kept to his side of the bed. It was strange lying with him and knowing that now there was no real alternative. It made everything less immediate and sharp. Then he said my name and came to hold me tightly, feeling me through my clothes.

'I want to *bury* myself in you,' he said later. We lay side by side watching the reflected light on the ceiling. 'And forget all this.'

'Yet you complained when I said the same, this afternoon.'

'Ah yes,' he said slowly, as if nothing had really changed. 'It's what I want.'

'Aren't you satisfied with me?' I asked, complacent.

'Yes. If this is what you mean.' He felt my breasts, almost derisively arousing me. 'Yet you and your body . . . they're miles apart.'

'I'm not aware of it.'

'Perhaps not.' He kissed me, and kissed my breasts, frustrated with himself. I pushed his head away, shy of his boyishness. His head sank down again with a sigh. 'There's always this barrier between you and me. I wonder if you'll ever let it down? It's almost a physical thing. I can feel it when we're loving. It comes into your movements as if somehow you begrudge giving all this. I can almost beat my fists against it.'

'I might want something more than your love of my body, of what I can give you.'

'A love of you, yourself? But you never let me see you. You're suddenly prim . . . with barricades up all round as if you couldn't even bear the thought of being hurt. You hold back something – and it's *that* which really makes me despair.'

'You're not sure what you *do* want from me. That's the cause of it.'

'I know what I want. I still don't know what I can get.'

He laughed and kissed me, but failed to arouse me, and laughed again at his helplessness. 'Don't you despise your "coolness" at times?' he asked.

'Is it very important, what we've got?'

His head turned towards me and I felt his long look. 'I've no values of that sort left,' he said. 'Have you?'

When I didn't answer he rolled on his side, away from me. I was imprisoned by him when he felt weakened and disappointed, as though we'd never be released.

I kissed him behind his ear, where his blond hair curled on his pyjama collar. He laughed at it, relieved. 'Go on,' he said, when I stopped.

'No, you're too erotic, Howarth.'

He laughed again, so stubbornly.

He had already made certain plans. Before he came to London he had paid a brief visit to secure the flat, made arrangements with a bank, and looked around for a job. He had arranged an interview with an advertising agency for the morning after our arrival. He got up while I was still asleep; I was vaguely aware of his movements about the room, and when I woke up he had gone. He'd left me a cup of tea with a morning paper on the cupboard beside the bed. The tea was cold. He'd left no message, and it wasn't until he came back, two hours later, that I knew where he had been. I was dressed and unpacking my cases. He came in disconsolately, carrying a large clean portfolio which he dropped on the bed.

'They have a job for me,' he said, after explaining where he'd been. 'It's not much, but I could build it up quickly.'

139

'What's in the portfolio?' I asked.

'The work I sent up a few weeks ago. I've brought it back ... it's all old stuff.'

I opened the folder and looked at the mounted sheets inside. The work was highly professional as far as I could judge, neat and very impressive. It was mainly designs for posters and book jackets and record sleeves, with drawings of machinery and several examples of typographic design.

'Are you going to take it?' I said. He watched me look at his work reluctantly: he was suddenly restless, regretting that I'd seen it.

'I worked in this agency before. When I came out of art school. But I left fairly quickly.'

'Why?'

'I disliked the work. It wasn't very well paid in those days. But now ... it's at least four times the size as I knew it. If I'd have stopped there I'd be a rich man now. They weren't slow to point that out.'

'Don't you think the job's good enough for you? This work, it looks tremendous.'

'It's very clever, isn't it? But it's quite a different thing doing that in an art school than in an agency.'

'You wouldn't like the hardness?'

'I don't mind that. Once I got used to *working* again ...'
He looked at me indifferently.

'The ethics of it, then?'

'I don't want to be pretentious about it at this stage, do I? Nay ... but it has worried me. What the hell am I going to do for a job? I've to pay maintenance to the family. Do you want me to talk about it?'

'Are you afraid to face that side of it on your own?'

'No ... But you're involved. My wife's filing the divorce and it's undefended. She's citing my desertion and miscon- duct with you.'

He watched my reaction without surprise. He'd been

140

waiting too long to tell me, and he was resigned to me. 'I'm sorry,' he said, almost ignoring my distress. 'It's the quickest and the cleanest way. I wanted it over with, quick.'

'But you never mentioned it. That I'd be involved.'

'It's the only way,' he pleaded, standing up and wanting to touch me. 'To get the thing over with as quick as we can. I can't bear the thought of it hanging over me indefinitely.'

'But you've pulled me in ... you've dragged me in without a word. You never asked me. I should have been given some choice. I never wanted it like this. ...'

'It can't be helped, believe me. She knew something about it and ... I told her everything. I wanted it all clean and open.'

'But you never *asked* me!'

'You wouldn't let me talk about it,' he almost shouted. 'I asked you to. ...' He gazed hopelessly at me, banging his fist into the palm of his hand. 'I'd have done anything to avoid something like this. It's been burning in my mind all the time.'

'Oh, Howarth. How could you? You knew I'd never want it like this. You knew. You've just used me, whatever else you meant to do.'

'I promise you I haven't done that.'

'But you have !'

We stared helplessly at one another, waiting for one of us to find something which would deny it.

Howarth picked up his raincoat and walked out of the room. I let him go. It seemed suddenly characteristic of him to walk out on a situation that had become unbearable. I was afraid that he had walked out on his marriage in the same way.

He hated to argue something out, to make something sound reasonable. He walked away from things. I began to dread that his weakness was in relying on others and on his technique of escape to solve anything that grew unbearable.

But he had nothing else to turn to. If he had been an artist as Michael insisted he was, he would have had something. But his portfolio of work had nothing to do with him: it was some mechanical process; nothing of Howarth himself showed in it. He had only a vast emptiness to turn to.

The difference between Michael and Howarth was now vivid and real. I kept remembering seeing them both together for the first time, at Christmas: Howarth standing aloof in the Professor's room, almost contemptuous and above it; and Michael, pouring himself passionately into his group, working within it.

Michael would go on, I knew, to a happy home life with Gwen and their children. His fatalism would be redeemed by his children in a way that Howarth had failed to find. Michael had waited for his children and not had them young like Howarth; he had given himself no time to overcome the force of their consolation. Michael would always be able to be consoled now. He was out of reach of my father's primitive conscience. It wounded him that he was, but he was safe. He was safe even in his work, protected on all sides by it, an instrument of his science, no longer a person. We'd lost him. My father had lost him as he had just lost me, and had cried out when it was all too late.

Howarth was an outcast from all this, I was sure. He'd been left behind; he'd been chased out. Coming to London was his acceptance of his situation. He'd declared his absence completely by withdrawing. He'd accepted it at last, declaring himself out of favour. Yet where had he withdrawn to?

It was no place at all. Around us settled the emptiness of London, the abyss. He couldn't retreat, like my father, to a hard, unquestioning conscience: the conscience that was his work, a miner's dolorous habit of thought and affection. He and my father had so much in common. But Howarth had stepped back into space, he had run back, and I had shared his lust for this freedom.

Only, it was a falling. A fall that neither of us knew how to end. The very area we'd moved to seemed steeped in our dilemma: the rot and the decay. It was a refuse area, full of detritus and rotting space. We'd come to it like so many others, with a bird's instinct, purposeless, drawn to it unthinkingly, like a natural migration. And what was to be its effect?

But he was surprised and secretly pleased to find me not angry when he came back. He may even have prepared himself to find me gone. I didn't ask him. My blood surged to him when he came in the room, his raincoat carried on his arm, his eyes questioning me. I held his hands to my face, warming him.

'Will you come shopping?' I said. He smiled in relief. We went down into Inverness Street market, and whatever he had hopelessly planned on his walk round he quickly forgot.

'I think I'll go down to the County Hall tomorrow,' he decided, 'and see what teaching jobs there are.'

'But you've just left teaching. Why do you want to go back? You said it was degrading.'

'Not the sort of teaching I have in mind. I wouldn't teach art. I'll teach in a secondary modern school where a specialist's not needed.'

'You're going back on yourself,' I warned him. 'I think you should keep to what you decided at first.'

'But I must find something to do, Margaret. Something that's not ruinous. I don't know. . . .' He rubbed his head wildly.

'I want you to be happy . . .'

He stared at me, uncertain of my change in meaning. He suspected I pitied him, now, and it made him nervous, and unwillingly dogmatic.

'You do what *you* think is right,' I said.

'Now you're talking like a woman,' he said, smiling. 'Uncommitted to work.'

'Don't worry. I'm getting a job myself. There's always a shortage of typists.'

'Ah, now that's what I need. A mechanical nature.'

'You make me sick,' I said, depressed by him.

He laughed cheerfully, and patted my shoulder. 'Do you know,' he said, 'I think I've given *you* all my conviction. Every little drop of it.'

In the afternoon he said he had some sort of surprise for me. He took me out of the house, and instead of walking down Inverness Street he took me in the opposite direction, walking between two rows of not unpleasant, heavily-painted houses. Within a few minutes a frieze of branches showed beyond the houses, then a broad stretch of grass and bare trees. He laughed at my surprise.

'But I'd never have thought,' I said, looking back at the roofs and chimneys, 'I'd never have guessed that this was here. It's like the sea ... in the middle of all these buildings.'

'It's only Regent's Park. Don't look too enthusiastic or they'll charge us to go in. There's still one more thing....' He put his arm in mine and kissed me and led the way up through the trees.

Down the side of the park stretched a row of beautiful terraces, white and glistening against the cold blue sky. Howarth explained their architectural uniqueness as we walked. But I didn't believe in the Nash terraces. They seemed again only a façade to the seething ugliness behind.

'There,' he said, and pointed at two strange birds.

Behind a fence two ostrich-like birds, dark brown, were pacing up and down; and then other features of a zoo came into sight: the low buildings topped by wire cages, and the noise of strange animals and birds. He was excited and loving at my surprise, pushing his face against mine, suddenly, and whispering, and kissing my ear. 'Do you want to go in?' he said. 'Or would you like just to walk round the side?'

'We'll go round the side,' I told him. I didn't want to look too closely at anything.

The zoo was in a low hollow, and as we walked down towards the lake in the distance we could see a few of the animals – llamas, deer, brown and white and black bears on their yellow, concrete hills. The menagerie was like an arena to the surrounding façade of glistening plaster and columns, as if everything had been flung out centrifugally. Or as if it were one large room, with its decorated walls. And the park – the park was strangely reassuring; worn and anxious like a mother: the place had a heavy maternity.

The lake had the same shallow artificiality as the zoo, stretching itself in its low hollow between the trees. Like the rest of the park it was deserted. The emptiness was a meagre, polite desolation, anxious not to be distressing. It seemed merely an absence of buildings, bare and thin with conceding too much. It was a big, empty park, sighing with the wind, its polite hand over its aching heart.

We came out on to Baker Street, and walked slowly towards the Oxford Street shops. 'I want you to buy some new clothes,' Howarth said. 'Make a complete change of yourself. It's very important.'

'What sort of change have we in mind?'

'Something sexy. Sex with restraint: that should be your new motif.'

'Something for you to play with,' I said.

'All right, then,' he said, angered. 'Just get some new clothes. I'll pay for them.'

'Do you know how much money I've got?'

He shook his head indifferently.

'I've enough to look after myself absolutely. And that's what I want to do.'

'What about food?'

'We'll halve it. If you haven't enough yourself I'll pay for everything.'

He grunted to himself as if he'd been amused. We went round the shops making plans for what I would buy. He had a passionate taste for clothes, strangely full of reason, and completely dominating me; then suddenly becoming bored with the whole thing.

We did nothing the next few days but walk around London, visiting places, eating out, like anyone on holiday. I never relaxed. I was afraid any moment of meeting Michael. I wrote a letter home, not giving my address, to try and reassure my parents, and for the first time told them fully about Howarth and his divorce plans. I didn't mention whether we intended getting married or not. I wanted to send them small presents, but it would have upset them, and been too ironical. I told them I would send an accommodation address for them to write to in the next letter.

I was worried by Howarth's sudden inability to settle on a job. He talked a great deal about doing manual labour, but it depressed him profoundly. His pride confused him. He was tremendously realistic about money and could measure its effect with great accuracy. When both of us had got used to mutual spending we pooled our accounts.

During the day he spent a great deal of his time on his own, often in the National Gallery, where he seemed to have sat for hours in front of only one or two of the paintings. Whenever he took me there he walked through rapidly, commenting on many of the pictures, but becoming impatient if I wanted to stop and look. It was as if we were trespassing on private ground. He came with me to buy my clothes, taking infinite pains to see that I found his taste acceptable. The two winter suits and the coat I bought pleased him. I was more feminine and stronger, much more a woman, and full of his male attention and flattery. I began to enjoy sharing my body with him, wanting to lead him and antagonize him. He was frightened: he was frightened of giving me a child. 'Why won't you let me use a contraceptive if you won't,' he complained.

'I can't bear it.'

'But it's only sense. . . . We *can't* have a child.'

'It's the thought of it,' I told him. 'Just the idea. It makes me feel sick.'

And it frightened and exhausted him. 'How can I make love to you?' he pleaded.

'With one of those – it makes it all artificial. As if we didn't believe in it for *our* sakes, but just for the sake of doing it. It's so premeditated. And crude.'

'Crude, crude ! . . .'

But I was ashamed for him. I refused, repelled and degraded the only time he tried it. Nothing had ever revolted me more. He tried interrupting his loving, and was dissatisfied and slowly ashamed of himself. I was much more aggressive towards him.

I was the first to get a job. Howarth was noticeably relieved. He relaxed, lazily, and took longer in choosing what he would do. I found the work easy, and more congenial: it was in the B.B.C.'s Overseas Department. I simply caught a bus from Camden Town to Kingsway and back each day.

I was astonished by my new confidence. It cowed Howarth. He knew I was immediately successful at work, and almost popular. The people in the office had a cautious respect for me; it had none of the familiarity and irony of my work up north. I liked working in London, and travelling through it in the early mornings and the winter evenings. When I wrote to my parents and sent them two presents for Christmas they must have sensed my relief: their return letter contained no reproach, and no warmth. I was extremely happy. Only Howarth wearied me. It became apparent how we were feeding off one another, and only I seemed to be thriving. He was cold at the ease with which I took to London. He had expected me to be difficult. But I thrived on the anonymity. I took my confidence from him, and was agressive.

In return he had a bated satisfaction; then a slow frustration that grew with the distance that suddenly sprang us apart. I struggled to keep with him. I relied on his sexuality wilfully; I loved his body and its fairness. It was so vulnerable, and bare to everything.

I gave myself to him like a child, thinking that it soothed him: the baby-talk and the baby-gestures. He accepted it, and gave all he could in return. He was in despair. I took his conviction away; and London took it away. He collapsed into his bitter, empty shell; that protective cynicism and disillusion which underlay his earnest nature. And he wouldn't let me help him. He made finding a job an act of pilgrimage, an atonement, a confession of his solitariness. He wrote twice to his wife, once at Christmas with a parcel of presents he bought for his children, and two weeks later, discussing the divorce arrangements. He didn't seem to care. We celebrated Christmas lavishly, reducing our small capital to a minimum. It passed him by unseen.

Yet, although he was despairing it didn't drain my enthusiasm: it drove me on. I was like a girl again, and full of a quiet sensuality. I had never been so alive. The moment he came into the room I was wanting to touch him, to watch his hands, and his mouth; to feel him touch me, casually, as he passed; to feel the heat of his body as he did something intently, reading or listening; the way his body curled in the chair. For a while the presence of Michael in London lingered over me, even after I knew he and Gwen must be back north. It faded slowly, and it vanished just at that moment when the novelty of London wore off.

After a month Howarth swallowed his pride and went back into teaching. I tried to discourage him at first, but he was peculiarly adamant, and resigned. He'd expected it all along. He went on Divisional Staff, and was sent to a secondary modern school in north London.

His unhappiness, the emptiness, began to depress me: he seemed to have no way to turn, no purpose in life that he could yield to, struggling with himself when I would have least expected it to provide a way out.

'I don't like doing this,' he said, the day before he was due to go. He spoke to himself, reprovingly. 'I shouldn't be doing this, I know. I'm throwing too much away.'

'You're not throwing anything away,' I reassured him. 'You're only tormenting yourself with it.'

'Why *should* I, though?'

'I don't know. . . . Some part of you – it must feel you've done wrong.'

'I know,' he admitted. 'But it can't be true.' He hung his head in his bewilderment. 'I'd never punish myself for leaving her and all that she meant.'

'What did she mean?'

He didn't stop to think. 'The uselessness . . . the inevitability of everything,' he replied quickly.

'But you can't escape that.'

He flushed, his fairness discoloured by his quick rage and regret. 'Don't tell me I've done it all for nothing. . . . No!' He condemned me with his fixed stare, urging me to judge him, to enrage him and free him from his fear.

'You tire me out when you torment yourself like this,' I said. 'I can't see why you must torment yourself all the time. You confuse everything with it.'

'But it's so simple,' he said. 'I didn't come here to feel like this. I came here for something fresh, a new start of some kind.'

'Didn't you come for *me*?'

'Yes.' He looked at me soberly.

'Because there's no new start to anything, is there? You're only making everything impossible for us.'

'But it should *mean* more than this. I should have something to show for it, besides you. You've gained a lot by coming here ...' He looked at me, full of jealousy. 'The truth is,' he went on, 'there's still this coldness between us. Of you having one thing in our relationship and me having another.'

'Then it's *your* coldness.'

'I can't believe that. There's something separating us. I can never feel *with* you.'

'You're being jealous and bitter,' I said. 'I've given you everything I have. There isn't any more. What else *can* there be? You have everything.'

'It's your pride. Yourself. You haven't given me *yourself* at all, you've only given *from* it. You haven't given me the thing itself, like I've given you.'

I shook my head. I couldn't understand. I thought he was merely urging his dejection on to me.

'Do you despise me,' he asked, 'because I've given you all *my* pride? I've given everything.... You've only given me bits in return.'

There was an air of nausea about him: it frightened me that I hadn't noticed it before, this plunging sickness. 'Then you shouldn't,' I said. 'You can't give all that to a person and then ask for it back.... And I don't think you have.'

'I've *sunk* it all in you. I don't mind that, though.... Yet I feel that you could leave me, Margaret, and I'd be the only one to suffer.'

'You don't believe I *can* love you, do you? I don't think you can believe anybody can love you.'

'I don't feel the love. It reaches me as different things – but never, it seems, as love.'

'Has your marriage destroyed so much?'

'I'm afraid of loving you, of finding that you love me. I've always been afraid of you because of that – because I feel you have so much love to give. But I can't feel your love. It all goes on outside me, on the surface. I *watch* myself loving you. It's miles away. I can never get hold of it, and feel: "*now*, that's it". There are just moments when I really know I'm loving and *in* love with you. I feel it in every part of me ... everything seems to feel it. I can't describe it. Then it goes. And I'm struggling all over again for it. It never *stays*. And I've been blaming you for that.'

'Do you want to go back to your wife? Is that what you're really trying to say?' I asked almost incoherently.

'No. This *is* something that I have with you. With her I I never had it. At least there's hope ... some hope with you. I can feel alive.'

'I'm glad,' I told him, tearful, weakened by him.

We lay down together, and curiously he didn't want my loving. I felt his relief. It burned in him that something had at last been resolved.

9

I wasn't sure why Howarth went back to teaching: it may even have been a longing for his own children. He was strong with himself in quite small ways. I knew he had a photograph of Sheila and Brian, torn from a family group, but I only saw it by accident when he pulled his wallet out. He never mentioned them. He gave me no direct cause for jealousy about the past. He urged himself on into the present all the time. It was a reluctant, staggered race.

He was already back from school the first day when I got home from work. He hadn't made my tea, which had been his usual habit. He was sunk with a deep muted depression in a chair, his figure illuminated by the glow from the gas fire. It was already dark and cold outside: the kerbs of the pavements were beginning to frost in Inverness Street. He'd still got his top coat on, but I could tell he'd been sitting there for some time. His smile turned his face into that clown-like remoteness, rejecting any direct sympathy.

'How did it go?' I asked, taking off my coat concernedly. I'd thought about him all day long, trying to imagine him in a classroom with his inevitable clumsiness and preoccupation. He stared up at my hair, almost as if he hadn't heard. He used to tease me about the pains I took with it.

'Don't you want to talk about it?' I said.

'It went all right. I haven't got the hang of it yet. I treat them like people.'

'Are they little horrors?' I laughed with relief.

'They're vile,' he said quietly.

152

'Do you want some tea?' I ignored his mood.

He stood up and took his coat off, and followed me into the kitchen. He helped me slowly with the tea, liking the way I did things, practical, smiling to himself, wanting to watch and to conceal his true feelings.

'We'll go out and celebrate tonight,' I told him.

He shook his head. 'I've some marking to do. I shan't have time,' he said.

'You are taking it seriously.'

'You want me to.'

'Yes . . . But don't forget me.'

'That's more how I like to see you,' he decided. 'Possessive.'

'I'm not immune to you, then?'

'You're not.' He laughed simply, revived and suddenly pleased with himself. He'd bought himself a light blue pullover since coming to London and he wore it all the time: it lit up his fairness and his pleasure. He looked very dear in it.

I read the whole evening, and watched him marking the ragged books. He surprised me with his conscientiousness, his head bowed stiffly over the table, working by the light from a red reading lamp. He was shut inside himself. All his force was turned inwards. It tormented me to resist him. When he was nearly finished I picked up one of the books.

'Are you teaching English?' I asked him, going near him. My hip touched his shoulder. He looked up, absorbed, afraid of intrusion. It burned me to touch him.

'Yes,' he said in an inquiring voice. 'English and History.'

'Have you ever taught them before?'

He shook his head. 'It doesn't matter,' he dismissed it. 'I can't think of any other subject to teach but English. It's useful and I don't have to distort it.'

'What about History?'

'That might be different. I've only had one lesson so far. I

153

think in the end I'll make it a vehicle of my own moral judgements. That's the most I can do, isn't it? The history books I have to teach from are full of the Nation and the Empire.'

'Yes. I think you've been wise,' I appeased him.

He listened to my voice carefully, as if it echoed inside him. Then he said, 'The French teacher's a German. The Geography teacher's a Frenchman. A little Belgian agnostic takes Scripture. I don't suppose they can mind me teaching English.'

He laughed to himself, resigned to his humour. I was glad that he was working. I stood close to him and felt him working. When I went to prepare supper in the kitchen I could feel his presence through the wall. It seemed to warm the air.

Afterwards he joked with me about writing my diary. He'd never seen it before: it was the first time since coming to London that I'd felt sufficiently comforted to write in it, and he was full of curiosity because I wouldn't let him see it. The next morning he was extremely quiet, too nervous to eat, yawning with his nervousness, his hands trembling slightly as if they were unusually cold.

Each morning during the next few weeks he would be silent and tense, pale, hardly aware of me, and unable to eat even a slice of toast, or drink a cup of tea. His nervousness affected me. I bore it with me on the bus to work, and I didn't feel safe or relieved until I was in the office. I wondered why he was so afraid and destroyed: in the evenings he would be full of excitement and high spirits, tremendously facetious, uncontained and lustful. He did little marking and no preparation at home now.

He told me several amusing stories of what happened in the classroom, and was never serious when he spoke about the school. There was just the white tension before he went, and that awful steeling of himself. Then the exhausting jubilance of the evening.

He reminded me of my father going to the pit, and coming back with that peculiar male hysteria and forgetfulness. He himself wasn't aware of the effect of his extreme appearance. He was still absorbed and conscientious: he disliked bringing work home to mark, or bringing anything that associated the flat with school, yet when he did bring books he marked them with great thoroughness and a care that was nowhere reflected in the work itself. The untidiness and the dirtiness of the exercise books made all his scrupulous correction look remote and out of touch. His neat, vertical writing in red ink on the black, scrawling mess was so striking that it suggested to me an insuperable barrier between him and the children. I said nothing. I was determined to allow him to build himself up in the same way that he'd allowed me.

One Saturday morning he came in from a visit to the galleries and said cheerfully, 'We've got visitors.' He enjoyed my surprise and anxiety, grinning at me and coming to hold me a moment. 'Try and guess,' he said.

'No. I'd rather not. I can imagine a lot of people I wouldn't like to meet. Is it one of those teachers from school?'

He laughed and shook his head. There was a dreadful simplicity and directness in his laughter now. It came out at the slightest opportunity. 'No. It's Ben. I haven't met him yet, but I bumped into that parson, Fawcett, in Charing Cross Road. He said they'd come down for the week-end to see the Cézanne exhibition. I gave him the address and they're coming along this afternoon around three.'

'Does he know I'm here?'

He patted me consolingly, and said, 'I suppose so. But I don't care. He won't dare show he's offended. He's tremendously formal, is Ben.'

'I think I'll be out, anyway. I don't want to see him.'

'But you can't go out. I want you to be here. I wouldn't have you out for anything.' He was so happy, happier than he'd ever been in London. I agreed to stay in. He hurried round tidying the flat, trying to conceal some of his enthusiasm. He made preparations to give them a meal, and as the afternoon wore on he glanced repeatedly out of the window, whistling softly to himself, hiding his agitation in endless little tasks he made for himself. I just sat down and watched him.

Even when it grew dark his spirit hadn't diminished. Ben was a notoriously late-arriver. Howarth's expectancy grew, raging inside him like an exile's. He stayed near the window, and once rushed down to Camden Town tube station to see if they had missed their way, to see if he could speed their arrival by a minute or two. He came back, his eyes still bright with expectancy. 'Isn't it just like Ben?' he said. 'The big stupid Ben. But he's good really.'

'That's not what you always thought of him.'

'Ah well, that was different,' he said, amused at my reservation, and apparently willing to appease me in anything. He clapped his hands together and shouted round the flat meaninglessly.

When it was completely dark and the street had emptied of all its Saturday activity, he suddenly became doubtful. His mood changed so quickly that I didn't notice for a while. I was half-aware of his silence for several minutes, and when I looked up at him he was sitting in the chair, his hands clasped in his lap, staring at the fire. I said nothing and went into the kitchen to get on with some ironing. The people overhead, an Italian and his family, were unusually noisy, with their wireless blaring and the frequent scolding of their child. I worked for half an hour before I went back into the room. Howarth was standing by the window in the dark, staring into the street. He smiled at me, his face lit up crudely by the light from the street lamps. 'Have you finished your ironing?' he asked.

'I'm just having a rest.'

I sat down by the fire. He stood at the window and began to hum to himself.

'It doesn't look as though they're coming,' I said.

'You could never rely on them, you know,' he said, as if reproaching me for having faith in them. 'Did you want to do anything particular tonight?'

'I wanted to listen to the play.'

'You and that play,' he said distantly. But he used to enjoy lying on the bed with me in the dark, listening to Saturday Night Theatre on the small portable wireless.

He stayed by the window. I waited to see if he needed me, then I went back to finish the ironing, wanting to forget him.

After I'd finished, I prepared a light supper, putting it on a tray to take through. I heard him crying. I stood outside the door and listened to him sobbing, muffled as if his head were buried in the divan or a chair. It was gasping and uncontrolled; the room was alive with his heavy breathing. I went back to the kitchen to wait, leaning on the table, wondering how long he would be.

When I went into the room he was sitting by the fire again, still in the dark, his face ringed with the red glow, his eyes liquid, but narrowed in disguise. He spoke naturally when I talked to him: there was no sign of his distress except the unusual swelling of his eyes and the way his hands held one another. He smiled and laughed occasionally, and was attentive to me. He lay stiffly with me on the bed to listen to the play: he didn't hear a word. He stared blindly the whole time at the reflected light on the ceiling.

In the morning we were still in bed when the bell gave three rings for us. I had the only dressing-gown, so I ran down while Howarth covered the divan.

It was John Fawcett at the door. He still had on his clerical collar.

'Margaret? Is Gordon in? I met him yesterday ... and I said I would call.'

'Won't you come up?' I said indifferently.

He ran his hand through his crew cut and smiled. He followed me agilely up the winding stairs. Howarth was standing across the room near the lighted gas fire: he'd quickly put on his trousers and shirt, but clumsily, and the room was roughly tidy. 'Oh, hello, Fawcett,' he said quietly. 'I thought it was you. We've only just got up.'

'Hello, Gordon.' Fawcett, conscious of his professional gestures, sat down with exaggerated confidence after briefly shaking hands. He smiled at us both. 'I'm sorry to come so early,' he said. 'But I simply had to explain about yesterday.'

'That's all right,' Howarth said, still cautious with our first visitor, and bringing himself reluctantly to sit down. He looked at me quickly to see how I was taking it. 'You needn't have bothered to come all this way round. I can guess more or less why you didn't come yesterday.'

'I know you're offended,' Fawcett said strongly. 'I don't blame you. I tried to get Ben to come, but he refused. I hate going back on my word like that, so I've come round to apologize, as the least I could do.'

'It's good of you,' Howarth said. 'I'm glad in a way that you have done. I'm sorry about Ben.'

'He said you misled him about the train times when you came down here. And he also thought you were going on your own. Of course I didn't know about any of this when I met you yesterday.'

'Ben can be naïve,' Howarth said quietly.

Fawcett rubbed the palms of his hands over his knees. 'I don't know. It's not often Ben takes offence. Though when he does it's generally in some unexpected way.'

'Did he have any other reason for not coming round yesterday?' Howarth asked, almost fiercely.

'He doesn't like you two living together like this ... I believe Ben thinks now that you were wrong to leave Joyce. He seems to think that by visiting you here he'll inadvertently be condoning it.' He looked at both of us frankly, and with deep curiosity.

'And is that what *you* feel?' Howarth said.

'We all understand the situation, of course, particularly since we don't have to live it. But even then, it's been a dreadful mistake, Gordon. I'm not just being crude – but you've both made a name for yourselves. With Margaret's brother being in the university, and you so well known there, it's been an inevitable topic for anybody with a couple of minutes to spare. Personally, I sympathize very strongly with what you've tried to do, even though I can't endorse any of it. I've never lost any respect for either of you.'

Howarth was silent, watching him minutely. 'Would you like some breakfast?' I asked Fawcett.

'I've had mine already.' He glanced at his watch, then rested both his hands again on his knees. 'At the hotel. But I'd welcome a cup of tea, if you don't mind.'

I went into the kitchen to put the kettle on, and when I came back Howarth was saying, 'I don't see why. We both want a divorce, and she won't put anything in the way. She's said so. I've got it in writing.'

'Well, that's all I can tell you. It's going to be quite some time before you can marry Margaret. They won't grant two people like you and Joyce a divorce as quick as that.'

'Still, I don't care.' Howarth quickly withdrew. 'It can't make any difference in the long run.' He drummed his fingers on the arm of the chair.

'What about your children?' Fawcett said, allowing some feeling to show for the first time.

'I reckon that's what you'd like to reproach me for most.'

'Not reproach. I believe reproach is an evil thing. But I have more sympathy for them than for anyone else involved. They are the most helpless.'

'I don't think you know what helpless means,' Howarth said darkly.

'But I can't understand you leaving two children like that. I've been to visit them, I ought to tell you. I thought with having known you in the past I had some privilege of that sort. Whatever the situation was between you and Joyce, the result has been that she's all the worse as a *mother* for your leaving. Perhaps you've affected the differences between you by leaving her. But what you've left behind – that's deteriorated too.'

'Are they unhappy ... the children?' Howarth asked dryly.

'They were very quiet when I went. Perhaps because I was a stranger, but I'm not sure. It was plain enough how impatient your wife has become with them.'

'She always was.'

'Well, she can't be any better. Her impatience with them now almost amounts to open resentment.'

'So you want me to go back to her.'

'It's the only sane thing left that you can do.'

'Would we be here like this if it were?' Howarth said incredulously.

'You know,' Fawcett said slowly, easing himself forward in his chair, 'I don't think you've *disgraced* yourself coming to London like this. If you went back to your wife it might even have all been to the good.'

'That's just the mercenary thing I'd expect from a parson,' Howarth said, but he was not embittered. '*Spiritually* mercenary, I mean. But what we've got here, Margaret and I – it's not just something you can pick up out of anywhere. And having got it – it's not something I could ever bring myself to spoil. It's permanent. For good.'

Fawcett withdrew slightly, within himself. He looked offended. 'I wish I could believe that,' he said. 'But I've seen too much of human nature even in my small experience to be as sure about it as that. There's no emotion so permanent that you can categorize it like that. I'm as convinced of that,

Gordon, as much as I'm convinced of anything. It's at the root of my belief.'

'I'm surprised you're not a Catholic,' Howarth said crushingly.

'I don't need to be a Catholic to be human,' he answered quietly, suddenly pitying Howarth. 'I'm ready to step down on what I've said, not because I don't believe it, but because I might not be the right person to tell you. I don't want to arouse your bitterness against me.'

'You're beginning to get just that bit too patronizing,' Howarth said, and stood up as the whistle screamed on the kettle next door. 'I think we ought to drop the subject. . . . They're only opinions, and I've experienced mine, as you say. You've only observed yours. I'm sorry we can't get nearer than that.'

'So am I,' Fawcett said, watching him go out of the room to the kitchen, then looking back at me.

He looked round at the walls, then again at me, searchingly and unashamed. 'Has he done any painting while he's been down here?' he asked, his voice slightly lowered.

'No. . . . Does he *ever* paint?'

'He used to. Hasn't he shown you his work?'

'He's never mentioned it.'

'No. He hasn't changed much. . . . He was very promising. Some drawings and paintings he did of the war. But after his first child died he seemed to forget it.'

'Why?' I asked with a sudden concern.

'I don't know. . . . Perhaps the war had something to do with it. He went into the army when he was twenty and didn't come out until 1946. Has he told you much about his wife?'

'No. And I don't want to know.'

'He blamed her for the death of their child. She seems to have left it too late in calling the doctor and the baby died of diphtheria. And when he doesn't blame her he blames himself.'

'And do you think this should affect me?'

'No. . . . And it doesn't explain anything. I just wondered if he'd told you. It's not something he'd ever talk about himself, though.'

'And it's not something you can do anything about,' I said, suddenly wanting to protect Howarth.

'No. . . . I believe he really does love you. And there's nothing I can do about that.' He looked at me expectantly. We could hear Howarth putting crockery on to a tray in the kitchen. 'I didn't believe it until I saw him looking at you just now when he was speaking.'

'And me?'

'I know how *you* feel. I knew when I first saw you with him at the literary circle . . . I felt frightened for you. It was obvious then he hadn't told you he was married.'

'I'm not sure he loves me,' I said.

'No?' He was full of a slow surprise. 'But then . . . you never will know.' He was silent, about to explain, when Howarth came back into the room and put the tray down, and looked at us both narrowly and suspiciously.

I went out to fetch the sugar he'd forgotten, and when I came back they were both talking about Cézanne: Fawcett with a brooding concentration and feeling.

When he'd gone Howarth tried to ignore him; he acted as if Fawcett hadn't been, or if his visit were merely a confirmation of his settled mind. He quietly made the bed, and while I cooked the breakfast he went out to get his three Sunday papers.

He was away a long time. His breakfast dried in the oven and I ate mine without appetite. I refused to go and look for him. I sat and read the Saturday papers through again, listening acutely for the door clicking in the well of the house.

When he came in he was excited. He might have been crying, his eyes watering with rage and disturbance. He had no papers with him; his hands were clenched. He came into the room and stood there like a puppet, suspended in the middle of the floor. 'I've just *seen* Ben,' he said. 'Would you believe it – he was stuck in a café at the end of the road all the time Fawcett was here.'

'Did you speak to him?'

'We were asked to leave the place – that's how noisy it got. There's no friend like an old friend.'

'Did he want to see you?'

'He'd no choice. I saw them both through the window and I went straight in. Fawcett at least made it clear he didn't like it. He never said a word the whole time. He just sat there looking at me thoughtfully, like a simpleton . . .'

'I don't think he's simple. He's sincere . . . and decent.'

'He's still simple. And I don't think he's sincere . . . whatever that means.' He sat himself impatiently in the easy chair, then stood up again to walk about the room. 'But Ben – he didn't want to come here because of you. He seems to think I've betrayed my "cause" by attaching it to you. He said I was a hypocrite, a masochist, self-pitying – everything in fact that I normally associate with him.'

'It sounds very childish.'

'Ben is childish. He talks about a black and white world, right and wrong. Fawcett thinks it's an institution world. Between them, one saying too much and the other nothing. . . .' He splayed his arms helpless in the air. 'What chance have I got?'

'You wanted to see them.'

'Oh yes,' he said impatiently, bursting within himself, and recognizing that this was just what he had expected and what he needed. He smiled awkwardly, knowingly, still angered yet half-amused at his anger. His face was contorted as he shook his head from side to side, biting his lips, clenching and unclenching his hands.

'You're glad it's happened,' I said.

'No. I could have done without it. It was what I expected, but I'd have been better off without all this disturbance. It rankles me now.'

'You're still unsure of yourself, at the bottom.'

'I always will be when I'm like this,' he pleaded. 'How can I ever be sure that there's not something other than just *our* faith in what we've done?'

'Are you still looking for some outside reassurance?'

'Aren't you?'

'It's been simpler for me to find it.'

'Oh,' he said mockingly, yet curious and perhaps surprised. 'Could you say that and at the same time imagine yourself living back up north? It's easy living like this down here. But would you still feel certain about it up there?'

'If you want to go back and live there, both of us, I wouldn't be depressed. It'd be more difficult, but it wouldn't change me.'

'Ah, I don't know. . . . I was beginning to feel some sort of security, that I'd got somewhere at last.'

'I don't think it's Ben who's upset you so much as Fawcett. What he said about feelings not lasting.'

'He's being superficial, isn't he?' Howarth said. 'Of course feelings don't last. They develop. He doesn't like the idea of feelings *breeding*, no doubt. He obviously thinks I came with you for that.' He pointed at the bed.

'No. . . . He doesn't think that. You torture yourself with what you've done. It's as if you've been looking round all your life for something like this. . . .'

'Is that what he said?'

'No.'

'What did you talk about when I was out of the room?'

'He asked me if you'd done any painting since you'd come down here.'

Howarth looked at me doubtfully. He had been standing in the middle of the room, but now he went to sit on the bed.

'He seemed to think you were a painter.'

'He would. He's an optimist, *and* religious.'

'Why should he be wrong?'

'Because he *is*. He knows nothing. There is *nothing* to paint now. Except paint itself.'

'But what *do* you want, Howarth?'

He looked at me soberly, as if he were no longer mystified. 'You,' he said. 'That's all there is . . . and all there ever was. You know, I always used to think I was a "real" person. But recently, now . . . I'm beginning to feel I'm only a figment of my own imagination. Isn't that odd? I've always charged myself with being down-to-earth, with being one of the un-feeling poor. But now, though . . . it's as if I'm floating in the air, that I've never once had my feet on the ground.'

'I think Fawcett has made you feel too lonely.'

He quietened. 'I don't know about lonely. . . . But I do feel really *alone*, now. Maybe it's better that way. It makes it all simpler at any rate. I was a joke, I know, in the university common room because I took some things seriously. Anyone who does that nowadays is suspect straight away. And it was in the common room there that I looked for the company I thought I needed.'

'To hunt with the hounds and run with the fox.'

'I am the fox,' he said, quietly amused. 'Didn't you know? And this is my hole.' He was full of his ironical amusement.

I thought a great deal about home. Having left it, I began to think of it with some nostalgia: I could only enjoy it in its absence. I was glad of its reassurance: in a way it measured the depth of things as they then were. Its severity became less imminent and destructive: a plant that had been pruned and now flourished more wisely. My mother wrote two letters to the accommodation address I gave her. But all along I had been expecting something from Michael, vehement, full of resentment and hurt. But nothing came. My mother described Michael's flat, describing it in the detached way in which she now seemed to accept me, as if the whole of her interest had been depressed. There was no reproach in her letter, no meaning in it at all: she told me how Michael and Gwen saved nearly the whole of Michael's salary, of their plans for an architect-designed house outside town, and the choice they intended of cars. It was factual and dead. She said nothing of herself, nor of my father. Neither did she mention Howarth. She had no curiosity; her letters were habits, but ones I would have suffered without.

I showed the letters to Howarth. He was extremely interested in them, reading them more thoroughly than I did, but saying little of how they affected him. Apparently trivial things of this nature interested him profoundly; almost as if he expected to discover the thing he wanted in them.

He received no letters of his own apart from the one from his wife. His isolation haunted him, more real than it had ever been before: he shrugged it off and tried to forget it in me. One evening when I came into the room unexpectantly he was looking at a photograph, his head bent towards the reading lamp, fair and reddened by the glow. He was so intent that his head came up involuntarily, in surprise as well as dismay, and he impulsively held the photograph out rather than show any sign of concealing it. 'Have a look at this,' he said.

'I'd rather not.'

'You don't know what it is.'

'They're your children.'

He nodded. 'Well . . .' And still offered them.

'I don't want to see them.'

'I'd like you to. They're to do with me. They're part of me.'

'Do you try and forget them that much?' I said hopelessly.

'I'd like you to look at them.'

I took the photograph, gazing at it blindly. But the two faces broke through. It was an early photograph: they stared up with simple, untouchable faith, as they might have stared at Howarth as he suddenly came in the room. 'It's not recent,' I said, relieved.

'No. You don't have to feel responsible. They're not as innocent as that now.'

'You're being sentimental,' I warned him, and handed it back.

'About these?' He was surprised.

'About their innocence.'

'But what do you know about it?' he said half in anger and in amazement. 'You've never had a child!'

He wanted to apologize. He held out his hand towards me, shaking his head.

'I want you to be strong without that,' I said quietly.

'I thought I had been.' He was conciliatory, and watched me carefully, his body tensed towards me.

'Yes,' I said. 'But with a thing like that – I'd rather you had it on the wall than catch you looking at it furtively.'

'I wasn't being furtive, you know.'

'You were afraid of them, though. You showed it. They make you afraid. It's better to have them on the wall.'

'If you don't mind then, I will,' he said, and the next day he bought a frame and put up the photograph as the only picture in the room.

The emptiness of London slowly shaped itself: we had an affection for certain places, for Regent's Park, the Embankment, Piccadilly. It was a conventional choice, pleasurable with its masses of unknown faces and the places we couldn't afford to visit. Our main pleasure was the walk we often took in the evening: down Camden High Street and Hampstead Road to Tottenham Court Road, round the West End, coming out by the Victoria Embankment, crossing Hungerford Bridge to the Festival Hall, and catching a bus back to Camden from Waterloo Bridge. We listened a great deal to the wireless, and went once a week to one or other of the two cinemas opposite the tube station. They were habits that Howarth at the most didn't resent. He needed the refuge, and he was too exhausted by teaching to attend to much else.

Even though we were so close he kept a great deal of his life to himself, partly at my insistence, as with the prospects of his divorce, but often because he guarded himself with an exile's jealousy. He told me little that wasn't anecdotal about school: I knew the whole of it numbed him, the dirtiness, the indifference, the compulsion to educate people who didn't want it, the obsessiveness of the staff. But he was determined not to give in to it. He didn't want me to help him. At school he could only succeed alone: his isolation there was as complete as it was at home.

But I could only look uneasily at the closing-in of life around him, the slow and meaningful intrusion of things he would have wanted to ignore, and I tried not to think of how he would act when he again felt that he must break out. I wanted to keep him: but it was an end in itself. He needed a vista to his life. At the moment he couldn't see it, and was too busy and too numbed to search.

He was usually happy in the evenings, seeking his relief from within himself against the heaviness of the day. He lived for the evenings, delaying our going to sleep in order to make them as long as possible. He was always exhausted with his tenseness in the mornings, unable to eat, deliberately numbing himself, almost afraid to move, it seemed, in case his fear would break out. When I asked him to apply to a decent school to teach in he refused. Strangely, he was suspicious of good schools: suspecting the same perverseness and uniformity that he thought he had found at the University and the Art College. He hated education, believing that its success was contained in its mundanity. He insisted on teaching in a bad school, believing that there his individuality glowed within him, lit up by the startling contrast.

The more he taught the more convinced he became in his hatred of education, tormented by his inability to accept such a simple thing or to see any alternative. It was the mediocrity and the depersonalization that wearied him: he seemed to use this restlessness to conceal that caused by the thought of his divorce.

All the time I was aware of this waiting: with Fawcett's visit and with his argument with Ben, I felt his reluctant admission that he needed to antagonize, to feel opposed. He forced his life apart with this restlessness. At times he seemed to me to be something that would inevitably be destroyed by its own personal civilization.

He was fully aware now of having carried me, of my prospering by the energy of his isolation. He made our domestic life as close to a married one as he could, treating me at times as the conventional wife, and acting with the imagined sobriety of a husband. He wanted an equality between us, thinking that he carried, by virtue of his sombre nature, the heavier load. It made me feel that there were things he hadn't told me about his wife, facts about their life together that would dissuade a divorce court. He spoke about it obliquely: reading aloud the divorce hearings in *The Times* mentioning certain divorcés who lived in the street or whom he came across in the poor backgrounds of the children he taught. It was no good resisting him.

On those days when my tea was not ready when I arrived home from work I was to know that something was wrong. Usually it was some defeat he had suffered at school, and it took his pride several hours of the evening to rid itself of its rancour. When he was content, or only mildly disturbed, he would have the tea waiting and sit down to eat it with me. One evening, half-way to Easter, I came home to find him with the tea not made but he himself in a state of suppressed elation.

'Read this,' he said, flinging down his cigarette the

moment I came in the door, and thrusting a letter at me. I could tell by the first sentence that it was from his wife, but when I made to put it down he insisted that I should read it.

I followed the large sprawled handwriting with a disembodied sensation, my chest burning at the surprise that my first glimpse of a person I had tried so hard to ignore and deny should be in the shape of a letter and the muddled hysteria of her thoughts. I had wanted something cold and thoughtful. But she was writing out of instinct: the words were confused remnants of her emotions. She wanted him to come back on any condition and without any rebuke.

'What do you think of that?' he said, calm now that it was shared.

'Is it what you've been waiting for all along?'

'I never expected it,' he said unwisely.

I sat down, handing the letter back to him, too shocked to take my coat off or even to bother wondering about him. His wife terrified me. My picture of her as a dislikeable woman had dissolved with the pitiable immediacy of her letter. She needed him back, not as a father or husband, but as a person, as someone she'd known.

'What are you going to do?' I asked him.

'I'll have to tell her what I said before, if I *do* write.' He was suddenly irritable.

'But you're not sure about it. Yet I can't blame her writing in that way. It's bound to affect you. It'd all have been easier if *she'd* have given some grounds for divorce.'

'That's a right nice thing to say,' he said, flushing and full of resentment.

'I meant some recognizable grounds, that everybody could have understood.'

'They can understand this plain enough. And so can she.'

'So you're going to tell her the same thing. Can't you see

170

she'll only write back if you do? She'll go on pestering us like this perhaps for ever.'

'You've taken it a bit too seriously,' he decided. 'It's only to be expected this sort of thing.'

'So you did expect it, after all,' I said wearily.

He sat down, sullen and resentful of my interference. 'You made me feel she wouldn't do things like this,' I said.

'How?'

'Your attitude: you seemed so confident that she wouldn't interfere, that this was what she wanted as well. That day at Lindley Ponds ...'

'That day at Lindley Ponds ... you're going to make it hang over the rest of my life.'

'It'll always hang over *mine*. ... You made it all sound so final then, as if you'd already agreed about it between you.'

He stared moodily at me, full of accusation. '*You* sound as if I might even consider what she says. Don't you see – this helps to clear the thing up. It gives it all a bit of meaning, and sense ... to me at least. And I'm the one who's been demanding these things.'

'She's admitting that you've beaten her. Didn't you know that already? This is only the start of her intrigue. You're flattered by it already: that she should ask you back in language like that.'

'It's not flattery, and I haven't *beaten* her. It wasn't a contest between us. That's *your* idea of sex. To me, it was a mutual thing, failing each other like this. At least this shows that there was some *reason* in what I did. I've been needing to feel that badly.'

'And yet, until now, you were content to rest on your own feelings.'

'Yes. But I feel safer now that I've got this. Don't worry. She won't write again. I'll make sure I tell her everything.'

'But *if* she does, it makes your divorce sound almost

impossible. She can't write like that and give you a divorce at the same time. And she sounds a woman who doesn't like to let go.'

He laughed, and came across to kiss me.

10

He was cheerful throughout the next week, suddenly friendly: it was a sexless friendship in which he was affectionately careful about the distance between us.

For a whole week he didn't write to her; he wrote to his solicitor and received a letter which he didn't show me. I didn't even know of its existence for several days, during which time his friendliness had changed into absent-minded humour. He was quietly amusing the whole time I was with him, teasing: it overlay the truculence and the moodiness of his nature. He was disturbed by the way things were going but did everything to conceal it. 'Why haven't you written to her?' I asked him then.

He looked up doubtfully from an evening paper. The main electric light was on, but he was frowning just as he did when reading by the light from the small red lamp. But his eyes were so alive. 'I got in touch with my solicitor first,' he said, uninterested. 'I don't want to spoil anything inadvertently by writing to her.'

'Is the divorce going to be difficult, like Fawcett said?'

He put the paper down, and crossed his legs: he frequently crossed his legs as a habit now. I thought it had something to do with his schoolteaching and his need for authority. 'As a matter of fact,' he said with a sudden frankness, 'her letter can change things. The solicitor's advised me not to acknowledge it. That's why I haven't written. I'm waiting for him to find out what the situation is.' He watched me unsympathetically.

'I've wondered all along,' I said tonelessly, 'whether we could ever carry off a thing like this. It's been so unreal to me. I wake up in a morning and I can't believe it ... at times it seems so artificial living like this. Like being on a tightrope in a nightmare all the time. I've dreaded something happening every minute ...'

'What's artificial about it?' He was cautious, looking at me only half-determinedly.

'Me. Trying to ignore that you have a wife and children, and that they still have a *right* to make demands on you.'

'It's immaterial. I thought you'd got just the right attitude to all this. I'd come to think you were right to ignore it.'

'Yes, and then this happens.... And what do you mean by the letter changing things?'

'The solicitor thinks she might be considering withdrawing the petition.'

'Out of spite?'

'She might even do that. But it'd be unlike her. No ... *he* thinks she's going to try and seek a reconciliation, and that she'll withdraw the petition as a first step.'

'But once she knows you won't go back, do you think she'll still refuse to give you a divorce?'

'I don't know ... that letter from her is quite a shock really: it makes her seem a stranger. Like a letter from an unknown woman. I just can't see her writing it.'

'Maybe it was the woman she used to be, the one you married. Did she love you then?'

'Yes.'

'And you?'

'... I could bring myself to believe that I did, or that I didn't.'

'It doesn't say much for me,' I said, trying to be amused. 'Don't you know whether you love me?'

'You're not asking me seriously,' he reproved me. 'I don't think I could answer you in a mood like that.'

'But I *am* serious. Do you feel for me now what you felt for her when you married her?'

'I suppose this sort of thing is inevitable,' he said heavily, almost with sarcasm. 'But I married her fourteen years ago, when the war was still on. How can it be the same?'

'You must have loved her to marry her.'

'I did.' He was about to leave it, but he added slowly, 'If anything it was that ambitious sort of love, of a young man – half attraction, half fulfilment.'

'Fulfilment?'

'Of all those *demands* ... surely you know. Haven't you ever felt all those demands made on you to marry? The obligation.'

'Was there an obligation in marrying her?'

'There must be in all marriage. It's when something like this happens that the obligation is suddenly ineffective, suddenly amounts to nothing. There's always some higher demand that either materializes or doesn't.'

'It sounds a rotten way of looking at it. It makes it seem hopeless when you talk like that.'

'As you like. . . . But all the same, with you I don't feel any obligation.'

'It's a kind of personal greed,' I went on. 'As though marriage is something only to get things out of, not to put anything into.'

'Well, that's the usual excuse. But marriage doesn't mean much really. You're made to think it does. With me – all I'm trying to do is to count more than I have done in my own life.'

'What sort of love do you have for me?'

He rubbed his hand across his forehead in a fit of nervous concentration. 'I can't say. I'm not used to thinking about it as coolly as this.'

'But what difference is there between me and your wife? Physically there can't be much. If anything, she must be better looking.'

'She is,' he said. 'But you affect me in every way. She only affected me in some. I feel more virtuous somehow with you . . . is that any clearer?'

'Don't you like looking too closely at me?'

'I've looked more closely at you than at anyone. If you ask me what attracts me most – then I reckon it's the difference there seems to be between your body and your mind. They're like two separate things in you. I can feel it tremendously when I'm loving you. It's a real thing. . . .'

'You're always exaggerating that, and it can't be true,' I said harshly, afraid of his struggle to approach me.

'You asked me,' he said simply, resigned. 'If you do know what it means then you must feel more for me than I thought.' He watched me with sudden care, hopefully, afraid and smiling. His concern stiffened his smile into that clown-grimace.

'At times you look at me so scornfully that I wonder if I count at all.'

He laughed out, gaily and threateningly, misunderstanding. His laughter fevered and emptied him. 'What do you feel's going to happen with the divorce?' I asked.

'Nay, forget it.' He was still playful. 'You've left it with me till now, so don't suddenly start interfering.' He wanted to be mild, but his expression was hard and brutal.

'You'll have to tell me,' I said quietly. 'If you don't tell me I shall leave you.'

He quietened, gazing disbelievingly at me, nearly smiling, but realizing my need to shock him. 'You're turning me over and over,' he said. 'Like a toy. Examining all the crevices, the details, how the eyes work, and why it squeaks when you press its belly. Do you think I should submit to that?'

'Have you any choice?'

'I shan't explain it. No,' he said, flushing, and turning his look away. His expression hardened.

'I'll take this as what it means,' I warned him.

'You can take it how you like.' The blood rushed into his face as if it burned him. 'I'm not giving in as easily as that, now or any other time. You can do what you like about it.'

'I shall leave you if you don't tell me.'

He knew I wanted to infuriate him, to *make* him submit. He was deriding me now with his secret and with my fear. 'Well you go, then,' he said. 'I'll never look back at you. I can tell you that.'

He watched this exaggeration of ourselves as I packed my suitcase. I did it coldly, but still raging inwardly at my help-lessness and his insistence on it. His anger grew as he watched in his stubborn silence. It was that final hardness that drove us apart, his eyes glinting at me as though I'd betrayed all that I'd promised.

When I walked down to Camden High Street I expected to hear him coming after me, not hurrying, but strolling with that slow gait, suggesting to me how ineffectual I could be. But there was no sign of him. I began to encourage myself towards the completeness of this sudden and unexpected break. I was too surprised to think. I caught a 68 bus down into Bloomsbury, noting the details of the journey with great care, and choosing a hotel in Cartwright Gardens as if it itself were a reflection of my sudden pride. I went to bed early, determined on sleep and oblivion.

I was wakened at eight, relaxed and feeling no remorse, only vaguely anxious as to what the parting had meant. Such simple actions always deceived me: my life seemed to have been made up of occurrences whose simplicity had misled me as to their meaning. I was curious about him, though coolly, waiting for a message that would explain everything.

At work I expected him to ring up. But I was nervously jealous of this strange independence. I wanted to tell my acquaintances in the office all about it, as if it were the achievement of some long secret ambition. It was a physical lightness, as if leaving him had freed me of a heavy load: my back was straighter and my fingers raced over the typewriter keys, as though they had been relieved of a binding pressure. I made a date with a girl in the office to go out that evening: we went into the West End to the Lyons Grill for dinner and then to a cinema. But I was bored by my own sex: I kept looking round for Howarth, convinced he'd appear at any moment. When each minute passed and he didn't come I grew increasingly bored, and was aching; I hated my friend for not realizing that to me *she* was Howarth. I couldn't accept her as herself. In the dark beside me she was confused with him. I was aware of him as a part of me, like my own legs and arms, all our senses shared. But she was foreign. The evening extended on all sides into that vast emptiness again, the emptiness of the cinema and the blankness of the film.

The following day a different, unknown weight descended on me. My immediate elation had vanished completely overnight. And this weight was more oppressive: there was no one to share it with.

The routine no longer had a purpose: before it had been a preoccupation, a relief; but now it was boredom itself, dolorous, ineffective, embalmed in its uselessness, cold with its uninvolvement of me. The letters, the contracts we had to type – everything we did was a yawning, shuffling silliness that was carried out with us as its apparently inanimate components. The typewriter was a disease, sprouting from my fingertips like a growth, and contaminating sheet after sheet of paper. Without love. Yet when I was called to the phone I was calm.

All Howarth gave me was the message. He said nothing about himself. He read the letter that had arrived that morning. It was only a note, he said, to tell me that my father expected to arrive at Kings Cross in the evening and wanted me to meet him there. I told Howarth I would bring him to the flat, but when I asked him what he thought he rang off.

My father looked already lost in the crowd as it swirled towards the barrier: his small, stocky figure resentful in the parade of bodies. He stared self-consciously towards the people on the other side, as if afraid of recognizing me among them. He seemed now to have all the bewildering warmth and strangeness he'd possessed when I'd seen him at the pit.

As he pressed his way aggressively through the barrier, he caught sight of me waving at him and his face lit up with immediate pleasure; then he quickly looked away, hiding himself. We shook hands clumsily, uncertain of what was expected, of what we should feel.

'How're you keeping, then?' he asked shyly, his voice so strange with its northern accent that I scarcely recognized it. I was afraid of him, but happy, relieved that he was alone.

'How're you keeping?' he said again. 'You got my note, then? I wasn't sure it'd get down here in time.' He walked quickly towards the street as if we had an immediate appointment outside.

'How's my mother?' I asked him.

'She's all right.' He paused and looked blankly at the evening crowds of Euston Road. It was almost dark and the lamps were early and still red, like rows of crude fruit racing to the distance. 'Which way do we go?' he said. 'It's the first time for thirty year I've bin down here, you know.'

I began walking up towards St Pancras church, talking with him about the family, not caring why he had come down, what it was he needed. He was satisfied with the warmness, yet strained by his first rushing impression. The train had dazed him: he hid his curiosity, staring straight ahead, talking rapidly and intimately, content with the strong feeling between us. I was continually surprised by the strangeness of his northern accent.

He quietened when we stood in the bus queue, opposite St Pancras church. 'Oh aye,' he reminded himself, hesitant after his stream of family talk and suddenly feeling himself under my care. 'Are you living close by, then?'

'It's only a threepenny ride away.' We were both silent, urgently aware of the dark traffic and the people around us.

'Did you want to come back home?' I said. 'Or would you rather get a hotel first?' He had no case, but carried a plastic mac rolled round something in his hand.

'Oh, I don't know. I don't know how long I'm staying. I thought I might stay Sat'day, you know. . . .' He preoccupied himself with his surroundings.

'What did you come down for, Dad?'

'Well – I thought we might have a talk, lass.' He was watching the bus anxiously as it drew up, and with deliberate politeness ushered me inside first. 'Will . . . this chap be at home, then?' he said, wiping his hand across his nose.

'I'm not sure. He might be out.' I was about to tell him of the quarrel, but I kept it back, dismissing it in my own mind as of no consequence now. My only impulse was to take him to the flat, to let him see how confident and undismayed I was, how successful everything had been. 'Didn't you want to see Howarth, Dad?'

'I don't mind.' He watched the drabness of the buildings with a nervous indifference. We began to wait for the bus to reach Camden. Inconsequential phrases repeated themselves in my mind, as if I were searching for some easy conversation. I prayed that Howarth hadn't taken malice and gone out. I seemed to be busily talking to myself.

He was angry, and afraid of the district, of its bustling crowds, the foreigners of Inverness Street market and the accents: it was all unreliable, the sounds alone weren't trustworthy. 'All them spivs,' he said, submitting to it, but drawing up hate and ridicule into himself at its strangeness.

Howarth was expecting us. The flat was very tidy, and he was serious and polite.

'Hello, Mr Thorpe,' he said, the moment my father went into the room, and strode forward and shook hands confidently. My father was prepared to submit: the bustle of London had already wearied and betrayed him. He was reassured, almost relieved, by Howarth's confidence, and by the confident tidiness of the flat.

'I'm going to leave you two to talk a while,' Howarth said. 'I can imagine why you've come, Mr Thorpe, so I shan't get in your way for an hour or so. I'll be back around eight, and we'll see if we can have some sort of meal together.'

My father murmured his agreement, uninterested, and Howarth went out. He didn't look at me.

We listened to his feet descending slowly, sensibly, to the street. My father was uncomfortable in the room: the bed itself might have distressed him. Subconsciously he avoided it, sitting across the room with his back to it as if it were another person. 'I wouldn't mind a pot of tea, Margaret,' he said quietly.

He couldn't bear to be alone. I was only a minute in the kitchen, but he followed me. He'd taken off his jacket and was in the green pullover I'd once knitted him. He wanted to be intimate and matter-of-fact. He watched me put on the kettle and prepare the tea things: he didn't look at the place at all.

'You've got two rooms?' he asked.

'Yes. We manage all right. We share a sort of bathroom downstairs.'

'Oh aye.' He nodded, pained but already prepared for any material surprise.

'Do you know why I've come down?' he asked with sudden, slow formality.

181

I sat down at the table, arranging the tray, and he sat opposite me, leaning on the table edge.

'Mrs Howarth came to see us,' he said. 'She came to see your mother and me.'

'What about?' For the first time I was embarrassed, and he was relieved by it.

'She asked us if we could do anything. . . . She doesn't hold any grievance against you. But she needs him back, she said.' He was aware of the emotions involved, but was determined not to be put off. His calmness admonished me; he stared at me with scarcely any concern, blinking with a vague tiredness. 'I got off work to come down,' he said.

'She's written to Howarth,' I told him, 'and said much the same thing. She won't admit to losing him, to letting him go. I think she's wanting to make him suffer for it.'

'Nay, I don't think it's ought like that, Margaret,' he said. 'She's a genuine woman, I could tell. She said she'd do ought to get him back. But she wasn't blaming anybody. As far as I can make out she takes all the blame on herself. . . . I don't know.'

He spoke as if he'd discussed what he'd say a great deal before he came down. There was my mother's sentiment in his voice, perhaps even Michael's. He leaned heavily on the table, secure in his righteousness. 'I don't know what you're hoping to gain, living like this,' he said, allowing his first aggression to fade.

'His divorce is being heard soon,' I replied. 'Then there'll be an end to all this, thank God, I shall have to go up . . .'

'Nay, I don't think so. . . . Hasn't this chap told you? She's withdrawn her petition or whatever.'

'I'm afraid so,' he added, watching me acutely and wearied by my look of shock. 'You can see what a position you're in now. Why don't you come away, once and for all, and leave them both to it? You can't step between a man and his wife.

182

You just don't know what goes on, what it is they have between them.'

'You know it's not as simple as that.'

He suspected that my agitation was a sure sign of my doubt. Standing up he turned off the already steaming kettle, and showed at last his full concern. 'There's nowt in it for you, lass. She's not going to divorce him, and he can't get one without her consent on it.' He sat down to watch the effect of his words, his hands splayed on the table.

'She *knows* Howarth won't go back. . . . So she's making as much trouble as she can. . . .'

'But this chap,' he said, still afraid of mentioning him directly, 'he's not going to wait for her if he's got ought about him. If he's a *man*. He'll have to go back. I've no doubt on that. And neither has she.'

'He won't go back.'

'Nobody can ever think ought of you for living like this,' he said. 'People don't look at muck if they can help it.'

'I can get the respect that I want. I'm respected down here.'

'Aye. You'll be running from place to place like a couple of filthy dogs,' he said, full of hate.

'That's not the life we have down here,' I told him quietly.

'Here? But what sort of life is *here*, pray? It's the back of beyond – I saw the sort of people as I came up. The scum of the earth. That's what you're living with. Just look at their faces. . . . Is that what you want?'

'There are other places. We don't have to live here.'

'Aye, and what places are those? Just like this one. What decent people are going to have you amongst them? You'll be dirt. Just dirt to them. What if you have a baby?'

'His wife won't always be like this. In seven years . . .'

'In seven years! Bloody hell, Margaret, just what do you think people are? For Christ's sake try and act like a grown woman. In seven years ... in *two* years you'll be just a wreck, a washed-up bit of rubbish.'

'I don't think so.'

'I've seen his wife. She's a determined woman if I know ought. You don't seem to realize she's got all *her* life at stake an' all. A*n*d her kiddies'.' He rubbed the edge of the table with the palm of his hand, watching me as if this insignificant action would persuade me. He did it unconsciously. 'Any road, Margaret, if you don't reckon that that's ought,' he said with difficulty, 'you might have some consideration for us. For your mother, if nobody else. God knows ... we've never demanded much in the way of what you did with your life. This's the first thing where we've had to ask you not to go on. It was your mother who was wanting to come down here. But I wouldn't let her ... But listen, you can't go on ignoring your family like this, Margaret. We even let you have some time down here, we didn't butt in, just in the hope you'd see some sense. We waited ... but nothing seems to have happened.'

He hated pleading for himself. He was suddenly young with his earnestness: it gave his face a youthfulness, and he stared at me as if it were a third person he was speaking to. 'I'd nearly to hit our Michael to stop him coming down here to settle this Howarth once and for all. I could fair kill him mysen. I mean that ...'

'Did *she* tell you she'd stopped the divorce? Or have you only heard?'

'She told us. I thought you'd have known. I'm surprised you haven't heard. I am.'

He was still waiting for me: the noise of other arguments and conversations penetrated from the well of the landings, suddenly threatening and resounding. My father was tired and pale. 'Haven't you listened to what I've said?' he asked.

'Yes.'

'And ... and you're carrying on.'

'I have to, Dad. It's not as simple and as one-sided as you make it. There's so much more. So much now.'

He nodded, agreeing quickly. 'What is there?' he said.

'Howarth's everything I've got, Dad.'

'He can't be ...' He shook his head, uncertainly. 'Man or woman, you've got to give up far bigger things in your life than that. Believe me, if it's only something like this you've got to give up in the whole of your life then you'll be a lucky woman.'

'It only wears me out when you talk like this.'

'Like what? ... It's all the truth, you can't get rid on it,' he said contemptuously.

'No. It's *not*!'

I watched his familiar anger rising as he suspected that I derided his emotions and his life. He had this secret fear. But he could see no scorn in my face, and he reluctantly gazed at his hands, feeling his ignorance of me, finally pained by it. He was so easily forgetful of his feelings.

'What can you hope to gain by carrying on like this?' he said, his fierceness controlled and more menacing. 'If you get shut on all of *us* what will you have got?'

'You're exaggerating it hopelessly. It's just hopeless talking about it like this.'

'If you'd only come and see your mother,' he said, staring at me in tears of frustration.

'You mustn't, Dad.'

'Perhaps *he'll* change your mind when he hears ...' He turned his head to a sound on the stairs.

But it wasn't Howarth. The Italian father tramped upstairs, and his arrival caused the usual crying out and shouting. 'Howarth's given up more than any of us. We could never go back now.'

'If he hasn't heard about the divorce you don't know. He'll have been relying on that all along. When he finds out ... What's he going to say?' His voice sounded empty and lost now, and he was coughing into his hand, from his lungs.

'It can't make any difference.'

He rubbed his face wearily. 'What's made you like this, Margaret? I'd never have thought it'd have turned out like this. Your mother feels it even more than me. We just don't know which way to turn.'

'You were only just saying that there were bigger things than this to suffer in life,' I told him bitterly. 'What things are they, pray? One minute it hardly counts, then the next you're making it like this. . . . Don't you see it's all to no good? I can't go back on what I've done, ever.'

'What do you want me to do, then? Get down on my knees and beg you? I'd do that if I knew it'd change anything.'

I stood up and hurried through into the next room.

He followed after a few minutes. He came in quickly and sat on the edge of the couch. His defeat hardly seemed to matter to him. It was his miner's resignation that gripped him; coughing, then gazing stonily at the floor, beyond hope, possessed only by his sense of endurance.

'Oh for God's sake !' I screamed. 'Don't be so *helpless* !'

He heard Howarth's footsteps and stood up. He looked round for his jacket, ignoring me, and hurriedly pulled it on, breathing heavily through his nose. He didn't care that I watched his preparation to appear respectable: it was too familiar and I knew its purpose.

When Howarth came in, his face set for opposition, he found my father polite almost to the point of warmness. It dazed me to see him performing like this, sticking to his pride whatever happened, to show no pain whatever he felt. I burned for him.

'Are you ready for something to eat?' Howarth asked.

'Oh, I don't know,' my father said. 'I've been thinking of catching a train back tonight. There's one just after ten . . . I think I'd better be getting down to the station.'

Howarth looked up at me casually. But there was an intense relief in his face. His eyes stared with it, almost haunted. 'But you'll have to have something to eat,' he said forcefully, and helped me on with my coat. His hands touched me for a second. 'We'll go out and get a bite, then come down and see you off.'

My father said nothing. His silence hurt him. Howarth led the way downstairs. Between Howarth and me there seemed to be no friction, no sign of what had happened. His politeness concealed everything, even his curiosity about my father. They scarcely realized they were merely being polite and proud with one another, each fearing the other's significance as if I weren't there.

As we walked down to the bus I again found my mind talking with itself, holding the remnant of some intense conversation of which only snatches came to me, irrelevant phrases like scraps overheard, made meaningless. It was the disturbance beneath the conversation that impressed me, like in a dream, beyond my control. 'I couldn't eat anything,' I told them, as we came to the High Street.

'Ah, but your father could,' Howarth said.

'I want nothing.' My father was small beside Howarth: he looked at me earnestly, and was angry. 'I don't want ought. I'll catch the next train.'

'We might as well take a trolley down,' Howarth said quietly.

We crossed the road. Howarth held my arm, possessively. 'What did you want to see Margaret about, Mr Thorpe?' he said, while we waited on the other side. 'I can imagine most of it, that you'd like her to go back. But why did you leave it until now?'

'Your wife came to see us,' my father said. 'She was desperate, I can tell you.'

'She shouldn't have done that. . . . But we knew as much. We had a letter from her.'

'Did you know she's stayed your divorce?'

'I heard yesterday from my solicitor.'

'Margaret didn't know that until I told her.' He waited for Howarth to show himself.

'I've purposely kept it from her, Mr Thorpe.'

'Aye, you have,' my father said, as if exposing a great deceit. He looked at me pointedly, his eyes tired but full of justification. 'How does it affect you, then?' he asked Howarth.

'It doesn't make any difference at all. She'll have to give me a divorce eventually. Sooner or later: it won't make much difference.'

'And you think all this is fair on our Margaret?'

He upset Howarth by the simplicity of his concern.

'Margaret makes her own decisions, Mr Thorpe. She doesn't have to rely on me in making up her own mind. I've seen to that all along. That's one reason why we've been apart like this.'

'Like what?' my father said, confused but indifferent.

Howarth looked at me. 'Haven't you told your father?'

I shook my head. 'No. I don't see that it's got anything to do with it.'

My father watched us suspiciously, like someone standing on the threshold of a private room.

'I'd have thought you'd have told him,' Howarth said.

'What's this?' my father asked. 'What's this all about?' He stood at the side of the road stiffly, his hands clenched at his sides.

'It's nothing,' I told him. 'It doesn't concern you at all.'

He suddenly stated: 'I don't know what to do. I can't go home to your mother like this.'

'Like what?' I said, wretched for him.

'I can't go like this . . . I can't explain anything to her . . .' The trolley pulled up beside him silently, and startled him: he winced as its shadow fell across him, jerking back his head. He climbed on mechanically and sat down beside someone. We sat across the gangway from him, Howarth on the outside.

'Is this to the station?' my father asked the conductor.

'What station d'yew want, mate?'

He looked at me to explain, avoiding Howarth.

'Three to Kings Cross,' Howarth said patiently, and handed the money.

'Are we right for the station?' my father said determinedly to me. I reassured him and he stared fixedly out of the window.

As we neared the station all the pretence disappeared. I yearned for him. I forgot Howarth, and wanted to comfort my father, to touch him. As I stood back to let him get out I said, 'We're all right, Dad. You'll see it was right in the end.'

'Right!' he whispered in the bus. 'You're dirt! Both on you. You're just bloody dirt.'

We got off and stood outside the station. The street glowed with the mellow orange of the lamps.

'Tell my mother that I love her,' I told him fiercely. 'And that I'm happy.' I was terrified of his suddenly turning on Howarth with his fists as I knew he might easily do. Howarth sensed it and said nothing, standing back.

'I wish to God I'd never come down,' he said, so coldly and full of hate that he seemed physically to drain away from me. He started walking into the station, and I hurried to keep up with him.

'You won't kill my love for you like this,' I said incoherently.

He stared gauntly at me. 'Love? What love have you? It's nothing but a selfish bitch's lust. You rotten slut.'

Howarth could bear it no longer. He stayed behind, and we left him.

'You've no right to say that to me,' I said weakly, panting to keep up with him.

'Go away, lass,' he called.

I walked dumbly behind him. There was a train already in, with twenty-five minutes to wait. He strode through the barrier without looking back. I bought a platform ticket and ran after him. There was nothing to say. He climbed into a carriage and walked down the corridor of the train.

I followed him from window to window. There'd been a time on holiday as a child when I'd hunted for him like this, burning and despairing at his loss. I stood patiently outside the carriage he chose. It had one other occupant. He sat the other side. I waited blindly, standing on the deserted platform afraid to stare in at him.

I stood close to the window hoping he would come out again, or make some sign. Other people drifted down the platform, hesitating by the open doors. One or two looked with interest at me waiting alone. When I glanced back at my father I found him staring at me through the two layers of glass. He looked away. I could scarcely see him for the reflection. At the front of the train there was some activity as the engine came down out of the tunnel and slowly backed on to the carriages. They jarred with a heavy crunching. Steam drifted from beneath them. A man wheeled a stall towards me, and parked it a few feet away, full of refreshments and snacks. My father suddenly got up.

He walked quickly down the corridor until he found an empty compartment. He'd found it unbearable to sit with a stranger. I followed him, and waited. At the next carriage door a couple were saying good-bye. My father could just see them. But he stared only across the compartment, containing himself. His eyes were red, as if he'd just come from work, and he was leaning forward, his arms on his knees. He was crying. It looked as though he was being sick. I looked away and waited for him. The station was unusually quiet and empty.

Suddenly he stood up and came to the next door down

the carriage. He lowered the window and when I came close he said, 'Nay, but come back with me, Margaret.'

I shook my head slowly. He stared at me with his old tiredness and defeat. He drew the window up slowly in front of his face as he might have done a mask, and looked out at me a moment longer through the glass. Then he went back to his seat. The station was full of the long emptiness of his journey north, the hours he would sit alone. The train was almost empty, and dark. We seemed to listen to each other's silence. He had withdrawn completely into himself now, no longer aware of his surroundings, enclosed in his underground cell. The train lurched heavily, but he didn't move. He looked up for a fraction, not at me but at the startled face of the man at the next door. A porter came down the train testing the doors. He met a second man coming from the opposite direction. An inspector waved his arm towards the rear of the train, then turned and lighted his green filter towards the engine. It whistled briefly, and moved smoothly, the thunder of the steam now echoing within the vault of the station. I watched my father intensely.

He passed by unseeing, the train carrying him along the platform without a sign towards the tunnel and out of sight. The desolation of the station was complete without him: the long emptiness of the track, the useless brightness of its steel, the disappearance of the last carriage into the tunnel; the whole useless efficiency of the train. I followed him in my senses, noticing each detail of the brickwork as the lights illuminated the wall.

Howarth was waiting at the barrier. He might even have watched me. He took my arm in his, holding my hand tightly. He was white with anger, his eyes staring and motionless.

I guided him off Euston Road into Cartwright Gardens. I collected my things from the hotel and paid my bill while he waited outside. He insisted that we walk back to Camden, he carrying the case, so that he could walk off some of his despair.

Soon I was clutching his arm ready to fall at any moment. He hailed a taxi, and we drove home.

I lay on the bed oppressed by my loneliness as by a physical thing: it was a suffocating weight on my lungs and stomach, stifling my life. Howarth covered me with a travelling rug and sat across the room by the gas fire. It hissed quietly. The chatter of the people in the house was tossed about restlessly beyond the door. The room seemed smaller, tiny. Things murmured in the street. I heard Howarth emptying my case, opening cupboards, and sliding drawers. A smell of cooking drifted up from the rooms below. Laughter rose from outside, climbing the walls of the house. They seemed to creak. It surged for a moment in the street. If only I could have *touched* him.

II

I had a habit, when I was lying on the bed and Howarth was across the room, of twisting my head into the sheets so that I could see him upside down. His face then appeared like a piece of apparatus, mechanical and amusingly inhuman. His big toyishness was emphasized by the silent shutting of his eyes and the clamp-like openings of his mouth. It pleased me to be able to turn him at times into a machine, the strange perspective reducing all his humanity to the automatic movements of a puppet or a doll.

Eventually this machine amused me less. For one thing, when he was inverted in this way, and unaware of what I was doing, the real sense of scale would be replaced by an almost infinite one, where his head was nothing less than a mountain, and the great apertures in its side were the features of an indescribable life. They continued to function unknown to him, their mechanism so crude and prodigious that they were unrecognizable: it was an unchallenged, unknown monster in the room with a bloodless, engineering appetite.

I began to be unnerved by this transformation that the mere twisting of a head could produce. Once, when he caught me looking at him in this way, he laughed: the horrible mechanics of it, the great split of his mouth and the huge cogs that were his teeth, the shutter of his eye, convulsed me. The nostrils opened and quivered, the cheeks creased back in thick folds, flushing with the effort of his laughter. The sound itself was transformed into a vibrant mechanical sobbing; the flanges of a great machine rasping together under a heavy load.

I was tormented by my association of Howarth with this infinite mechanism: what *was* Howarth? When I righted my head and looked at his familiarity, his identity was more elusive than ever. In what way did Howarth occupy this peculiar machine? Where did *he* end and the impersonal features of his mechanism begin? His physicality depressed me. There was no indication of the margin of his huge male physique, none that I knew I could cross to feel myself in the real Howarth, to be in his individuality, where it lay like a single, hidden egg in the nest of his body. Where was Howarth in all this? And why could he never indicate this division between himself and the mechanism that contained him?

After my father's visit it was as if he took advantage of this obscurity to protect himself. There was a new warmth and intensity between us. Yet there were moments now of deep withdrawal, when I couldn't feel at all that he was with me, as if he wished desperately not to burden me with the thing that he was. My father had exaggerated the wall of confusion and antagonism surrounding Howarth: but at school and now at home he had experienced this open resentment and abuse. One day, when we were out walking in the park, he pointed out a group of children coming towards us, and laughing slightly said they were ones that he taught. They smiled at him as they passed and he called out cheerfully to them. When they were behind us I heard their abuse called after him, full of obscenity and filth, bringing my heart into my mouth. I looked at him. His face had stiffened, and paled. I could have fallen on the ground and wept for him. But he showed no sign except that weariness round his eyes. And we never went in the park again.

Perhaps he wanted to assume all the responsibility for defending me as well as himself. The collapse of the divorce suit, the visit of my father, even Fawcett's coming, had all reduced the sanctuary wall. His need for a vista, for a view in his life, only increased at this sudden widening of his horizon. As I watched his moodiness increase, and that hunted look come into his eyes, I felt that he was concealing himself more and more behind that mechanistic barrier, as if he wished it to be absorbed indistinguishably into the vast mechanics of the city around.

When I asked him about this, telling him that I was beginning to feel like some object discarded in his wake, he was immediately warm and disbelieving, coming to hold me tightly, and assuring me physically that there could never be such a thing. 'How could I ever leave you?' he said, laughing at the impossibility.

'Because I was the means of you doing this, of being alone. And now you've achieved it you want to get rid of the means.'

'But that's utter nonsense,' he said with his schoolteacher vehemence. 'Have I ever shown one sign of going back on you? I just couldn't do it. And remember it was you who left me a few days ago. You drove yourself to that.' He was so confident and hurt that I had to be dissuaded from my feelings.

Later I asked him, 'Are you sure she will re-petition ... *can* she petition for divorce again?'

But his confidence had already subsided.

'How long will she make you wait?' I insisted.

'I don't know.' He moodily showed he was no longer indifferent to her hold over him.

And within a few days he was saying, 'I never thought I'd be waiting on her beck and call like this ... I've been thinking – I ought to go and see her and *make* her realize she must change her mind. I'm certain I could by talking to her....'

'How long would it take? How long would you be away?'

'I might do it in a day, in two days,' he encouraged

himself, seeing that I wasn't offended. 'Would you want me to do that? To go and have it out... Would you like to come with me?'

'I don't ever want to see her. If you go I'd rather you did it quickly.'

He went the following week-end, as if he'd been waiting a long time for this opportunity. I wasn't sure why he went. There was something more to it than just the need to convince her.

I saw him off at Kings Cross still full of the memory of my father's departure: both of us were afraid of the separation, of what there was in it that we couldn't see. For a moment, after the train had gone, disappearing sickeningly into that great tunnel, I thought I'd never see him again. I sobbed wildly as I walked down the platform, with a sudden and brief hysteria: by the time I reached the barrier I was calm. He was making every effort to come back that night, and I knew he meant it. I filled in the day as best I could, walking about town, afraid of waiting alone in that empty flat.

In the evening I went back, and turned the wireless up loudly to hide all the sounds from outside. All the time I was listening for the creak of his footsteps in the well of the house. At eleven he hadn't appeared. I went out and caught a trolley down to Kings Cross and waited for the last evening train. I searched the crowd carefully, sensing he wouldn't be there. But it tired me. When I got back to the flat I was able to sleep without a wakeful torment.

In the morning there was the familiar deadness of Sunday in the air. The street was silent, the house made no sound.

I cooked my breakfast slowly, desperate at the thought of filling in the whole day, wondering if he might have caught a morning train, if in fact he was already on the way, speeding towards London; wondering where he had slept. I was pulling at him; he was a weight inside me, drawing at my body with that dead, tearing dullness. I ached for him. Everything was waiting for him, needing his noise and smell and sight. The buildings waited. The street, still mounded with rubbish from the previous day's market, was empty and still. He would come up it. I hurried about trying to fill the silence.

But he invaded everything.

I dreaded him coming, the shock. I wanted it over, without the doubt of his waiting. I filled the morning with a score of unnecessary jobs, turning the wireless loud for 'The Archers' so that I could hear it in the kitchen; even cleaning the outside grime of the windows, and sitting over my diary unable to write a word. I couldn't bring myself to the boredom of reading the Sunday newspapers: they were a weariness in themselves, overfull and bloated. There was the same deadness about them. They filled the flat with their unread neatness. I watched out of the window for him, and saw him turn the corner several times. Each time I burned at the resemblance, flaming with the disappointment. And at lunch time, unable to cook a meal just for myself, I caught a trolley to Kings Cross and waited for the arrival of the afternoon trains. They were three hours apart, the next one not arriving until the early evening.

I left the station and caught a bus outside to Greenwich. It was a long rambling journey, through the fringe of the City and across the river. But I tolerated the bus: it was an imprisonment sitting there. I raged at myself for this helplessness, determined that I'd never let Howarth leave me again. I hated him for this. I exploded against him, raging at his callousness, hating and writhing at him for his indifference. I choked, and burned at him. I struggled up the steep hill of the park, pained with the effort of moving. My body had no will to move. But I scrambled up the hill as unseeingly as I'd scrambled up the cutting at Lindley Ponds, hating him.

I walked down with long, aching strides, sitting in the bus unable to keep still, changing seats while I waited for the bus to leave. The journey back was better. I hated him less. We were coming together now, rushing towards one another, to meet one another. I hugged and kissed him, and laughed with him. The bus sensed our closeness, rushing on through the late afternoon streets towards the City as if it too belonged to Howarth, to the completeness of him. My body leapt inside itself, glowing and throbbing as we neared Kings Cross in a darkening river mist.

There were thirty minutes to wait. I bought a Sunday paper and read it enjoyably, looking up occasionally from the pleasure of the full print to the even greater pleasure of the clock. The engine came in slowly, as if afraid of the station. It nosed its way down the groove of the station so cautiously, like a shy lover. The crowd teemed out of the carriages, the porters standing like markers, engulfed, the length of the platform. I looked first for Howarth's fair hair amongst the denseness of the crowd: I saw it, recognizing him with a raging heat inside my chest. The sense of him burned me. But he didn't appear. The crowd thinned, trickling down from the back of the train, meeting relatives with a short, eager intensity. The train had emptied.

I went to the indicator board and found the arrival of the next northern train. It arrived late in the evening. I couldn't think of anywhere to go. I was maimed by Howarth's desertion. I couldn't move without him. There was nowhere to go: the flat no longer belonged to me. I came out of the station and saw the cinema opposite. I went in and bought the cheapest ticket: a wooden seat in the gallery. It was a converted music-hall; the crowd was young, and a left-over from the hall's vulgar days. They called out their obscenities at the old films, making crude noises with their mouths, going on and on almost dolefully, by habit, hardly aware of themselves, just calling at the screen.

I endured it, cowering in the narrow seat as if the abuse were directed at me. I couldn't see a clock. The attendant flashed his light ineffectually at them. I thought of the outside of the cinema all the time, the growing darkness, the mistiness, the deep premature red of the lamps. The film frightened me by its incoherence, the senseless passage of events, the steady reverberation of obscenities, louder and louder. On the screen people were kissing, and the noises and screams were now almost hysterical, a crescendo; and the lights flashing, and the shouting. The people kissing.

When I came out the street was ghostly and the silence of it deafening. I went across to the station and waited for the train. I hated relying on the place, on its brickiness. And I was already afraid of the engine as it coasted in, slow as before, with the same reluctance, seemingly the same black engine, the same deserting crowd flooding towards the barrier. The shouts of the cinema throbbed in my head. I didn't want to look for him; I searched half-heartedly, standing where I knew he must see me. The crowd thinned; there were bursts of greeting amongst the waiting people, intimate explosions. The engine stood close to me, black-nosed, gleaming, steaming uselessly. I waited in the hope of having missed him, then hurried out to the trolley-bus stop. No one waited there either.

The trolley came and I got on. It purred up to Camden like a dead thing, tugged by habit on a string. I rushed up the street to the flat, suddenly sure that he was there. I knew he was. I could hear the wireless playing as I came up the stairs. I pushed open the door already laughing at him. The emptiness yawned at me. I knocked open the door of the kitchen: it was as I'd left it. When I touched the wireless it was hot. It had been playing to itself all day, emptily filling the room, filling the house. I turned it off, lying down on the bed in despair.

I wanted to go out for a meal, but I was too exhausted. Everything was useless now but the waiting. I had to be still and wait. There was no rushing about. I listened to the house, lying on the bed waiting for the sound of him. The house seemed to empty itself. The wireless had driven everything out throughout the day. Its electric heat and burnt rubber filled the room. I cried for a long time, urging myself to it, shuddering for his body and his touch. I undressed and got into bed and cried again. I hated him. I hated him now more than I'd ever done. My body throbbed with it, my legs aching with hate, my face burning. I needed to kill him. I needed him dead and absolutely destroyed. I burned everything that was him in my mind. My body was shattered and flung apart by its desire.

I woke early. I looked forward to seeing him. I couldn't go to work. It wasn't even important to ring up and tell them I was ill. I lay in bed until it was late, watching the pale sunlight and the slow heaving of the clouds over the street. I felt hungry. I cooked myself a good breakfast, cooking it slowly, talking to myself, as if for a stranger who would inspect it. I took every consideration with it. It was no more to me than that I should please the stranger and do my very best. I watched him carefully as he considered my work. I ate it with the stranger's relish, enjoying every mouthful, lingering over it to read the newspaper. I tidied the flat again. The day lengthened. I was determined not to go down to Kings Cross. The burning slowly returned with the noises and the bustle in the street. I felt sick at having eaten. I couldn't bring myself to clear the table, to touch anything. My hands were lifeless. I waited for the sound of him, feverishly at first, then with complete silence, sitting in the chair in the middle of the room. Each sound on the stairs burned me. I longed to go and see, to rush out into the street and see him before he reached the door, then to the corner to see him before he reached there, then to the station to enjoy the surprise and longing of his arrival.

I clung rigidly to the chair. Footsteps rose through the house, ascending to the door, passing, and clambering upstairs. Footsteps descending. The outside passed by. The inside raged. I hated him. My legs and arms ached. His nearness, his absence inflamed me. I clung to the chair, vehement at my stillness. I waited with the bricks and the stones; everything was in flames if he didn't come soon, the sound of him. Nothing moved from me. It clung to me. My body was racked with the burning. Then it shattered, leaping wildly apart. There were his quick footsteps on the stairs, coming up interminably. Rising and rising. The house rose with his ascent, creaking with it. He opened the door and stared at me strangely, half surprised.

I stayed still, calm, smiling at his arrival. I loved him for his presence, for the vision of him. He was old and famous to me. More familiar than anything in the world.

'I thought there was something the matter,' he said, suddenly smiling and holding up an envelope. 'You haven't picked up my letter downstairs.'

'I only went down for the papers, before the post came,' I told him quietly.

He looked at me shyly. He didn't ask me why I wasn't at work. I was aware for the first time that I'd dressed myself in my best clothes. The surprise livened me. He put down his bag and shut the door. He came across and knelt by the chair, suddenly feeling my body. I leapt up in flames at him, flinging my arms round him and crying out, gripping him with all my shocked strength. He hugged and rolled me against him, murmuring and caressing. There had never been such greatness before. His touch bemused me, the smell and warmth of him, until all my aching was absorbed in him, and we were together.

'What is it?' I said, as he got dressed to take me out for the evening. His quietness was meant to impress me. I went and put my arms round him as he tried to pull on his shirt. He laughed and tried to shrug off my embrace, but I clung to him, feverishly prolonging his warmth.

'You haven't even asked me how I got on,' he said.

'I don't care.'

He smiled soberly, looking down at me from beneath his lowered brows. He hadn't shaved for two days. I ran my fingers over his lovely, fair bristle. It was almost invisible.

'Come on. You've had enough,' he complained, drawing his head away. 'I want to talk.'

'I'm not stopping you talking,' I said, still holding him and grinning at his massive helplessness. He tried to push my hands down hopelessly, then shrugged.

'Oh, if you don't want to hear what she said.'

'But you'd better tell me.'

I let him go and he sat down on the bed. I fetched his shoes, and knelt down and fitted his small feet into the clumsy shapes, pulling the laces tightly, securing them.

'It was just about a waste of time,' he said, watching my hands intently as if they were his own. 'It only gave her a chance to let her mouth off.'

'I could have told . . . I knew she'd be just like that.'

'You were very noisy about it, then, for you never told me.'

'I had to let you find out for yourself. You don't believe she's scheming. You won't believe me when I tell you.'

'She won't give me a divorce. . . . At least, she says that now. It might be different in a year . . .' He moved his feet inside his shoes, undulating the bright leather and turning up the toes: he enjoyed them. I kissed them, wanting to touch him all the time, weak with it, my head faint.

'You spent all that time up there just finding that out.'

'I went to see Ben, and Fawcett too. And I dropped in at the college.'

'Oh, Howarth. You are a big fool. You shout about them one minute, and you go cap in hand the next.'

'I don't see why I shouldn't see them.'

He sat quietly, nursing the sensations of his visit.

'I'm glad you went.'

'Why?' He looked at me with simple, relieved curiosity.

'I didn't know I'd miss you. It makes things clearer to me.'

'Did you miss me?' He watched me closely, stooping towards me.

'How long did you see your wife for?'

'I saw her twice. Saturday and Sunday. I spent the whole of yesterday arguing with her. . . .'

'Will you *ever* become aware of people, Howarth?'

'How do you mean?' He was offendedly amused.

'You're such an awful judge of people. You never see them clearly for more than a moment. I'm sure . . . and that's because you're always wanting to see what *you* want in them.'

'You think that Joyce is playing around with me?'

'Does she still love you?'

'She wants me to go back to her. That's all I know.'

'You aren't sure about her at all, are you? What did you go up for? . . . Didn't you make her see that it's hopeless for her to hang on like this?'

'Her idea is that if she waits long enough I'll go back to her.'

'What did you say to that?'

'What could I say? She believes it. . . . She *wants* to believe it, so she does.'

'We can admire her confidence if nothing else.' I gave a sound of despair and moved away from him. He gazed keenly at my clothes, then at my face.

'Don't fight her, Margaret. You were right at the beginning to have nothing to do with her, so let's keep it that way.'

'But she's fighting me. Aren't I supposed to do *anything*?'

'Just be what you are.'

'What is it that makes a woman like me live with a man I

can't marry? A year ago I'd have shuddered at the thought. But now ...'

'It's no good having those sorts of thoughts, looking backwards all the time.'

'I'm looking *outwards*, not backwards. Can *you* be as indifferent to these things as you're trying to believe?'

'I endured the sight of my children.' He still sat facing me, glancing occasionally at his shoes, and moving his feet in them. 'They were so pleased to see me.'

He loosened his collar with a quick, impetuous action, and went into the kitchen to shave.

When he came back I was ready with my coat on, waiting for him. 'Did you want to leave them?' I said.

'Yes.' He nodded confidently at me. 'I was glad to leave them.'

'Because it would have been too much to stay longer?'

'Yes.' But he wasn't sure what he meant.

His visit north pleased him where I was concerned. Looking back, he enjoyed the thought of me waiting, and the new response in me since his return. 'Did you miss me a lot?' he kept asking, provoking me, amused and pleased with himself. He was beside himself to console me. He indulged in it for several days.

Later, when I asked him how long his wife would keep him waiting, he said, 'She thinks she's the one who's doing the waiting. Still ... she is so practical, she must surely begin to see sense in a year. ... She'll come to terms, don't worry.'

'Will you marry me as soon as your divorce comes through?'

'Yes. As soon as ever I can.'

'Wouldn't it be falling from one trap into another?'

'Are you a trap as well?' he asked with veiled innocence.

*

He had settled down at school to a quiet, concealable disillusion. The Headmaster had praised his work, and he tried hard not to be unhappy in it. One evening he brought home a young Welsh teacher who taught Maths and P.T. in the school. Between them they unfolded a miasma of horror and disgusting detail that comprised their daily life. Howarth was reluctant to confess it, ashamed that he'd exposed it to me in this way. With the two of them together, and listening to them, I saw Howarth's teaching slowly eroding his spirit. His inner hardness seemed exactly the measure of that reduction.

'We must be child-men to be able to deal with them at their level,' the Welshman said. 'Any person of feeling or intelligence wouldn't even understand them. And worst of all, *they* wouldn't understand either feeling or intelligence.'

'They're human,' Howarth said.

'That's not our bloody fault. They don't serve any use by being either human or alive.'

Howarth smiled at him bleakly, as he might have done at Ben, or Fawcett. 'Why do you teach them, then?' he asked.

'I was *sent* there, man. I was given no option.'

'You can leave.'

'And be sent to another asylum? I've been *educated*, I have. But what for, man? Just to paste the lugs of those lousy shits?'

'Everybody at that school's like you,' Howarth said. 'I don't know why you do it.'

'Not everybody.... Look at Jackson. He's the best teacher there. And why? Because he's small-minded. He makes them stand up when he comes in. He sees that their hands are clean, that their pen nibs aren't bent, that they walk out of the left side of the desk, that they sit up when they're not writing. That they call him "sir". You've *got* to be small-minded to spend all your life doing that sort of thing. If you want to be a good schoolteacher you've *got* to have a mind the size of a peanut. You just haven't a cat in hell's chance if you don't.'

His anger wearied Howarth. After the Welshman had gone, he said, 'People like that: they make me feel so lifeless. As if it's a weakness of mine, a lack of life, that makes me try to fit in with it all and try for something worth while. I'd hate to be like that Jackson. But he *is* a good teacher, and he *is* small-minded. And I can see myself getting more like him every day. Do you think I haven't the strength to complain, to object?'

'You've got the strength, and you know you have.'

He shook his head in bewilderment. And he didn't bring the Welshman home again, he didn't even mention him, and his information about school diminished.

He didn't care. He was doing a task which someone else could have done, a little better or a little worse. There was no privilege or uniqueness in it. Yet although he tolerated it like this, it wore him away, slowly, closing up channels, reducing him to that hardness of spirit that must either crack or go on being exhausted. He had an inexplicable affection, that had no pity in it, for those schoolteachers who had endured this process, and not broken. He would point them out instinctively in the streets. They were little more than children, their spirit shrivelled to nonentity, unconsciously miming and reproducing the mannerisms of the children they taught. It was as if the final hardness only reflected their outside-world of infancy, and their adult bodies disguised the crumbled residue of a man. They were children themselves, Howarth would bitterly insist, tormenting himself with the inevitable result of teaching.

One moment I wanted to laugh at him, and the next to cry. But these images haunted him, the images of reduced people, as if they were a strange and threatening race, childmen who wandered about the streets and in and out of the schools. I pleaded with him to leave teaching, but he couldn't find any alternative. 'There's nothing left for an educated person to do,' he said, 'except, under the excuse of earning a living, deliberately to distort things. In teaching I'm the only one to suffer distortion – isn't that fair enough?'

'Don't you distort the children yourself?'

'Hardly,' he said, outraged. 'Their distortion of me is far more merciless and instinctive.'

He wouldn't be moved. There was that proud silence in him at the root of it. The silence of someone waiting and assured.

His waiting unnerved me: it was for something he needed to receive, something he expected to be given to him. And yet he didn't seem aware of it himself. He carried on teaching as if condemned to it from birth. But I knew it couldn't last. There was that awful straining of his spirit, when he would sit opposite me in the evening, suddenly look up, and begin to half-laugh, half-cry with a mingled frightened ecstasy. He would come to tap my knee or my shoulder, sometimes my face, with a great, visible suppression of his strength, as if he might have wanted to crush me with his one blow hadn't something quickly intervened. Then he would stroke me for a second, with the same movement. There was this tightening suppression about him. He waited, and wondered why I was mystified by him, and physically so possessive.

Just to see him move was enough: his big stillness stirring a moment, his head moving just for a second and his hair creasing, and the gentle pressure of his breathing. He pursed his lips when he was sleeping, pouting. Every small part of him held me: the passion of his life, of his body being alive to the smallest movement. His stillness was frightening, the suppression: he was helpless as his head rested on the pillow, confident and blind, unaware. How could he be so unconscious of himself?

But I was always entranced by that stillness when I woke up before him and raised myself to look at him: the idea that he *could* be still, all that energy and feeling moulded into one. It was permanent: he was so complete. He ceased when he moved; he broke into those bewildering fragments. I loved to see him move, just that moment before his limbs broke apart: the stillness broken slowly, by a slow stir, and his head turning, his eyes empty of themselves, then seeing me, and filling with me, coming to life with that full movement of his body, smiling at the pleasure he gave me. I ached to possess him always in this silence. It was the confidence and the quietness of our coming together, as if in the stillness we had fused, and he smiling, and our eyes emptying into one another without that fear and resignation.

12

I was walking up Inverness Street from the bus, late home from work, when a hand gripped my arm viciously.

Michael walked along beside me, not interrupting my stride. His face was sullen, unfrightened: there was none of the alertness of being in a strange place. 'Are you coming home?' he said almost wildly.

His grip was deliberately painful on my arm. He squeezed the muscle with uncaring strength, and I tried to hide my feelings. 'What are you doing here?' I asked, my surprise and the strangeness blunted by an outrageous sense of pain.

'Are you coming home?' He gritted his teeth, ignoring the concern of passers-by.

'No. Of course I'm not.' I stopped myself from arguing with him: I only wanted to show my determination, and my confidence that I couldn't be hurt.

'I'm taking you home,' he said. 'You've nearly killed my mother.'

'If you don't let go my arm I'll call for someone to help.'

'Call them.' He was wild. I didn't recognize him. Nor what it was that enraged him.

He tightened his grip, the flesh crunching against the bone, so that all blood and strength drained from the limb. He looked me bitterly in the face, holding his head close. 'You're *coming*!' he said, and shook me violently.

'You can do what you like. I won't come.'

'Do what I like?' He shook me wildly again, so that my brooch dropped on the pavement, and something fell from my hair. It was as if he were bullying me as a child again. 'You're coming back with me. We're not having any more of this.' He began to propel me down the street, forcing me in front of him with all the strength of his hand on my arm. I was driven along with him. He was breathless, breathing heavily behind me. My weakness excited him; he was ecstatic in his determination. My arm lost all feeling, hanging limp and dead from his hand. He stood me on the congested pavement, searching for a taxi. The grip on my arm weakened as his hand tired. But it was still strong. When I tried to pull away he held me firmly, his face taut and white with the strain, and his eyes staring ferociously about him.

'I'm not going with you,' I told him calmly. 'You can't hold me like this all the way, and if you take me to the station I shall call a policeman.'

He stared quickly at me: there was a certain madness about him. He gave my arm one final, grating squeeze until it felt in two, then released me. He was unmoved by my cry of agony as feeling returned to my arm. I massaged it, blinded by the circle of pain, my eyes shut to him, and started back up the street.

'I'm coming with you,' he said whitely. 'I'll kill that louse.'

'I'm not going home,' I told him, walking along in a daze.

'I've got the address. I'll find out this stinking little hole you've got. . . .'

'You shan't come near us.' I couldn't understand – the intensity of his anger, the wildness. He was like a wild animal. And needing Howarth to kill and tear.

'It's no good following me. I'm not going in until you've gone.'

'What kind of rotten man is it that lets you go on like this?' His feelings bled inside him. His face was still white, his mouth open.

At the top of the street I waited at the corner, uncertain

what to do. He brought a piece of paper from his pocket with a roughly drawn plan, and looked up at the name of the adjoining street. 'This is it,' he said. 'You stay here. You're going back with me, d'you hear?'

'It's no good,' I told him quietly. 'You can't do it.'

'You'll have no choice.' But just as he started looking up at the numbers, Howarth himself came striding urgently down the street. He must have been looking out, concerned at my lateness, and seen me at the corner with Michael. He came down, his coat open, his face already flushed.

Michael saw him a moment after me, and started towards him. But Howarth came straight to me. 'Are you all right?' he asked, looking intently into my face.

I nodded and said, 'Yes.'

'You're white.' He peered anxiously at me, not sure of his fear.

Michael waited a few yards behind him. His lips were compressed and trembling. When Howarth turned towards him he said, 'I'm taking her back with me.'

'You've come a long way for nothing, then,' Howarth replied. 'Because you're not taking her anywhere while I'm here.'

He could have swamped Michael. He stood facing him calmly, not even surprised, as though he'd been expecting this all along.

'Her mother's seriously ill,' Michael said bitterly, his face so threatening that in a moment I thought he would have to throw himself on Howarth.

Howarth watched him, then turned back to me. 'Is it true?' he asked.

'I don't know.' I shook my head, my eyes widening and blinded with tears.

'Come on, we'll go in,' he said, taking my arm. I winced, and he stared suspiciously at me. 'Are you sure you're all right?'

'Yes . . . But I won't go back with him.'

'No,' he said quietly. He had already sensed something, but I wasn't sure; I couldn't have known what it was.

Michael followed, so close that he pressed against me as we went up the stairs. Howarth was purposely slow then, making Michael wait when we reached the landing. He blocked the doorway a while, standing there just looking into the room, before letting him in. He turned to Michael as he came in, and said, 'What are you doing down here?'

'I'm taking her back. Even if I have to drag her.'

'Well, you can't do that, can you, while I'm here? So what then?'

'I'll wait.' He sat down quickly, on the couch across the room. He puzzled Howarth. 'She knows she has to go back.'

'Well, I'll give you time to cool off,' Howarth said. 'Then I'll throw you out.'

'Why do you lie about my mother?' I asked him bitterly.

'How long is it since you've seen her?'

'It's unbelievable. You'd use even her just to get your own way.'

'It's *she* who wants you back,' he said calmly. 'At least, away from here. That's why you're coming back with me.' He gazed at me with a brotherly confidence, excluding Howarth. There was something in it more than just his personal hate of Howarth. And it involved more than just the three of us.

'You all know what I feel. I told my dad when he came down. So what's the use of you waiting?'

'Yes. I *know* what you told my dad. He hasn't been back to work since.'

'That's his fault, not mine. I *told* him.'

'And you think that's enough? . . . Tell me, what do you see in Howarth, Margaret?' He said it so seriously that if I hadn't known him I would have taken it for sympathy. Howarth seemed almost amused by him; but he stared at him soberly.

'What do you see in Gwen? Isn't that enough for you? Or would you like to destroy this for me too?'

'Gwen didn't happen to be married with two children when I met her. She'd have *told* me if she had.'

'This sort of baiting,' Howarth said. 'It won't get us anywhere. Can't you talk sensibly now that you're here?'

'I forgot,' Michael apologized. 'You're an authority on "sensible" things. I ought to leave it to you . . . like this set-up here. Living in this hole. . . . You're a crank, Howarth, and the least you say the better.'

Howarth was silent a moment, looking at Michael. I knew he was deciding whether to hit him. Then he said, 'That doesn't help much, either.' He knew that there was something more than Michael's personal hatred, and he looked at me strangely. 'What Margaret wants to know is whether her mother is ill, or whether you've just made it up.'

Michael didn't answer. He wouldn't answer. I knew that my mother must be unwell. But not that she'd sent him. Instead it seemed like some personal vengeance of Michael's, on life, on those round about him. He didn't believe in Howarth.

I could hardly breathe, seeing Michael so obsessed with his hate. It seemed the hate of many people. I wanted to ease and soothe him. But he rode on my feeling, of being stretched between them. He watched me for it, wanting to use it.

'Why must you try and spoil everything now?' I asked him.

'How can I spoil any of this? The whole thing is just an absolute ruination.' He was surprised and hurt.

'You seem to have destroyed every single thing in my life.

Maybe it's not true. . . . But I feel that you've tried. Everything that I've ever thought worth while you seem to have gone out of your way to disillusion me about.'

He looked at me distantly, withdrawing. 'You aren't a child, Margaret,' he said with confident and quiet contempt. 'What do you think you are, talking like that?'

'I want you to go.'

'You're relenting already,' he said deeply. 'You know you can't go on living like this. It's not in your nature. It's not in any of our natures. Not even Howarth's.'

'I'm not going back,' I moaned.

'You'll have to, Margaret, whether you want it or not.'

Howarth went across to Michael, standing over him, but calm. 'You've got to be *absolutely* truthful about this,' he said. 'It's not a game that we're playing. What *are* your reasons for coming down here like this?'

'Please, Howarth,' I told him. 'Don't argue. That's just what he wants.'

Howarth looked back at me, across the room. 'Don't you want to know what his real reasons are?'

'I know what they are. . . . He hates you and all that you stand for.'

'But why?'

'Why? . . . Because you aren't what he is.'

'Have we all to be like him?' He was nearly smiling at me, knowing full well what I meant.

'No. You've just to be *nothing*. That's how he wants you. And if you're not. . . . This! This is what he does!'

I pulled off my coat. The bruise was thick and purple, swelling the arm. The muscle looked almost distorted. 'That's what he does!'

Howarth hadn't moved. He looked at my arm, then slowly back at Michael. 'You are a brave man.'

'I made that mark,' Michael stated, as if it explained everything. 'That's what I felt.' His eyes looked small and empty. 'How can you go on, Margaret, when you see this sort of thing happen? It's against *everything* in us.'

'It's against everything in *you*!' I cried at him. 'In you and my mother and my dad. But this is *me*. This what I've got. It's got nothing to do with you.'

'You're wrong.' He shook his head, looking up at me, past Howarth, with half-fearing eyes. 'It's not only you it concerns. And it's not all you've got left.'

'It's all I've got.'

'I think you'd better go,' Howarth said to him.

'I can't go!' Michael flung his fist against the back of the seat. 'Don't you see? I *can't* go without her!' He dazed me with his blazing frustration and demand. 'I've got to take Margaret back with me. You can do what you like about yourself. But don't go crawling to some suffering woman for support. I've never known a man condone his own weaknesses as you've done, Howarth.'

'You don't *have* to be like this,' Howarth said. He was still patient, but there was a heaviness in his voice. I could hardly understand the control that he had. 'Why don't you try and help us instead of being so bitter? Surely *you* could have consoled your parents. I'd have thought, if you had any feeling at all for Margaret, that you'd have tried first to help her in the way that *she* wanted. . . . Instead, you give us both the impression that all this is only an excuse for some sort of private revenge. God knows on what.'

'I've simply got to take her back,' Michael said, deep in his frustration. 'My mother and father *won't* be consoled by me. It was my idea to leave you alone down here. But Margaret – she's the closest thing they've got to their understanding. Somehow you've crumbled all their lives for them. They're *my* parents. I can't stand by and do nothing.'

He stared up at Howarth. For a terrible moment there seemed to me to be a bond between the two men. They examined each other's eyes, then Howarth looked away.

'And there's your own wife and children, Howarth. I don't know how much was disappointment in her, or how much in yourself. But you're crushing just too much. Margaret has to come home. It's absolutely essential.'

Howarth shook his head, as if he were denying something to himself. 'She has her own choice to make,' he said.

'Then it's settled,' I told him.

Howarth was looking plainly at Michael. 'But you must come, Margaret,' Michael said.

'Back to that *prison*? Don't you credit me with *any* feeling, Michael? Any at all? I must be like a lump of stone to you, to be thrown from one person to another whenever anyone feels like it.'

'You don't have to stay,' he said slowly. 'Just come back. I'll leave it to you what you do then. I promise that. When you see my mother and dad you can make your own mind up. . . .'

'Do you think I didn't make up my mind before I came down here? I don't understand you. . . . I'm wedded to Howarth in every possible way except for that rotten bit of paper.'

'I promised my mother I'd bring you back.'

Howarth had said nothing. I couldn't feel him. Then he suddenly took hold of my shoulders, turning me round. His eyes were wide and still, as if with shock. 'I think you'd better go back,' he said.

'But I can't!'

'Nay, I don't mean for ever. I mean just to show them.' He smiled strongly at me. 'If your brother can't help them, then you must . . . I think it's best at least to try.'

I listened to him helplessly, pounding with love for him. 'I'm sure you can do it. You've changed a lot since you've been down here. Just be yourself. That's all you have to do.'

'But you've never had any care for my family.'

'I know. . . . But it doesn't matter.'

Michael stood up, rigid and aloof. 'We ought to go straight away,' he said. 'Before we have time to think again.' He'd got his own way, again; but now for some reason he resented it.

'Yes,' Howarth said. 'The sooner we've got this thing settled. . . .' He brought my bag out from under the bed.

'Howarth,' I asked him, 'how can I?'

He straightened slowly, to look at me. 'You didn't stop me from going to see Joyce.'

'Do you hate *her*?'

'No. . . . It's not *hate*.'

'I hate my family now. I could never go back.'

'You can do something for them, Margaret. That's all it amounts to.'

'Do you want me to go, Howarth?'

'Yes.' He put my bag on the bed and opened it.

'Why? . . . I don't understand.' I looked from him to Michael.

But Howarth was already packing my bag. Their faces showed nothing. Then Howarth, recognizing my feeling, came to hold me. 'You're making it far worse than it is,' he said. 'But that's your brother's fault. Take no notice.'

'I don't understand it, that's all. Not any of it.'

He helped me pack my bag: a nightdress and my cosmetics. It hardly held anything else. I was trying to think, but it all confused me. Why was I going?

'Aren't you coming to the station?' I asked him with a sudden dread. He'd stopped at the top of the stairs behind me. Michael was ahead of me and looked up at us both.

'No. I'll say good-bye here, and wait for you here.'

I went back in dismay. 'But why aren't you coming?'

'Don't you know what it's like to wait?' He was smiling and ridiculing me.

'But I won't be so long,' I said, kissing him and hugging him.

'I'm glad.'

'Oh, I'll be back in no time. I'll be back tomorrow, the first moment.'

I couldn't leave him. Even for a second. 'Go on, Margaret,' he said, pulling my arms down.

'You won't go away and leave me?'

He shook his head at me, smiling with contempt. 'After all *this*?'

I kissed him again. He held me tightly a moment. 'You'll never leave me, will you, Howarth?' I whispered.

'How could I ever leave you?' He began pushing me away. 'Go on. You'll have to go. You'll be here all night if you don't.'

I turned down the stairs, warm with him, waiting for the last sight of him with his feet astride, smiling and waving, bending down so that he could see me on the stairs. He looked so certain and strong.

'Take care of yourself, love.'

'Oh, I will,' I called back.

Michael said nothing. At the station for some reason he booked first-class tickets and we had a compartment to ourselves. But the train was empty. It was the slow last train of the night, cold and makeshift, with not a sound of anyone aboard.

There was the blackness outside, and Michael, and nothing else on that aching journey north. I cried for Howarth, aching for the return, wearied by the thought that all I was passing took me away from him, that it would all have to be travelled back. It dragged at me. I hated the greed of my parents.

The shock of the evening was at last heavy on Michael. He was white, and hardly spoke. He smoked continuously. I felt sick with it. The train spluttered on through the darkness. There was a terrible shrouded whiteness outside: the snow was plastered against the window frame and glazed the darkness with its white bands. It crusted against the window, thawed, and was flung off. It came swooping past, flickering and flashing, swirling with smoke. At one point it rained: the coldness seemed to shatter the train, tearing through it in long gusts and torrents. It seemed hollow and empty, eerie with its coldness, swaying through the damp desolation of stations and the heaving darkness. Its monotonous struggling drove into me. My arm still throbbed. I was gladdened by it. The pain was luxury and warmth and comfort.

13

The darkness of the estate was broken up by the small yellow pools of the lamps. The roads were empty; there was not even a parked car or a cat. But a solitary light went on upstairs when the taxi re-started its engine and moved off down the road. Its noise drowned the place, sending back waves between the houses.

We heard my father's nasal panting down the stairs. The light glowed dimly through the frosted panels, then my father opened the door carefully, wide-eyed, and flung his arms round me. I fell between them, frightened by him, by his closeness. We held one another silently, but I couldn't return his warmth. 'Where's Mum?' I said.

He pulled back, and Michael shut the door behind me, then went into the living-room and put the light on. I sensed some betrayal on his part.

'Where's Mum?'

'She's upstairs,' my father said. 'Go on up and see her. Go up and see her.' He let me pass. He was still in his pyjamas, and so small and pleased that he seemed a child. 'Go on up, love.' I climbed hurriedly up the stairs, and he didn't follow me. He was already talking to Michael in the living-room when I reached the landing: the low growl of their voices seemed to come from the roots of the house.

My mother was sitting up in bed, waiting for me to switch on the light by the door, away from her. I could hear her moving nervously on the bed; then she blinked in the sudden burst of light, shy and uncertain, and not familiar.

I went and held her for a moment, but I could bring no surge of feeling into me. There was a coldness in her, too; inexplicable and puzzling to her. She was strangely self-contained. 'But I thought you were *so* ill from what our Michael said,' I told her.

'I haven't been too well,' she said finally, looking at me, still shocked, and strange with sleep. She suddenly burst out, 'Oh, Margaret, love,' and held me again, sobbing to herself and trying to speak.

'It's all right, Mum. You can see I'm all right.'

'Yes, I know. It's been so bad.'

I drew back from her, and we looked at one another, pleased; she was still shy of her emotion.

'Mum, I've to tell you now. I've only come for a visit. I'm going back to London. I've only come to let you *see* that I'm all right.'

'Yes,' she said disbelievingly, without interest, pushing it from her mind.

There was so much between us now, dividing us; and it was solid. I was glad of its protection, that I needn't care, and was only mildly angered at Michael's exaggeration of her illness. I began to think of Howarth more and more intensely. The silence of the estate outside was terrifying. My body sobbed for him. 'Michael said you were ever so ill – he seemed to make it like that.'

'He's always exaggerating,' she said lightly. And suddenly pressed me against her.

'Doesn't it make you feel better to see me like this?'

'Oh, yes. I feel better already, Margaret. Just the sight of you.' But there was still the coldness and strangeness. When I tried to talk about Howarth she said, 'Please, not tonight. I can't cope with any more, love.' She shook her head wearily.

I talked with her a while longer, then she insisted on getting out of bed and padding in her bare feet to my room to make sure my bed was aired. They'd been relying on Michael.

There was a hot water bottle barely cooled in the bed, and a pair of my old pyjamas. They'd expected it of me all the time.

I was shocked by the preparation. There was no recognition of my sacrifice. Only the old blindness and wilfulness. My father came up and encouraged my mother back to bed. There was something worn and useless about them both now. Irrelevant. I felt betrayed. I would have gladly gone back, even walking. But Howarth had wanted me to come. I fell into a broken sleep, yearning and empty, resting in a huge hollow. My body ached for him, every limb feeling for him. My body curved to his in the bed. We'd lain here months ago. I rested against him, sobbing at his absence, filling my dreams with the nightmare of my journey from him.

In the morning my mother treated me with the privilege of a stranger. She was up early – if she'd even slept – and when I came down the fire was burning brightly and the table set for our breakfasts. Michael had gone home and was coming back at lunchtime. My father came down shortly after me, and we had our breakfasts together, quiet, and with already an air of futility. I told them about the job I had at the B.B.C. and the sort of people I met, the odd glimpses of well-known people. They listened distantly.

'You've got nice clothes,' my mother said. She hated liking them, not sure what they meant. 'You seem quite changed. I hardly recognized you last night.'

'Howarth chose the clothes.'

She was pale, and did look ill. Her skin was like ivory, so damp-looking and smooth. Neither she nor my father ate much. Shortly afterwards my father went upstairs and was sick. We listened to him in silence, sitting at the table with the three half-eaten breakfasts. He came down gaunt and smiling, and made a joke about his greedy appetite, and went to sit by the fire. He shivered in its heat.

I helped my mother to clear the table. When I mentioned

Howarth she hung on to my words grimly, not listening, only hearing the implication. She looked at my stomach once or twice, suspiciously. I despised her for her silent narrowness. 'Is my dad still off work?' I asked. 'What's been the matter with him?'

'There's something wrong with his back,' she said tonelessly.

'Won't you *ever* be reconciled to me living with him? Either of you?'

She sat in the easy chair away from the fire. She looked supremely old, as did my father. 'Is that what you really want, that?'

'We'll be married in a year. I'm sure of it. Will that be so terrible?'

'You'll never be married to him.'

'She'll have to divorce him. She can't leave him dangling like that. She can't even want it for herself.'

'She said she'd never divorce him,' my father said lifelessly.

'We'll have to wait longer, then. But it'll change. It can't go on like this for much longer.'

'What about the children you'll have?' my mother said weakly. She had tired quickly, and now seemed on the verge of absolute exhaustion, devoid of any argument or reason. 'What sort of life can you give them? They'll be worse off than you are: afraid of anybody asking questions. What will they do when they have to give the names of their parents?'

'Those things don't matter,' I told her fiercely. 'It doesn't even come into the immediate future.'

'That's a right old one,' my father said. 'We weren't going to have any children for two or three years, but our Michael was born afore we'd been wed one. If you live with a man like that ...' He broke off in distaste, sickening within himself.

'You know you can't go on,' my mother said. 'It's not right. Not to any of us.'

'Nobody's turned their back on us yet, and we haven't made it a secret. People take you as you *are*.'

'Do they? Well they haven't done round here. They couldn't have been more shocked,' she said. 'You can't realize how it's affected folk here. It's just hell for me and your dad to step into the street . . . a decent girl like you.'

They were so worn and faded. I could hardly believe in their feelings and their concern. They were no longer wanting to help me, but for me to help them. Only they wouldn't admit to that, through habit. We were each helpless to one another, and drawing away from one another.

'I only came back because I thought you really needed me, to see me . . . and because Howarth wanted me to. I'm well. And I'm fit and happy. I've never been so happy in my life before. Can't you see?'

'Aye, you're prospering,' my father said.

'But there's no reason to fret over *me*. Why do you do it? You can see just by looking at me.'

My mother, for a moment, was too tired to talk. She lay back in the chair breathing deeply, staring at the fire as she concentrated on some physical discomfort. We both watched her guiltily, my father gripping his chair with barely concealable remorse.

'Mother, you do see that this is the only thing I want, don't you? I've always done what I thought was right. Would I ever have done this if it wasn't everything to me?'

'You're a grown woman, and you've done what you wanted, Margaret. I can't see that there's ought we can do.'

'But why must you be ill like this?'

'This's how we are. We can't change now. We've lived through life . . . I'm sure, you see, that you'll live to regret it – *and* to come at us for not making you see sense. You've done it always before as children, blaming us like that. There's nothing worse in a mother's life.' She held her chest with her hand, her face twisted as she breathed. She tormented us both.

'I don't think we ought to talk any more about it for now,' I told her. 'I'll stay today, and go back tomorrow morning. You want to rest now, Mum.'

She closed her eyes, and turned her head sideways on to the back of the chair. Her skin was tight and unusually smooth, with the veins deep blue under the paleness. My father looked at her, shaking his head hopelessly from side to side. 'Why won't you give o'er worrying, Mother?' he said to her dismally.

Michael didn't bring Gwen at lunch-time. He came along expecting almost anything. 'Have you cleared it up yet?' he asked tensely, the first moment he got me alone.

'I'm going back tomorrow morning. There's nothing I can do. . . . How ill *is* my mother?'

'The doctor's been calling once a week. He just says she's tired and run-down, and should go away for a rest. She's got a tonic, and some pills.'

'It absolutely exhausts me seeing her like this. It's almost as if it were all deliberate. It's terrible.'

'She's much better since even yesterday. Your coming back has made a difference already.'

'And when I go back to London?'

'I don't know.' He was cautious. 'It depends how well you convince her.'

'She won't be convinced.'

'No,' he said lifelessly. 'I didn't think she would. She can't see anything to hope for by it.'

'What can I do?'

'Can't you leave Howarth?' he asked suddenly, carelessly.

'How can you *ask* me, after yesterday?'

His face clouded: he became absorbed in himself. 'It's

almost a straight choice,' he said thickly, the blood rushing to his face. 'Between him and my mother.'

'It's not like that at all. It's . . . *evil*, you saying that.'

'I don't know,' he warned me. 'We can't do anything for her, except you. She's not really ill. She just wants you out of all this. Every little bit of it's wrong to her.'

'She's not fair to me. She's always run the home, and now she wants to be treated like a queen in it, doing just what *she* wants. She doesn't give me a chance. She's made it so I *can* only hate her.'

'It's only the particular circumstance of you and Howarth. How can you expect them to stomach him? If he'd been single they'd have minded less.'

'Yet even then they'd have disliked him, wouldn't they? You gave them all that artist nonsense. They believe he's just a callous man, with no feelings for anyone but himself. . . . Why *do* you hate him?'

'He's useless.'

'But he's tried . . .'

'All those like him – they're just useless. All this sub-culture nonsense. Art ! . . . He's simple. He tries to be honest with himself. But you believe he's far more than that.'

'I only know we need one another. I don't think you'll ever understand that. It's something that I don't think you have with Gwen.'

'That's not a very wise thing to say,' he decided, without any frankness.

'I'm going back to Howarth and never coming here again,' I said bursting into tears at the finality and hopelessness of it all. 'Nothing on earth can stop me. I don't care if they die.'

My mother sensed the inevitable result. During the after-noon it seemed to strengthen her: now that there was no hope at all and she had to face it, she gathered herself together with a visible determination, and even managed to smile once at Michael's joking insistence.

I wanted to leave them then, and catch an evening train to London, but Michael was determined that I should stay just one more night. 'I think she's coming round,' he said. 'Don't go just yet. Give her a good chance.'

Gwen came in the evening and we played cards together. In the middle of the game my mother suddenly burst into tears and ran from the room. We heard her crying upstairs. My father listened dourly, looking at me with murderous eyes. But we were relieved. It seemed she had released herself. She came down later, at the limit of her exhaustion, and sat in the easy chair, her eyes glazed, her arms dropping down beside her. We tried to be natural. But we couldn't ignore the final tearing apart of the family. There was nothing to be said. We looked at one another like ghosts.

I missed Howarth more than I could bear. I was incomplete and lifeless without him: I had no existence. I would have gladly trampled on my parents to reach him even for a moment. But I lay still in bed, my body cold with absence. It was unbearable to lie still and wait, to wait for the morning, for the train, for the long journey. It was a separation from life itself: the silence of the estate around was that of an entombment, a graveyard, booming and flaming in its emptiness.

In the middle of the night I got up and made a cup of tea in the scullery. I could hear my mother and father moving about upstairs, and when I opened the curtains there was the patch of light from their bedroom flung across the narrow lawn, spreading out into the darkness of the road. It was a big patch of light, broadening as it extended from the house, and falling aimlessly over the simple shapes outside.

Soon my father came down, in his bare feet, his pyjamas too large for his small muscular body. I poured him his pot of tea, and he sat stiffly on a wooden chair, staring at the coarse matting on the floor, and coughing at the dust in his throat. 'Shall I take my mother a cup of tea?' I asked.

He shook his head. 'She's only just got off. I've made her take three of them pills. She's just beginning to get her eyes shut.'

We sat in silence, unsure of one another. The light deadened everything, cheapening all the colour, reducing all the pans and crockery to shadows. The scullery was emptied by the light and by the thing between us: we were two shadows, with acres of sleeping bodies around us. The place had a dead harvest, the stillness. And in the middle of it was this aching, a solemn convulsion of my inside, as if Howarth had been ripped away from within me.

'Won't you come away, Margaret?' he said, as if the silence had been a long conversation which he was now ending. 'You could go away for a holiday. We'd manage it somehow. We've always stuck together before.'

'No. It's no good, Dad.'

'Wouldn't you do it even for me?' he asked quietly. But he was so full of distaste at this that his face twisted wretchedly. We watched ourselves retreat from one another. 'Can't you see what it does to all of us?' he said. 'It knocks out everything we've done for you. . . . And I'd do ought to get your mother and things right again.'

'I can't argue about it,' I said miserably, and suddenly too tired by it. 'To me it only makes everything you have done for me seem worth while.'

He continued to drink his tea out of habit: to slake his throat. Everything was an obligation to him now. His eyes drooped and were familiarly reddened by fatigue. 'Your mother wants you to leave him. More than anything in the world. You know that.'

'I know.'

'Then . . . Don't leave it too late. That's what I'm asking you.'

'You mustn't blame me like this!'

'No. All right. We'll blame nobody. We're all to blame. But only you can do ought about it.'

'My mother won't die,' I told him.

'You don't know what your mother might do ... I'm asking you, Margaret.'

'I can't. I can't!'

'Nay ... Margaret.' He shuddered at me.

I was too tired. The night was a weight on me, its silence. I went into the hall and for a moment stood there to look at the living-room. It was dark, but the ashes still glowed, faintly illuminating the room, casting those great russet shadows on the ceiling. The room was lived in. It was warm and cosy, and its familiarity was something that couldn't be spoiled. It was unearthly, its glow coming from within itself, concealing and revealing things indiscriminately. I went upstairs. As I lay in bed I listened to my father moving about downstairs, restlessly from the room to the scullery and back. All around the house was still. The estate. I ached for Howarth, longing for him to take me away from this thing for ever.

It was my father who wakened me.

He had a letter, and as if he sensed its significance, he brought it into the bedroom, woke me, and stood by the bed a moment while I tore open the envelope.

I had already recognized Howarth's neat handwriting. The letter was long. I stared at it blindly, suddenly hot and stifled, disbelieving as my eyes tried to plunge amongst the first few words. 'I've called an end to it and I'm going away. . . .

'I only hope this reaches you before you catch your train to London. But your brother understood. . . .

'Although what I've done has always to me been the hardest way, it has still been weak. Even when I've been strongest with myself.

'I just haven't been strong enough. That must be it. I haven't a chance of achieving any of those things I set my heart on. I don't know whether your brother came at the right or the wrong moment – but it must have come in the end. We'd have been hunted out.

'This is the cruellest thing of all. Writing to you like this. But I could never push you away even for your own safety while you were near me, and I could touch you. Even when your finger touches me I'm in flames. I could never turn away when you were there.

'If our love has counted then it's as a purgative, for me. I'll always have it here. It's helped me to reconcile myself finally. You might say the hounds have got me at last. I wish at times I was a hound like you. Doing things together, in groups, never useful if he's alone. That's what your brother means. But – it was wrong of me to share my uselessness with you. Your brother must be right after all. When he hears of this I imagine he'll pat himself on the back. It can't be helped. People have spent their lives patting themselves on the back at my expense. I still need you, Margaret. You're life to me. But I can't destroy everything merely because I want to live. . . .

'In a way it solves everything, doesn't it? Things still go on. I can't believe that the clock is still ticking as I write this, when everything else has stopped. It's still ticking. I've tried to stop too many things, to call a halt too noisily. And look what's happened. I couldn't go on teaching in that school. I can't throw myself overboard and end it all. But another twenty years – It doesn't seem much, in a strange way. I still love you, Margaret, with everything I've got. You're still with me in the room, where we've been together so much and I'm crying that I can't just see you and touch you. Those evenings when I came home from school feeling the bottom had dropped out. And then *you*! So optimistic. All the time.

'You're everything that was worth while. I'll just go on and on repeating it. The freedom and the peace I found through you. But I see I'm not the person to demand those things outright. I've either to steal them or do without. I can't steal any longer. I'm the worst thief there ever was. I don't know what it is, but I just can't steal. I suppose I'll end up in a cage now as an oddity. "Look what happened to old Howarth", will be the caption, and people will look at me with that funny smile. What makes a man like me? It's a useless question, isn't it? I'm just there, without use or purpose. So I end up as a decoration. The only way I can be accepted on my own terms is by being inconspicuous. . . .

'I can't stop you coming back to London. But I won't be here. I've already let the flat go, and arranged for your luggage to go north. I couldn't bear to think of you alone in this flat. That would be too much. I'm leaving London. I'll be gone by the time you get this. I've no idea where I'm going. I'm just going – perhaps one more run before the hounds really get me. You never know. I'm glad you've got a brother like yours. He'll know just how to help you now. But please don't let him crow. My death was only pointed out, not accomplished by him. He might even understand what it's all been about. . . .

'I'd made my mind up when we said good-bye yesterday. I knew as I watched you go down the stairs that this was the last time. I know you'll never forgive me that deception. I can't describe my feeling as I watched. I'll never want to remember it – the loss of everything. If you can ever bring yourself to forgive me I shall know that I wasn't completely a failure to myself, that there was a little bit of dignity in it somewhere. Without that I suppose everything will have been useless.

'If I'd been an artist as I wanted to be when I was young, my work might have taken the place of you. But I'm not creative in that way. That part of me was deadened. You've been my art. I've punished and loved and struggled with you. I can never reject you now. And only you can show what I've really been. You're the test of my deepest character. I've never shown myself to anyone as I've shown myself to you. I seem to have put all my faith and ambition into you. And if there's any failing then it's not your fault. You must go on.... At least I've shown you that if nothing else. You must go on and on. There's nothing more important than that: it's magnificent....'

My eyes strayed over the remaining words: it was a steadily rising crescendo, of waves, of water, of a depth that finally reached my throat, my mouth, and I gave out a drowning cry, collapsing into that endlessness of space, that suffocation that blinded and choked and ruined everything.

Michael stretched himself out in his deck chair in the middle of the lawn. Gwen, gently rounded with her first pregnancy, sat closer to the back door of the house, in the shade. Both of them were pleased and really taken with John Fawcett. His unspoken curiosity roused Michael, almost distressing him one moment with his urge to blunt it, then amusing him the next with its seeming invulnerability. It was the first person I'd seen him overtly respect.

Both the men screwed up their eyes slightly in the heat of the afternoon sun, but Fawcett's short-clipped hair gave him a sharp, forceful appearance, swamping the more hesitant and perhaps heavier power of Michael. I liked seeing them together – they were so oddly contrasted. Their liking for one another may have sprung from that. They went on talking in the slow, easeful sun, while I drowsed on a blanket, close to the flowers.

Voices came from nearby houses, and overhead an aircraft lumbered through the tiny, fractured clouds. The hill and the low wood beyond the garden hid the first approaches to town. 'We'd planned on an architect-designed house,'

Michael was saying. 'But Gwen soon put a stop to that. She was pregnant within three months of us getting married, so we had to rush into this place.'

'This place isn't so bad,' Fawcett said, amused by Michael's impetuosity.

'It's very fine,' Gwen called from the doorway, quickly chastising Michael whenever he showed his peculiar blindness to things.

'Yes,' Fawcett said, 'I'd count myself a very lucky man if I ended up in a house and garden like this.'

'It does. It does. It's a bit like a vicarage in any case,' Michael said mockingly, glancing at Gwen and shaking his head. 'Why she had to get into that condition so early beats me.'

Fawcett laughed to himself, and softly glanced at me. 'Are you comfortable stretched out there?' he asked.

I nodded, staring across at the two men as a mutual silence overcame them. Fawcett was openly anxious, but Michael had a certain furtiveness about him. 'I'm very comfortable,' I said, and closed my eyes.

A moment later I was only drowsily aware of their murmured voices. I was overwhelmed by the scent of the flowers, the heavy scent of the newly mown grass.

I wakened to the sound of tea things. Four chairs had been brought out and a tea table. Gwen was laying the tea things. The two men watched her careful handling of the crockery.

'... He was a conscience was that man,' Michael said wearily.

'Did you know that he's gone back to his wife?' Fawcett's voice was very distant, and unfamiliar.

'Has he?' Gwen leaned over him and put the sandwiches down.

'But poor chap. He must have been human after all,' Michael said.

He laughed carefully, but without derision. 'Still. That's

enough of that. . . .' He must have glanced at me, but by now I had re-closed my eyes. Even Gwen's rattling stopped a moment. 'You must tell me exactly what your Belief is, Fawcett. . . . And let's see if I can break it down.' He laughed challengingly.

When I opened my eyes Gwen was staring slowly at me. 'Margaret? . . . Won't you come and have some tea? We've been waiting for you, love.'

More about Penguins and Pelicans

Penguinews, which appears every month, contains details of all the new books issued by Penguins as they are published. From time to time it is supplemented by *Penguins in Print*, which is our complete list of almost 5,000 titles.

A specimen copy of *Penguinews* will be sent to you free on request. Please write to Dept EP, Penguin Books Ltd, Harmondsworth, Middlesex, for your copy.

In the U.S.A.: For a complete list of books available from Penguins in the United States write to Dept CS, Penguin Books, 625 Madison Avenue, New York, New York 10022.

In Canada: For a complete list of books available from Penguins in Canada write to Penguin Books Canada Ltd, 41 Steelcase Road West, Markham, Ontario.

Penguin Fiction

The Midas Consequence

Michael Ayrton

In a restaurant in the south of France, an old Italian
sculptor holds court. He has climbed to the
pinnacle of his art, received the bounty of the gods; all he
touches turns to gold.

'There are flickers of thunder and bursts of lightning, and
real myth horror . . . this is one of the few
novels about an artist which rings true, and rings with a drama
which will still clang in the reader's mind long
after he has finished' – *Books and Bookmen*

No Place Like : Selected Stories

Nadine Gordimer

'A magnificent collection worthy of all homage' – Graham
Greene in the *Observer* Books of the Year 1976

With this collection of thirty-one stories Nadine Gordimer
displays all her descriptive power and acute insight,
pinning Africa to the page like a butterfly for our
inspection.

'This dazzlingly rich, impressively solid selection . . . The
scrupulous intensity of her regard shouts from the
opening sentences' – Valentine Cunningham
in the *New Statesman*

Foreign Affairs

Sean O'Faolain

'The finest collection of stories to come out of Ireland for
many years' – *Hibernia*

Eight stories from the acknowledged master of Irish letters.
They deal in love and strangeness, from Dublin to
Brussels to the crumbled remains of ancient Sybaris, delineating
with wit and colour the silent spaces between lovers.

Changing Places

David Lodge

'Not since *Lucky Jim* has such a funny book about
academic life come my way' — *Sunday Times*

Rumpole of the Bailey

John Mortimer

Horace Rumpole is sixty-eight next birthday; with an
unsurpassed knowledge of Blood and Typewriters and a habit
of referring to his judge as 'the old darling'.
He now takes up his pen in the pious hope of making a bob
or two. In doing so he opens up some less-well charted
corners of British justice.

Memoirs of Hadrian

Marguerite Yourcenar

This is a reissue of Mme Yourcenar's magnificent recreation
of the young, ambitious Spanish soldier who rose to
be an outstanding ruler of the enormous and far-flung
Roman Empire.

'An astonishing work : I have read nothing that
surpasses it as a sustained and convincing
exercise of historical imagination' — *Sunday Times*

Something Nasty in the Woodshed

Kyril Bonfiglioli

The Hon. Charlie Mortdecai, that dubious art dealer,
is faced with witchcraft and rape in the ancient ritual manner
in Jersey. His reaction is craven, the jokes are as
hysterical as ever and the rapes themselves are
quite, quite horrible.

Aspects of Love

David Garnett

David Garnett's novel is set in France and has all the
delicacy and flavour of a ripe peach.

In it he explores all the nuances of feeling and the
freedoms, sexual and otherwise, that four closely knit people,
who are concerned to keep the taste of life on
the tip of their tongues, can allow each other.

The Ice Age

Margaret Drabble

Margaret Drabble articulates the anguish of thwarted
hopes, the disappointment and spiritual hangover
of the seventies with a rare mastery.

Anthony Keating is middle-aged. His undoubted talents
have brought him a dodgily prosperous living as a
property developer, an estranged wife, a devoted mistress,
several children and a heart-attack.

He is paralysed by his situation. As are his friends
by theirs. The Ice Age is upon us.

The Village Cricket Match

John Parker

As the last ball is bowled, the stumps drawn, and the
shadows lengthen over the field of play, spectators and
players adjourn to the village pub to relive the
game over good, strong ale . . .

The same gentle, sun-drenched atmosphere is beautifully
evoked in *The Village Cricket Match*: the common
rustic swing, the rare and truly elegant late cut, the demon
fast bowler and the lucky six into the village pond, are all here.

and

A Temporary Life

David Storey

This Sporting Life

The world of professional Rugby football is a tough world, and Arthur Machin allows little sentimentality in telling the story of this sporting life. It is a physical life, fouled by the grime, sweat, intrigue and naked ambition of a northern industrial city. From pathetic Mrs Hammond, who suffers Machin's crude affection, to Weaver and Slomer, the game's backers, David Storey's characters are drawn from the raw side of life.

Saville

David Storey

An absorbing and evocative saga of a Yorkshire mining family – at its centre, Saville, a boy whose growing-up in the forties and fifties forges a powerful conflict in his nature, and a destructive resistance to his environment.

'Certainly a major achievement . . . a definitive and liberating statement' – *The Times Literary Supplement*

Pasmore

A young university lecturer is in the grip of a nervous breakdown, struggling to resolve a disintegrating marriage in a chaotic and meaningless world.

Radcliffe

The story of a passionate relationship between two men and its tragic and terrible consequences.

'A brainstorm of a book; it boils in the mind long after it is done' – *Sunday Times*